PRAY FOR DEATH

Center Point
Large Print

Also by William W. and J. A. Johnstone
and available from Center Point Large Print:

Tyranny
The Doomsday Bunker
Ride the Savage Land
The Range Detectives
Dig Your Own Grave
Hang Them Slowly
Too Soon to Die
Rope Burn

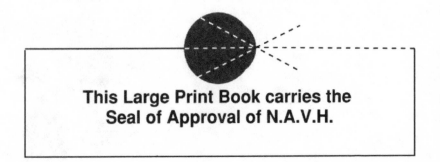

**This Large Print Book carries the
Seal of Approval of N.A.V.H.**

PRAY FOR DEATH

A WILL TANNER U.S. DEPUTY MARSHAL WESTERN

WILLIAM W. JOHNSTONE

AND J. A. JOHNSTONE

CENTER POINT LARGE PRINT
THORNDIKE, MAINE

This Center Point Large Print edition
is published in the year 2020 by arrangement with
Kensington Publishing Corp.

PUBLISHER'S NOTE
Following the death of William W. Johnstone, the
Johnstone family is working with a carefully selected
writer to organize and complete Mr. Johnstone's outlines
and many unfinished manuscripts to create additional
novels in all of his series like The Last Gunfighter,
Mountain Man, and Eagles, among others. This novel
was inspired by Mr. Johnstone's superb storytelling.

The text of this Large Print edition is unabridged. In other
aspects, this book may vary from the original edition.
Printed in the United States of America
on permanent paper.
Set in 16-point Times New Roman type.

ISBN: 978-1-64358-676-2

The Library of Congress has cataloged this record
under Library of Congress Control Number: 2020934764

PRAY
FOR
DEATH

CHAPTER 1

Jim Little Eagle reined his paint gelding to a halt on the bank of Muddy Boggy Creek about fifty yards upstream of the log building bearing the crudely lettered sign that identified it as MAMA'S KITCHEN. The Choctaw policeman had been watching the comings and goings of the typical clientele of the dining room and gambling hall just recently built three miles outside of town. And from what he had observed, there was no doubt that the owner, a man calling himself Tiny McGee, was selling whiskey and employing a prostitute as well. Jim figured it was time to remind McGee that it was illegal to sell whiskey in the Nations. There was little doubt in Jim's mind that the recent complaints from the merchants in town were caused by patrons of Mama's Kitchen. On more than one occasion in the past week, three white drifters had amused themselves by racing their horses through the center of town, firing their firearms and scaring the people. He was not confident that his visit to Mama's Kitchen would stop the harassment of the citizens of Atoka, because his authority was limited to the policing of the Indian population. He knew that McGee knew this, as all outlaws did, but he felt it his duty to give him notice, anyway.

Inside the log building, Bob Atkins and Stump Grissom sat talking to Tiny McGee at one of the four small tables. A door that led to several rooms in the back of the building opened and Bob's brother Raymond came out, pretending to stagger as he hitched up his trousers and buckled his belt. His antics caused a round of guffaws from the table and a loud response from Bob. "I swear, Raymond, damned if I don't believe Mama's Baby done wore you out!"

Coming out behind him, Ida Simpson commented, "Don't pay no attention to him. He's as rutty as a bull in matin' season." A working girl with signs of wear, but uncertain age, Ida had adopted the name of Baby because it was so appropriate for Mama's Kitchen. Although Mama's was, in effect, a saloon, there was a kitchen and Tiny did sell meals. His cook was a well-traveled woman named Etta Grise, now too old to do the work Baby did. Tiny hoped the name of his establishment might disguise his actual business interests. His plan was to make Boggy Town, the name already given to it by outlaws, a separate little town where outlaws on the run could hole up. And, so far, he had not been visited by any deputy marshals out of Fort Smith.

"I expect Baby's up to givin' you a ride now, Stump," Raymond japed as he sat down at the table.

"Not me," Stump responded. "I ain't thinkin' 'bout nothin' but supper right now." He was about to say more but stopped when he realized everyone was looking past him toward the door. He turned then to see what had captured their attention.

"Well, well," Tiny said, "if it ain't Jim Little Eagle." He sneered openly at the Choctaw policeman standing in the doorway, his rifle cradled in his arms. "What brings you down to Boggy Town? Course, I expect you know I don't serve no Injuns in here."

"I think you sell whiskey to Indians out your back door," Jim answered him. "I come to give you notice that it is illegal to sell whiskey in the Nations, to white man or Indian. I think you already know this. I don't want to put any more drunken Indians in my jail. I think you better stop selling whiskey."

"Damned if he ain't mighty uppity for an Injun," Bob said. "You gonna let him talk to you like that?"

Tiny laughed. "He's the local Choctaw police-man. He knows damn well he ain't got no say-so about anything a white man does." He sneered at Little Eagle. "Ain't that right, Jim?"

"I think you would be wise to take my warning and stop selling whiskey," Jim insisted. "Maybe it would be best if you move your business someplace else. Atoka is a peaceful town."

"This ain't Atoka, this is Boggy Town, and I got as much right to be here as any of them stores in town," Tiny said. "Maybe it'd be best if you take your Injun ass outta here before somebody's gun goes off accidentally." His warning prompted the other three at the table to push their chairs back, preparing for a possible shooting.

With no change in the solemn expression on his face to reveal his frustration, Jim Little Eagle replied, "That would be an unfortunate thing to happen, because my rifle fires by itself when accidents happen. And you are such a big target, white man, you would be hard to miss." When Stump Grissom started to react, Jim whipped his rifle around, ready to fire.

"Let him go, Stump," Tiny warned. "You shoot one of them Injun policemen and there'll be a whole slew of deputy marshals down here." He looked back at Jim. "All right, you've said your peace, so get on outta here and let us get back to mindin' our own business."

Knowing there was nothing he could legally do to close the saloon, Jim backed out the door. With a keen eye still on the door, he climbed on his horse and rode away. He had at least accomplished one thing by making the visit. He verified the suspicion he had that Tiny McGee was operating a saloon. There had been no attempt to hide the whiskey bottle in the middle of the table. He would now notify the marshal in Fort Smith.

Behind him, the four men filed into the kitchen to eat supper. "Soon as we finish eatin'," Bob Atkins suggested, "why don't we take a little ride into town and make sure all them folks are awake."

"Good morning, Will," U.S. Marshal Dan Stone greeted his young deputy when he walked in the door of his office over the jail in Fort Smith. "Are you ready to get back to work?"

"Yes, sir, I surely am," Will replied, and took a seat across from Stone's desk. It was a truthful answer, for he had spent the last three days in town, most of it sitting around Bennett House drinking coffee and listening to Sophie Bennett and her mother talking about the wedding coming up. Out of desperation, he had excused himself from their discussions from time to time, telling them he had to check on his horses and tack. He found himself longing for the hills and open prairies, and that was something that troubled him. His on-again, then off-again, engagement to Sophie had been due to his job as a deputy marshal and the fact that it caused him to be gone most of the time. When he thought about it, he couldn't really blame her for wanting him to go back to the ranch in Texas, a ranch she had never seen. That was another thing that upset her—he had promised to take her there three weeks ago but had to answer a call from Dan Stone to ride with eight other deputies to capture a gang of train robbers targeting the MKT Railroad.

Noticing a look of distraction in Will's face, Stone commented, "You look like your mind's off someplace else." He flashed a smile and asked, "You thinking about that wedding? Is that where your mind was?"

"Yes, sir, I expect it mighta been, but it's back on business now," Will said. Stone had guessed right, but Will felt no inclination to tell his boss that he wasn't sure about getting married. He knew he would, however, because he had asked Sophie to marry him, and she had said yes.

"Good," Stone said. "I'm sending you and Ed Pine down to Atoka to arrest three men who've been terrorizing the town." When he saw Will's questioning expression, he paused before continuing. "I know, you're thinking that sounds like a job for one deputy with a posseman and a cook, but Ed's been pushing me to send him back in the field. So, I told him I would, but only in partnership with another deputy. He feels like he's ready to ride again, but I think he's still a little weak from that chest wound. He just won't admit it." He shook his head as if exasperated. "So, you're the best man to ride with him. He likes you and he's still beholden to you for going after him when he was left for dead over near Okmulkee. If those three men were in jail, I'd let Ed go without you, but you're gonna have to arrest 'em." He shrugged. "That is, if they're still there by the time you get there, considering it's gonna take you damn near a week." He waited to hear Will's objections, knowing how he disliked being slowed down by a wagon. When Will didn't protest, Stone continued. "Ed's getting the wagon and said he was gonna take Horace Watson to do the cooking." That was fine with Will. He had worked with Horace before, when he was cooking for Alvin Greeley. Greeley was a useless sod, but Will had no complaints about Horace.

"I expect you want us to get started as soon as we can," Will said. "Is Ed takin' care of all the supplies we'll need?" Stone said he was. Will nodded and commented, "Looks like I'll just be his posseman on this trip."

"Pretty much," Stone replied. "You see any problem with that?"

"Nope," Will answered. "Ed oughta know what he's doin'. He's been ridin' with the Marshals Service longer than I have."

"Good," Stone responded. "I knew I could count on you." Will stood up to leave. "Ed's probably still over at the stable, if you want to check with him."

"I'll do that," Will said, and walked out the door.

Will found Ed talking to Vern Tuttle, the owner, when he walked down the street to the stables.

"Here's Will Tanner now," Vern announced when Will came in the door.

"Howdy, Will," Ed Pine greeted him cheerfully. "Have you talked to Dan Stone about ridin' with me?"

"Just came from there," Will replied. "He told me I was fixin' to go to Atoka, that you were in charge on this job, and that I damn sure better not mess up."

Ed chuckled. "Well, I'm glad he laid it on the line for you, so I won't have to do it." Serious then, he said, "I'd appreciate it if you'd check over that list of supplies I loaded on the jail wagon. See if there's anything else you think we'll need." Will took a quick check of the pile of supplies Ed had acquired and found them adequate. "Horace Watson's gonna meet us here at six in the mornin'," Ed informed him. "We can pack most of that food in his wagon."

"Are you plannin' to drive that jail wagon?" Will asked. " 'Cause I ain't. Whaddaya say we let Horace pile his cookin' stuff on the jail wagon and he can drive it, instead of takin' two wagons." That sounded like a good idea to Ed. Like Will, he'd rather sit in the saddle than ride on a wagon seat. "It'll take us just as long to get to Atoka, but we'll be free to scout along the way for fresh game, or smoke out any trouble ahead."

They talked with Vern for a while afterward, then Will had a quick visit with his buckskin

14

gelding before telling Ed he would see him in the morning. Ed walked out of the stables with him to say a final word. "Will, I 'preciate you goin' along on this trip. I know Dan don't think I'm ready to ride again."

"Oh, I don't think Dan thinks that at all," Will quickly assured him. "He's just concerned about these three jaspers raisin' hell in Atoka. I think he figures they're more than three harmless drifters. They might be wanted somewhere else and they might be a handful for one man to handle."

"I reckon we'll see, won't we?" Ed declared.

"I reckon," Will responded. "I'll see you in the mornin'."

As was their usual custom, Ron Sample and Leonard Dickens were sitting in their rocking chairs on the porch at Bennett House when Will walked up from the street. "Ain't it gettin' a little too cold for you boys to sit outside?" Will asked the two elderly boarders as he came up the steps. Never mind the coming of chilly fall weather, it seemed it might take a blizzard to run the two of them inside to smoke their pipes.

"There is a little nip in the air this afternoon," Leonard conceded. "But thanks to Ron, Ruth ran us outta the parlor."

Ron looked at Will and chuckled. "Yep, it didn't set too well with Ruth when I burned a hole in that carpet by the davenport. She made us go set out here on the porch. It wasn't much more'n a little scorched place in the carpet, was it, Leonard? I told her she could pull that rocker over a couple of inches and you wouldn't even notice it. She went on about tryin' to keep the house lookin' decent for your weddin'."

Will glanced at Leonard, who was looking at him, grinning like a Cheshire cat, and he knew there was a little needling coming his way. "No, sir," Leonard said, "we'd best not mess up that weddin'. Right, Will?"

"Hell," Will shot back, "you two ol' buzzards ain't even invited."

They both laughed at that. "Which one of us are you gonna pick to be your best man?" Ron asked.

"You'd be better off pickin' me," Leonard said. "I can still get into my suit I bought for my wife's funeral. It's just like new. I ain't wore it since."

"Maybe Leonard's right," Ron jumped in again. "There ain't much difference in a weddin' and a funeral, anyway. A feller gets his wings clipped at either one of 'em."

He could still hear them laughing after he went inside and closed the door behind him to find Sophie coming down the stairs. "Oh, Will," she said upon seeing him. "Good, you're home. Supper's about ready, so if you have to wash up, you'd best get about it." She paused on the second step, so she could look him in the eye. "Did you go to see Dan Stone today?"

"Yep," he responded. "I reported in, just like I was called to do."

When there was no more from him beyond that simple statement, she gave him that accusing look that he had come to recognize. "You're riding out again, aren't you?"

"Not till tomorrow mornin'," he answered, hoping she would think that at least they had tonight.

"Does he know you're getting married soon?" she asked. "We have so many things to do before then, and it would be nice if you were here to help."

"Sophie, there ain't anything I know to do to help plan a weddin'. You and your mama are goin' to plan everything, anyway. And in the meantime, I have to earn a livin'. So, I can't just sit around Fort Smith every day. When we get married, we're gonna go to Texas, like I told you, and live on the J-Bar-J. And I'll be home all the time." He gave her a smile. "And you'll most likely wish I was back in the Marshals Service."

She shook her head as if perplexed. "Just go wash up for supper." She gave him a quick peck on the cheek before continuing on her way to the kitchen. After supper, she would find out where he was going in the morning and how long he could expect to be gone. In spite of her efforts not to, she was following right along in her mother's footsteps. In love with a deputy marshal, she feared she was destined to realize the same heartbreak her mother suffered when Deputy Marshal Fletcher Pride was murdered by outlaws. Those thoughts brought her mind back to her mother. A strong woman, Ruth Bennett had operated her boardinghouse ever since the death of Sophie's father with never a sign of dependence on anyone. But lately, her mother didn't seem like the determined woman Sophie was accustomed to. Margaret, who had run the kitchen ever since Ruth took over the management of the boardinghouse, noticed a difference in Ruth's demeanor as well, and had commented to Sophie about it. They decided that Sophie's mother was probably working herself into a case of nerves over the upcoming wedding and would recover her old spunk when the knot was tied. Sophie's thoughts were interrupted then when she walked into the kitchen and almost bumped into Margaret coming out into the hall to ring her little dinner bell.

"Where's your mama?" Margaret asked, since Ruth was usually ready to help her set the food on the table.

"She's upstairs," Sophie said. "She was feeling a little tired and decided to lie down for a while before supper."

"She's been getting tired a lot lately," Margaret commented. "I wonder if she's feeling all right."

"I still think the wedding is giving her a case

of nerves," Sophie said. "She'll be all right when that's finally over."

Will was up and ready to leave at five o'clock the next morning. Margaret was in the kitchen, just getting ready to start breakfast when she saw him coming down the back stairs. "You leaving before breakfast?" she asked, and when he said that he was, she insisted on fixing something quick for him. "I've already got the coffeepot on and I'll throw a couple of eggs on the stove for you. Biscuits will be a while yet, but there's some cold corn bread from last night."

"That would suit me just fine," he said right away, and dumped his saddlebags and rifle by the kitchen door. Glancing toward the dining room door, he half expected to see Sophie. They hadn't visited very long after supper the night before because she complained about a headache, so they said good night at half past eight and retired to their separate rooms.

"How long you gonna be gone?" Margaret asked, breaking into his thoughts as she filled a cup for him.

"Couple of weeks, I expect," he answered. "Gotta take a wagon to Atoka and back."

"Well, you be sure and take care of yourself. You won't have much time left before that wedding when you get back."

"I will," he replied, thinking the whole world

seemed to revolve around that wedding. It would have been so much easier to simply go to the preacher and let him tie the knot without all the ceremony that was driving Ruth and Sophie crazy. He was willing to bet that Sophie wouldn't have so many headaches if they did. It was with a definite sense of relief that he ate his quick breakfast and was on his way to meet Ed and Horace. "Tell Sophie I'm sorry I missed her this mornin'," he told Margaret as he walked out the back door.

Horace Watson was already at the stable when Will arrived. A few minutes later, Ed appeared, eager to get started. As Will expected, Horace objected to driving the jail wagon instead of taking his chuck wagon, which he had modified to accommodate his every need. He finally surrendered and agreed to do it, but warned them both that this would be the only time. When the jail wagon was loaded up with supplies and Horace's cooking utensils, they started toward the ferry slips down by the river, with Horace and the wagon setting the pace. His regular chuck wagon was left parked where the jail wagon usually sat. A brisk breeze blew in their faces as they set out on a trail that followed the Poteau River to the southwest. Will and Ed rode side by side a little ahead of Horace in the wagon, Will aboard his buckskin gelding named Buster. Ed was riding a horse he had just bought, a big gray he called Smut. The day was bright and sunny. It was chilly, but it was supposed to be this time of year, so none of the three thought much about it.

Since the Sans Bois Mountains were just about the halfway point in the roughly 120-mile trip, they decided to make a brief stop there. Will knew the location of a hideout well known to outlaws holing up in Indian Territory, and Ed was interested in checking to see if it was currently occupied. The hideout had come to be known locally as Robbers Cave. Will had actually made an arrest there on one occasion, but Ed had never been there, and he thought it might be of future use to him if he knew how to find it.

"I used to know an old fellow who had a cabin not far from that hideout," Will said. "His name was Perley Gates, and he was the one who showed me where that cave is. But Perley was gone the last time I went to his cabin. He left a sign on the door to tell anybody who was interested that he was leavin' it for good, and welcome to it." He paused to think about the elflike little man, and it brought a smile to his face. "I ain't run into Perley since. There's no tellin' where he ended up."

"Maybe he changed his mind and came back," Ed said.

"Knowing Perley, he just might have," Will said. The thought served to spark his interest, so he replied, "I wouldn't mind goin' by his place, just in case he did. It ain't far from Robbers Cave. Matter of fact, it's on the way, so it wouldn't delay us much. We could rest the horses there." So that's what they decided to do.

CHAPTER 2

It took two and a half days at the wagon's pace to reach the Sans Bois Mountains and the trail that snaked its way through the narrow valleys that eventually led to a green meadow. On the other side of the meadow Will pointed to a log cabin built back up against a steep slope, and hard to see at first. They pulled up at the edge of the meadow when they spotted a sorrel horse in the small corral next to an open shed on the other side of the cabin. Will recalled that there was no corral there when he had last visited Perley, and his horse was a dark Morgan. "There's somebody in the cabin," he said to Ed, "but I don't think it's Perley. We'd better make sure." He rode ahead a few yards and called out, "Hello, the cabin!"

"Hello, yourself!" a voice came back. "What's your business here? And just so you know, I've got the front sight of a Henry rifle lookin' right at you."

"No need to shoot anybody," Will said. "We were lookin' for a friend of mine, name of Perley Gates. He built that cabin, but it's plain to see Perley's gone. We're U.S. Deputy Marshals on our way to Atoka. Just thought we'd cut through here to see if Perley mighta come back. We won't trouble you any further." He wheeled Buster around and started back out of the meadow but stopped when he heard the man yell behind him.

"Hold on!" the voice called after him. He turned to see a short-legged little old man come up from behind a large boulder at the corner of the porch and proceed to run after them. They pulled up and waited for him. Still holding his rifle as if ready to shoot, he asked, "How do I know you're deputy marshals? I don't see no badges." Both Will and Ed pulled their coats aside to reveal the badges they wore. He looked from one of them to the other, then back to Will, obviously trying to decide what to do. Finally deciding to take the risk and believe the badges were real, he lowered his weapon. "You come lookin' for them two jaspers up there in Robbers Cave?" When he looked again at Ed and Will to see puzzled expressions on both faces, he said, "I hope to hell that's what you came up here for."

"Like he said," Ed replied, "we're on our way to Atoka. We don't know anything about anybody holed up in that hideout. Are they causing some trouble?"

"Well, I'll say they are," the little man responded, as if it was a stupid question.

"What kinda trouble?" Will asked. He couldn't help thinking the new occupant of the cabin reminded him of the original one, even down to the curly white whiskers.

"They've raided my cabin three different

times. They'll wait till I go off huntin' and come in here and turn my cabin upside down, lookin' for anythin' they can steal. Last week they stole a four-point buck I was fixin' to butcher, came right up to the house and took it. When you boys showed up, I thought it was them comin' back, and I had my rifle ready for 'em this time."

"What's your name, friend?" Ed asked.

"Merle Teague," he replied.

"All right, Merle," Will said, "we'll take a look up at that cave and see if they're still there. We had planned to stop by there, anyway."

"Horace needs to rest his horses," Ed said, "so while he's doin' that, me and you can go up to that hideout."

They left Horace to unhitch his horses and let them graze while Merle Teague looked over the jail wagon. "You got any coffee on that wagon?" they heard Merle asking as they rode up the ravine next to his cabin. Horace must have said he did, because they heard Merle say he would build up the fire. Will had to laugh when he heard him, for he remembered that every time he had stopped to visit Perley, he was always out of coffee. It got to the point where he brought extra coffee every time he rode this trail.

Will led Ed up to the base of one of the higher hills where nature had formed a corral made of boulders. The opening that served as an entrance to it had three timbers across it that functioned as a gate. Inside were three horses. The two deputies looked the place over from the cover of a thick stand of pine trees. Will pointed to a solid-rock opening up near the top of the slope. "That's the front entrance. The cave is about forty feet long and has a back door. That stream you see runs right through the cave. It's hard to beat for a hideout. One of us can stand near the front and yell for 'em to come out and surrender, while the other one can cover the back door and arrest 'em when they run out the back. You're the lead deputy on this job. Which do you wanna do?"

"What if they don't come out?" Ed asked.

"Then I reckon we'll go in after 'em," Will answered. "Either that or we could steal their horses and make 'em come after them. So, what you want, front or back?"

Ed thought for a few seconds. "I'll stay in front and call 'em out. I don't know exactly where that back door is, so you might be better at that. Is that all right with you?"

"Fine by me," Will said. "You just give me about fifteen minutes to get in position behind that cave." He turned Buster to leave, then paused to warn Ed. "Be sure you've got some cover before you go hollerin' up at that cave. Be careful you don't get shot."

"You don't have to warn me about that," Ed assured him.

Will circled around the hill to come up from

26

behind the stone tunnel. He left Buster in a clump of small trees and climbed up through the rocks until he came to the opening to the small passage that led back into the cave. *If I had forgotten where it was, I coulda found it anyway,* he thought when he approached it and saw smoke drifting up out of the opening in the rocks.

He hadn't been in position longer than a couple of minutes when he heard Ed yell out his warning. "You, in the cave! This is U.S. Deputy Marshal Ed Pine. Come out of there with your hands up!"

There was no response from the cave, so Ed repeated his orders. Inside, Zeke Bowers whispered, "What the hell . . . ?" He gaped, wide-eyed, at his brother, Ike.

"How'd he find this place?" Ike whispered back. "The law ain't supposed to know about this place."

"That bowlegged little rat got the law up here," Zeke said. "What are we gonna do?"

"We need to see if he's by hisself," Ike said. He dropped the piece of venison he had been chewing on and crawled up near the front of the cave to try to see if he could spot Ed. Zeke crawled up behind him.

"Can you see him?"

"Nah, I can't see him," Ike replied. "I can't see the bottom of the cliff unless I crawl out in the open, and I ain't gonna do that."

"Can you see anythin'?" Zeke insisted.

"I told you, I can't see him, but I can see that there ain't no posse settin' down there waitin' for us to come outta here. He might be all by his lonesome."

"There's no use in stallin'," Ed called out again. "You're surrounded. I'm givin' you a chance to come on outta there and make it easy on yourself."

"You got no business botherin' us," Ike shouted back. "We ain't the ones that robbed that store in McAlester."

"Damn, Ike," Zeke whispered. "You shouldn'ta said that. He might notta even knowed about it."

"Come on out with your hands up and we'll talk about it," Ed yelled.

"He's by hisself," Ike said to Zeke. Then he turned his head toward the opening again and yelled, "We ain't comin' out! Looks like you're gonna have to come in and get us!" Back to his brother again, he said, "Let him come on in. We'll fill him so full of holes you can use him for a strainer."

"Hot damn!" Zeke exclaimed. "We ain't never shot a lawman before. Tell him to come on up here and get us."

"That ain't a good idea today or any other day," Will said, standing twenty-five feet behind them. Both brothers froze for a moment before they were sure, then they spun around, reaching for their guns. Ike was the quickest, so he caught Will's first shot in the shoulder, the result of which knocked him back flat on the stone floor of the cave. His pistol bounced off the solid rock as it dropped from his hand. With a new round already cranked in the chamber of Will's Winchester 73, Zeke found himself looking at sudden death. He wisely dropped his weapon.

"You all right in there, Will?" Ed Pine shouted from in front of the cave, already running toward the entrance after he heard the shots.

"Everything's all right, Ed," Will answered him. "You can come on in." He pointed his rifle at Zeke and motioned with it toward Ike, who was sitting on the floor of the cave holding his arm, a .44 slug in his right shoulder. "You can give your partner a hand with that wound," Will said to Zeke.

"He needs a doctor," Zeke said after a quick look at his brother's wound. "He's bleedin' awful bad."

"Take his bandanna off and stuff it over that wound," Will said. Ed walked in at that moment. "These are the two outlaws that held up that store in McAlester," he said to Ed, hoping Ed would realize he was bluffing. They had received no notice of a store robbery in McAlester before they left Fort Smith.

"Right," Ed came back right away, picking up on Will's bluff. "We figured they'd be here." He

29

holstered his .44 and picked up the two dropped pistols. "Good thing we brought the jail wagon. These two are gonna have plenty of company, but Horace is gonna have to pick up some more supplies in Atoka," he said, thinking about the three men they had actually come for.

"I expect so," Will said, then directed a question to Zeke. "How much of that money have you got left?"

"Ain't got none of it left," Zeke replied.

Still bluffing, Will said, "What? That fellow said you two took over two hundred dollars outta his store."

Both Ike and Zeke reacted immediately. "He's a lyin' horn toad!" Ike exclaimed. "There warn't but thirty-seven dollars in that drawer and we spent all of it that night."

Ed looked at Will and shook his head. Both men were thinking of the cost of transporting the two petty criminals back to jail in Fort Smith. It would amount to more than the two of them had stolen. The temptation to just run them out of the hideout and tell them to get out of the Nations was great. But they had foolishly confessed to the robbery of a store, so they had to arrest them and give them a day in court. "All right," Will finally ordered, "pick up your belongings and we'll walk on outta here, nice and peaceful. If you've got any sense at all, you won't risk your life tryin' to make a run for it."

They marched them down to their horses and waited while Zeke helped Ike up on his horse. Then with each deputy holding the reins of one of the two brothers' horses, they led them back to Merle's cabin, where they were transferred to the jail wagon. Horace Watson's reaction upon seeing the two petty thieves was the same as Ed and Will's. "It's gonna be nice and cozy on the way back to Fort Smith," he observed. "I'm gonna have to have some more food if we're gonna eat on the way back."

Standing by while the transfer to the jail wagon was taking place, Merle could finally hold his comments no longer. "You're lucky these two lawmen came to getcha 'cause I was fixin' to shoot your sorry asses next time you came stealin' around my place."

"You ain't got nothin' worth stealin'," Zeke responded.

Ike, confident now that he wasn't going to bleed to death, saw fit to join in. "I don't know, Zeke, that deer was pretty good eatin'. We was waitin' for you to go huntin' again."

"Get them two skunks offa my property," Merle demanded.

"That we will," Ed said, and closed the lock on the jail wagon. Will climbed up into the saddle, led them out of the maze of hills that hid Merle's cabin, and picked up the trail to Atoka again. The extra horses were on a rope tied to the back

31

of the jail wagon. Their owners were already complaining after finding they were going to Atoka before making the trip back to Fort Smith.

As they had anticipated, it took them two and a half days to reach Atoka. At the end of each day, they found a stream to camp by. Horace took care of the cooking and the prisoners were released from the wagon and shackled to a long chain for the night, with one end locked around the axle of the wagon. It was the typical fashion in which prisoners were handled, but not the way Will Tanner preferred. He had always felt hampered by a slow-moving wagon and had a running argument with Dan Stone about using one. On this occasion, however, he didn't complain, especially since it was possible they would end up transporting five prisoners back to Fort Smith.

They rolled into Atoka in the early evening and Horace picked a spot near the creek to park the jail wagon and set up his camp. While Ed stayed with him to guard the prisoners, Will rode up Muddy Boggy Creek to Jim Little Eagle's cabin outside of town. The Choctaw policeman walked out of his barn as Will rode into the yard. "Will Tanner!" Jim greeted him. "I thought maybe they send you." He was always glad to see Will. They had worked together many times in the past. "Mary!" Jim called toward the cabin.

In a minute, Mary Light Walker stepped out on the small front porch. "Will Tanner!" She repeated her husband's greeting and stepped off the porch to join them.

"Mary, Jim," Will greeted them in order and stepped down from the saddle. "Stone sent me and Ed Pine, too." When both Jim and Mary looked past him toward the road, Will explained. "Ed's back in town with Horace Watson and a jail wagon. He's set up camp on the other side of the railroad tracks." He went on to explain the acquisition of two prisoners he had not planned on and the need to do something with them while they investigated the problem Jim had wired Fort Smith about. "Anybody in that jail of yours?"

"No," Jim answered. "The jail's empty, has been for a couple of weeks."

"Good," Will said. "Maybe we can put these two jaspers in there for safekeepin' till we come to some kinda answer to your problems here in Atoka."

"You no stay for supper?" Mary asked.

"I reckon not this time," Will replied, "and I surely am disappointed, too. But I've got Ed and Horace and two fellows in the jail wagon back in town. So, I reckon I'll just have to miss out on enjoyin' one of your fine suppers." He shook his head and smacked his lips. "You know when I'm workin' up this way, I always try to hit town here in time to get invited to eat at your table."

She laughed, delighted. "You know you always welcome, Will Tanner."

"I'll saddle my horse," Jim said, "and go back to town with you. Maybe those three drifters will give you a show tonight like they do on some nights." He looked at Mary and said, "You might have to keep my supper warm in the oven till I get back."

"We'll try not to keep you from your supper," Will said. "Just open up that jail for us, then Ed and I can watch the town tonight. If they don't show up in town tonight, maybe we can find out where they're holed up tomorrow."

"No problem there," Jim said at once. "I know where they stay, where every no-good outlaw troublemaker stays. They stay at Mama's Kitchen in Boggy Town."

"Say what?" Will responded, not sure he had heard correctly.

"Mama's Kitchen," Jim repeated. "Big fellow named Tiny McGee built it about three miles east of town on Muddy Boggy Creek. He named it that, so the law might think it's a place to eat, but it's nothing but a saloon."

"Well, I'll be . . . ." Will started. "It wasn't here the last time I rode through, and that ain't been but four or five months. And I ain't ever heard of Boggy Town."

"That McGee fellow started calling it that. I think he's planning to start his own little town for outlaws on the run. He put some buildings up fast," Jim said. "He's selling whiskey to outlaws coming up from Texas, and he's selling rotgut firewater to my people at the back door. He's hauling whiskey in by the barrel, fills his bottles out of the barrels. That's for his white customers. The Indians have to bring a fruit jar to hold their firewater."

"Sounds like your problem is more than three hell-raisers shootin' up the town," Will said. "And it sounds like some big trouble for me, if this Boggy Town catches on."

"That's why I send for marshals," Jim said. "I wanted you to see for yourself."

"This ain't no damn jail," Zeke complained when Jim Little Eagle unlocked the door to the converted storehouse. "This ain't nothin' but a smokehouse. You can't lock us up in there."

He was not far off in his appraisal, but the storehouse had been fixed up to accommodate prisoners, complete with one small window and two straw pallets. Will had used it before to hold prisoners for a short time. "It'll do for you two hams," Will said.

"What about my brother?" Zeke asked. "He's still bleedin' like a stuck hog. He needs a doctor."

"I'm goin' to the doctor's office right now," Will replied. "Then we'll see about gettin' you some supper. Before long, you'll be so comfortable here you won't wanna leave." Will hoped it was still early enough to catch the doctor in his office, so he hurried up the street to get him while Horace filled a water bucket for the prisoners. Ed stayed behind and put an empty bucket inside the jail for the prisoners' convenience. Jim Little Eagle went with Will.

Dr. Franklyn Lowell's office door was locked when they arrived, so they walked around the building and knocked on the back door. In a few minutes, the door opened and Dr. Lowell stood there, glaring down at the two lawmen. "Jim Little Eagle and Will Tanner," he called back over his shoulder to his Choctaw cook and housekeeper. Turning back to Jim and Will, he complained, "It's always suppertime when you two come looking for me. Don't you ever shoot anybody when I'm not fixing to sit down to eat? Who's shot this time?"

"Howdy, Doc," Will greeted him. "Good to see you again, too. We've got a prisoner down in the jail with a bullet in his shoulder. I'd 'preciate it if you could take a look at him." He had used Dr. Lowell's services on other occasions and he couldn't remember a time when it wasn't inconvenient to the stocky little white-whiskered physician.

Recognizing Will's playful bit of sarcasm, Doc snorted to show it didn't bother him. "It's about time you showed up around here," he said. "It's time somebody did something about those three saddle tramps that take delight in shooting up the town. It's just a matter of time before I'm gonna have to take a bullet out of somebody who catches a stray shot."

"Yes, sir," Will responded. "I've got another deputy with me. We're gonna see what we can do. These two men we've got in the jail didn't have anything to do with shootin' up the town and one of 'em needs a doctor. Of course, I'll pay your fee."

Doc turned to face his housekeeper. "How long till those chops are done, Lila?" She told him she had not put them in the pan yet. "Well, wait on that till I get back. I won't be long. Get me my bag." He put on his coat while she hurried to fetch his bag. Will turned to Jim and suggested he might want to ride back and get his supper. Jim agreed and said he'd return after supper.

"You think your three hoodlums are gonna put on a show tonight?" Will asked Jim when they walked back to the jail with Doc Lowell.

"Maybe, maybe not," Jim Little Eagle answered. "They got to get good and drunk first." From what Jim had told them about the three men before, it appeared there was no motive behind their mischief other than the pure enjoyment of scaring the peaceful citizens of the town. His concern was that in their drunkenness, their shots were often wild, causing damage to windows and doors. As Doc had complained, he feared it was only a matter of time before someone was struck by a stray bullet.

"From what you've just told us, there's grounds enough to arrest 'em," Will said. "So, we'll just wait to see if they're still around. Ain't that what you say, Ed?" he asked as they arrived at the jail. Ed smiled and agreed. He knew Will was trying to remember who was supposed to be in charge. "Like I said, you might as well go on home and eat your supper," Will repeated to Jim. "Course, you're welcome to eat with us. Horace is fixin' to fry up some bacon right now."

"Thanks just the same," Jim replied. "I'll go to the house now. I'll be back after I eat." He jumped on his horse and rode back up the creek.

As Doc had told Lila, he didn't take long to remove the .44 slug from Ike's shoulder. He didn't concern himself with his patient's comfort. Ed Pine commented to Will afterward, "Hell, I coulda done that with my skinnin' knife." Will agreed with him but pointed out that there would probably have been a higher risk of infection. He then reminded Ed that he was just a posseman on this job. Ed was the deputy marshal and, as such, it was his responsibility to pay the doctor. "So that's the way it's gonna be," Ed joked. "All right, I'll pay Dr. Lowell and I'll make sure Dan Stone remembers to pay you a posseman's pay."

"Hey, Doc, I'm gonna need some medicine for my pain," Ike called after the doctor when he went out the door and Ed locked it.

"They're fixing to give you some supper," Doc

38

answered him through the door. "That'll do you just fine."

"He's eat-up with compassion for his patients, ain't he?" Ed commented aside to Will. "I'm glad he didn't do the job on my wounds."

Doc paused to complain before he started back up the street. "Next time you shoot one of these outlaws, bring him to my office instead of dragging me down here." He started again, but stopped to add, "And don't bring him at suppertime."

"Whatever you say, Doc," Will responded.

By the time Doc had finished and collected his fee, Horace had a fire going back at his camp by the creek with side meat in the pan and coffee working away. When it was ready, he brought it up to the jail and Will went in with him to guard the prisoners while Horace laid dinner out for them on the small table in the center of the cell. After the Bowers brothers were fed, Will and Ed went back with Horace to get their supper. The town seemed quiet enough as darkness began to set in, but there were still lights on in a few of the shops. Tom Brant had not taken in his display of long-handled shovels he had in front of his store, and Lottie Mabry's dining room was still busy. The two deputy marshals and their cook sat by the fire drinking coffee, enjoying the peaceful night. Horace produced another coffee cup for Jim Little Eagle to use when he returned to join them.

CHAPTER 3

Their pleasant evening came to a close, however, signaled by a single shot that sent two boarders on the porch of Mabry's boardinghouse running for their lives. As Jim had predicted, that shot was followed by an explosion of gunshots, accompanied by drunken whooping and hollering as three riders galloped the length of the main street. With nothing and anything as targets, they fired at the shops and stores as they passed, sending anyone caught on the street diving for cover.

Dropping their cups where they sat, Will and Ed scrambled to their feet and sprinted toward the street, leaving Horace to take care of the camp. They stopped at the corner of Brant's General Merchandise, which was about the halfway point in the street. Down at the end, the three bullies wheeled their horses and prepared to make another wild pass back up the street. "First thing we need to do is get their attention," Will said. He stepped up on the porch and grabbed one of the shovels from Tom Brant's display, then hopped back down beside Ed. "If you'll stand ready with that rifle, in case they don't wanna talk, I'll see if I can get their attention." He was watching the three closely as they picked up speed, pushing their horses to gallop. The rider he picked was Bob Atkins, since he was closest to that side of the street, then Will remained hidden behind the front corner of the store. He knew his timing was key in what he was about to attempt, so he held back until the riders were almost even with him. Then with only seconds to spare, he stepped out to the edge of the street. And in one motion, he set his feet solid under him and swung the shovel with all the force he could muster.

The back of the metal shovel blade caught Atkins square on his chest with his gun hand up over his head as he fired a shot in the air. The impact of the shovel against his chest, plus the speed of the galloping horse, was enough to stop Atkins right where he was while his horse continued on up the street. For a brief moment, Bob was suspended in midair, his feet kicking like a swimmer treading water, until he landed solidly on his backside. Still not sure what had happened because he got only a brief glimpse of Will at the edge of the street just before the blow, he blinked rapidly at the muzzle of the Winchester in his face. A couple dozen yards up the street, Raymond and Stump reined their horses back hard when Bob's saddle was suddenly emptied. When they wheeled their horses to come to his aid, they found themselves staring at Ed Pine, his rifle aimed in their direction. "Drop 'em," Ed ordered. "I ain't gonna say it again." There was not enough intelligence between the two drifters to fill a whiskey glass. But they had enough sense to know that one of them was going to lose in a shoot-out with the one rifle, and it was hard to tell which one of them Ed had his sights on. They dropped the pistols. "Now climb down off them horses. You're under arrest for disturbin' the peace and threatenin' the lives of everybody on this street."

They did as Ed ordered, but Stump protested. "We ain't threatened nobody in this town."

"That's right," Raymond Atkins said. "We was just makin' a little noise. You ain't got no cause to arrest us."

"I reckon we'll let the judge decide that," Will said, and took the six-gun out of Bob's hand before he had a chance to realize he was still holding it. "Now get on your feet," Will directed, and stood back to give him room.

Bob made a painful effort to comply, complaining as he did. "You damn nigh broke my back. I ain't sure I can walk."

"You'll make it, all right," Will said. "It ain't a long walk to the jail. Maybe you can lean on your friends for help." Bob got on his feet then and wobbled over to stand next to his brother. "All right," Will ordered. "Unbuckle those belts and let 'em drop to the ground." When they did so, he told them to take a step back. As soon as they did, Ed moved in and started picking up the gun belts.

Seeing a chance to make a move while Ed was bent over picking up the belts, Raymond nodded to his brother. Understanding what he was about, Bob took a step forward in an attempt to block Will's view, so he couldn't see Raymond reach for the pocket pistol he carried in his vest. It was a poor attempt to surprise the deputy, for Will took a step to the side when he saw Bob step forward. When Raymond drew the derringer from his vest and pointed it at Ed's head, Will had no option but to cut him down. It happened so quickly that he had no time to place his shot to simply wound him. Consequently, he shot Raymond dead center in his chest, killing him instantly.

Not sure what had happened, Ed hit the ground and rolled over to level his pistol at the prisoners. He gaped in surprise as Raymond Atkins dropped the little two-shot pocket pistol and slumped to the ground. He almost shot Bob when he dropped to his brother's side, but Will stopped him with a sharp warning not to shoot. "If either of you two have one of those on you, you'd best get it out now," Will advised. Stump opened his coat wide to show that he wasn't carrying one. Kneeling beside his brother's body, Bob glared up at Will after he realized Raymond was dead. The intense look of fury in his eyes told Will that he had made a deadly enemy at that moment. In the next moment, he heard the sound of galloping hooves as Jim Little Eagle charged into town.

"I heard all the shooting," Jim exclaimed when he pulled the paint gelding to a stop. He slid off the horse and walked over to stand in front of the three. "I told you somebody was gonna get killed one night," he said to Bob Atkins, who was still kneeling by his brother. "Lucky it was one of you three."

"Go to hell, you damn Injun," Bob snapped back at him. "I shoulda shot you the day you walked in Mama's Kitchen."

"Take it easy, Bob," Stump cautioned. "Right now, they ain't got us for nothin' but disturbin' the peace. Raymond shouldn'ta tried it."

"That's right, white man. Looks like you ain't got much luck at all," Jim replied. He turned to Will and said, "I'll go get Ted Murdock and tell him to come get the body."

" 'Preciate it," Will said.

"What for?" Ed asked. "He don't need a haircut."

"It's been a while since you were in town," Jim answered him. "Murdock's not just a barber anymore. He took on the job of undertaker. He say not enough business for his barbershop." He looked at Bob and smirked. "He say Indians don't get haircuts." He climbed on his horse again and rode up the street to the barbershop, guiding his horse through the small crowd of curious spectators that had gathered once the shooting had stopped.

"I expect we'd best escort our two new

customers to the jailhouse," Will said. "Then we can take care of these horses." He looked over at Horace, who had come to join the other spectators. "How 'bout tyin' their horses up at the hitchin' rail, Horace? After we take these two to jail, I'll take 'em to the stable."

"What about him?" Horace asked, pointing to the late Raymond Atkins.

"I expect Jim will be right back with Ted Murdock," Ed answered him.

"I ain't goin' nowhere till you take care of my brother," Bob Atkins snarled, looking up, much like a badger cornered by hounds. "You ain't leavin' him to lay out here in the street with all these strangers gawkin' at him."

"He's your brother, huh?" Will asked. "Well, I can see why you're grievin' so much now. It's a shame he tried to use that pocket pistol on the deputy, but I had a choice, and I chose to save the deputy's life. Your brother made a choice and it was a bad one. I'd advise you not to make one, too. Anyway, Horace, here, will take care of your brother's body till the undertaker comes to pick him up. So, get on your feet and start walkin'."

"I ain't leavin' till I see that undertaker," Bob said, and dropped from his kneeling position to sit on the ground defiantly.

"I think you've got yourself a little mixed up in the way these things are done," Will said patiently. "Let me set it straight for you. We're the arresting officers, so we decide what you'll do and what you won't do. Now, I'm gonna tell you again real politely, get on your feet and walk to the jailhouse."

Like a pouting child, Bob crossed his arms in protest and continued to sit beside his brother's body. "I reckon you're gonna have to shoot me, like you did my brother."

Still patient, Will said, "Believe me, I'm considerin' it." He turned to Ed, who was watching the debate between the lawman and the prisoner with some degree of amusement. "Deputy Pine, I wonder if you'd be so kind as to fetch me the rope offa that horse, there?" He nodded toward Stump Grissom's horse. Ed did so at once, eager to see what Will had in mind. Will took the rope and said, "Keep your gun on this fellow." Then he took the rope and quickly tied one end of it around Bob's boots, before the determined outlaw could deter him. Then Will tied the other end to the saddle horn on Stump's horse. "Now, Deputy Pine, if you'll walk our other prisoner, we'll take 'em to jail." That said, he took the horse by the bridle and started toward the jail, dragging Bob Atkins, protesting and cursing, over the deep wagon ruts of the street. It was only for a distance of about forty yards but seemed three times that far to Bob before Will stopped the horse in front of the jail. He untied Bob's ankles and stepped back to let him get to his feet, his .44 covering him, while he unlocked the door. He waited for a few seconds to throw the latch until Ed walked his prisoner to the door.

"Stand back away from the door," Ed ordered. "We brought you some company." Ike and Zeke Bowers stepped back to the back wall of the one-cell jail, gawking at the two new arrivals. They, in turn, stared back at them, wondering what manner of outlaw was occupying the makeshift jail. Noticing the silent scrutiny from both sides, Ed commented, "Now, you fellers can introduce yourselves. Give you a chance to make some new friends. If you behave yourselves, we might feed you some breakfast in the mornin'."

With the back of his coat and trousers tangled and dirty from his trip to the jail, Bob Atkins turned to look Will in the eye. "You dirty skunk," he threatened, "you've got the upper hand right now. But you shoulda shot me when you shot my brother. This ain't over between you and me. Don't matter how long they send me to jail, I'll come lookin' for you when I get out. And I'm thinkin' it ain't gonna be for long for doin' nothin' but disturbin' the peace."

" 'Preciate the warnin', Bob," Will responded. "I'll remember to keep an eye out for you." He looked at Ed and said, "Now, I reckon we can tell the judge that Bob, here, threatened the life of an officer of the law."

With the four of them locked up, Will and Ed

led the three extra horses down to the stables to see if Stanley Coons had locked up for the night. Jim Little Eagle rode along beside them. Coons was in the process of locking the back door to his barn when they got there. He knew both of the deputies and was happy to take care of the horses, knowing he would be paid for them. After that was done, the question of dealing with Mama's Kitchen and Tiny McGee was next on their agenda. "Now's as good a time as any," Will suggested. "Everybody oughta be through with supper and we can see what kind of business McGee is doin' now. If he's runnin' a saloon, now's about the time the drinkin' really gets started." Ed agreed, so they went back to the wagon to get their horses. Jim was of a mind to accompany them, but Will was not sure that was a good idea. "I don't know what we might run into in that place, but if it's trouble, I don't wanna risk havin' them out after you, tryin' to get even. Ed and I will be goin' back to Fort Smith after this, but you'll still be here with a wife and your home to worry about. And I wouldn't want you to suffer from any acts of revenge, just because they couldn't get to me or Ed." Ed agreed and Jim appreciated their concern. Although he was ready to make the visit with them, he saw their logic and decided to wait to see them in the morning. He told them how to find Mama's Kitchen and wished them good hunting.

After Jim left to go home, Ed looked at Will and asked, "How many do you think that jail wagon will hold?" It was said as a joke, but both deputies were thinking of a possible situation where they might arrest Tiny McGee for selling whiskey in Indian Territory.

They pulled their horses to a stop about forty yards short of the path that led down to the little cluster of log buildings sitting on the bank of Muddy Boggy Creek. From there, they could see the front of the main building and what appeared to be a long addition behind it. "What the hell is that on the back?" Ed asked. "It almost looks like a bunkhouse," he said, answering his own question. It raised a suspicion with both lawmen of the possibility that McGee was expecting to provide accommodations for anyone on the run from the law outside the boundaries of Indian Territory. If so, it was a pretty brazen move on McGee's part to locate it so close to Atoka. The typical outlaw hideout was located in a remote area, like the Arbuckle Mountains west of the MKT Railroad, or the Sans Bois to the east. "There are two horses tied at the hitching rail in front of the building, so it looks like he's got a little business."

"Let's ride on down there and maybe Mr. McGee will be glad to tell us what his plans are," Will said, and gave Buster a nudge.

The rough sign that said MAMA'S KITCHEN was just barely able to be read in the light coming from the window. "Has a nice homey feel to it, don't it?" Ed quipped as they dismounted and stepped up on the porch. They paused by the door to listen for a minute or two before entering. Other than the occasional raising of someone's laughter, it sounded pretty quiet. He pushed the door open and Will followed him inside, where they paused again to look over the smoky room. The thought struck both deputies that it might be claiming to be a dining room, but the most prominent fixture that greeted the customer's eye was the twenty-five-foot bar on one side. And the bald little man wearing an apron behind it looked very much like a bartender. "I expect we could buy a drink of likker here if we was inclined to," Ed commented.

"I expect so," Will replied, and they walked over to the bar, as Bud Tilton looked them over very closely.

"Evenin', boys," Bud greeted them. "Always glad to see new customers. What's your pleasure?"

"Well, we'd probably enjoy a drink of whiskey," Will answered him. "But you ain't allowed to sell whiskey in the Nations. Ain't that right?"

Bud's sallow face lit up with an impish smile. "Well, that's a fact, all right, but I think I can fix you boys up with a little firewater."

"How can you do that?" Ed asked. "It's against the law, ain't it?"

His response served to make Bud suddenly nervous. He called out toward a table where two men who looked like cowhands were sitting, talking to a woman and a huge man. "Tiny, you might better wait on these two gentlemen." Tiny looked up to give Will and Ed a quick look, then got up and came over to the bar.

"What's the trouble, boys?" Tiny asked.

Will brushed his coat aside to reveal his badge. "We're U.S. Deputy Marshals and it looks like somebody forgot to tell you that it's against the law to sell alcoholic beverages in the Nations."

McGee drew himself up to emphasize his unusual size, obviously accustomed to intimidating people. "Well, now, Deputies, I'm damn sure aware of that, but Mama's Kitchen is a dinin' room. And the kitchen is closed right now 'cause supper's over. We ain't sellin' no whiskey."

"Your bartender said he could fix us up with a drink, and that's sure as hell a whiskey bottle settin' on that table," Ed said, and nodded toward the two men sitting there with Ida Simpson.

Tiny gave his bartender a quick frown, but quickly turned back to the lawmen, smiling as he replied, "Those two fellers brought that with 'em. I didn't sell it to 'em. They eat here all the time, and they like to take a little drink after supper. So they bring a bottle in with 'em and I let 'em set at one of my tables if they want to. I figure it's against the law to sell it in Injun Territory, but it ain't against the law to drink it in Injun Territory. Besides, we're a good way from town where we ain't botherin' nobody. Just sorta mindin' our own business, you know." He paused to judge the reaction of the two lawmen, then continued. "Bud probably just meant he'd ask 'em if they'd give a couple of strangers a drink. So, like I said, supper's already over and the kitchen's closed, so I reckon there ain't nothin' more I can do for you boys."

"What's the bar for?" Will asked.

Tiny's smile gradually took the shape of a smirk, with no attempt to hide his irritation. "This ain't a bar," he said. "It's a sideboard to hold dishes and napkins and tablecloths and such."

"So, if I looked behind that sideboard, I wouldn't see any whiskey bottles and shot glasses?" Will asked. When Tiny didn't answer right away, Will motioned toward the table. "And I reckon that lady sittin' with those two fellows wouldn't jump in the bed with me for a couple of dollars."

Clearly struggling to hold on to his composure, Tiny replied, "That lady is a waitress, and I ain't got no idea if she'd jump in the bed with you or not. That ain't none of my business." It was becoming painfully clear to him that he was not fooling the two deputies, and he was uncertain if an offer of a payoff was what they had really come for. He decided to drop the bait, just in case. "If I *was* runnin' a saloon here, which I ain't, I expect you'd figure I'd offer a little money for you to look the other way."

"If you were to do that," Will said, "then we'd have to haul you off to court for tryin' to bribe two law officers. Wouldn't you say, Ed?"

"I expect so," Ed replied at once.

"Good thing I ain't offerin' no money, then, ain't it? Like I said, I'm tryin' to run a dinin' room here. I ain't runnin' a saloon."

"You wanna tell him?" Will asked Ed.

"You go ahead," Ed replied at once, content to let Will do the talking.

Will nodded and continued. "Here's the situation, Mr. McGee. We've had reports in Fort Smith that you were sellin' whiskey down here." That was not true, but he figured it carried more weight if it appeared that Tiny's activities were well known. "Deputy Pine and myself were sent down here to verify it, and I think we have. Now, you are guilty of breaking the law, but I think the Federal Court for the Western District of Arkansas is willin' to cut you some slack if you close your liquor business down today. Deputy Pine and I will be watching your place pretty close from now on to see who's comin' and goin'. We'll be arrestin' your customers who have been drinkin'. There's two of your customers in jail right now for drunken, disorderly conduct and disturbin' the peace. It's unfortunate that one other man with 'em decided to resist arrest and now he's dead. We mean to stop the sale of alcohol, so if you don't think you can make it as a dinin' room, I think the best thing for you to do would be to move on outta the Nations. We're givin' you this chance to clear out, even though you've already broken the law. Save us the trouble of transportin' you all the way back to Fort Smith. So, you close this place down and you won't have to go to prison, and we won't have to haul you back to Fort Smith. Everybody wins. Now, that's a fair deal, and one that the Marshals Service don't offer very often."

Tiny didn't respond for a long minute. When he did, it was with a high degree of skepticism. "Just the two of you, huh? You're gonna do all that arrestin' and jailin' all the customers I'm expectin' to show up here? You can make a helluva lot of enemies when you stand between a man and his whiskey."

"No," Will replied. "We wired Fort Smith a couple of days ago, after so many of the folks in Atoka complained about what was goin' on down here. There's a posse of deputies already on their way, and a company of Texas Rangers have offered to come up to give us a hand if there's any trouble." He took care not to make eye contact with Ed for fear he might give the lie away.

Tiny was not sure he believed it, but he was a little fearful not to. He had spent a lot of money to get his buildings up in a hurry and he built them in an agreement with Ward Hawkins, who was going to sell cattle in Texas for whiskey to sell in Indian Territory. The cattle would be stolen cattle, of course. That was Ward's specialty, and he would get the word out that the place to hide out was Boggy Town. And then these two lowdown-snake deputy marshals came along. He was expecting Ward to show up here in Indian Territory any day now. It might not be a good thing if all those lawmen arrived when Ward did.

It occurred to him that, if they were bluffing about the posse and the Rangers, the best thing to do was to put the two of those deputies in the ground. Fort Smith would never know what happened to them. That was bad news about Stump Grissom and the Atkins brothers. He now knew why they had not returned from town yet. He was familiar with their work, and he might have had them take care of these two lawmen, although, if what this deputy said was true, they didn't come out too well with their earlier encounter this evening. He glanced over at the two men still sitting at the table. They rode in from Texas this evening with warrants on their heads for armed robbery and shooting a bank teller. *Hell,* he thought, *this oughta be right up their alley.* If he could interest them in taking care of the two lawmen, that might be the end of the threat. And if the deputies weren't bluffing, there wouldn't be any way the murders could be tied to him. He decided that was the gamble he would take, and with that in mind, he said to Will, "You win. You can tell your bosses in Fort Smith that I'll close my business down. You can give me two or three days to load up all my stuff and get outta here, can'tcha?"

"You're doin' a smart thing," Will said. "Course, we'll be keepin' a watch on you to see that you keep your word."

"Like I said," Tiny replied, "it'll take me a little time to get all packed up and shut the place down."

Will took a good look at the two men sitting at the table before he and Ed walked out the door. He wanted to make sure he would recognize them if he ran into them after this. "Man, what a tale you made up in there," Ed commented when they rode back up to the creek trail. "You think he believed a word of it?"

"I doubt it," Will answered.

"He said he'd pull up stakes and move out in two days," Ed said. "Maybe he did believe it."

"He just wanted us to get out of his hair tonight," Will replied. "He's thinkin', if there really is a posse already on their way, they'll be here in two days. If they don't show up, then he'll know he's just got you and me to deal with.

And I've got a pretty good idea how he intends to handle the problem of you and me. We'll see what he does tomorrow, see if he shows any signs of movin' outta that saloon."

CHAPTER 4

"What's the matter, Tiny?" Dave Harley asked when the big man came back to the table and sat down. "Who were those two jaspers? You didn't look like you was enjoyin' the conversation, did he, Tom?"

"I reckon not," Tom Freeman answered, and pulled his hand out of his lap to reveal the .44 he had put there when they saw Will open his coat to show his badge. "Me and Harley figured they looked like lawmen that mighta been askin' about us."

"Well, you're halfway right," Tiny said. "They was lawmen, all right, two deputy marshals outta Fort Smith. But they didn't know nothin' about you boys. They came in here to order me outta business for sellin' whiskey." He poured himself a drink out of the bottle on the table. "They expect me to pack up and move away from town just like that."

"Damn . . . U.S. Marshals," Harley drew out. "You gonna do it? Move out?"

"Hell, no, I ain't gonna move out," Tiny spat, getting madder by the moment. "After I built this place and spent every dime I had to fix it up for customers like you and Tom, I ain't shuttin' it down. No, sir."

"Well, ain't that some luck?" Tom remarked. "We hit town and the first thing we see is two deputy marshals where there ain't supposed to be no law a-tall. Ward Hawkins said Boggy Town was the place to go. Said there weren't no law but a Choctaw Injun, and he didn't have no jurisdiction over white men a-tall." He cocked his head and gave Tiny a sideways look. "You sure those two jaspers weren't lookin' for two fellers that shot a bank teller in Fort Worth?"

"I wouldn't lie about a thing like that," Tiny answered. "They were after me for sellin' whiskey and havin' a whore." That prompted him to ask, "Where'd Baby go? She was settin' here when they came in."

Harley laughed. "She got up and hightailed it to the kitchen when me and Tom pulled our .44s out and stuck 'em under the table."

Etta Grise came out of the kitchen at that moment. "You want anything else from the kitchen?" When no one said they did, she asked, "You want me to save anything for them other three? That little short feller, the one they call Stump, he had me save him a biscuit after supper last night."

"Nope," Tiny said. "He won't be eatin' no biscuit tonight. Those boys ended up in jail"—he paused—"at least two of 'em did. One of 'em got shot. It was one of the Atkins brothers, but I don't know which one."

"Well, now, that surely is a sorry piece of news," Etta said. "I reckon I'll throw them cold biscuits out. That is, if there's any of 'em left. Ida was workin' on 'em when I came out here."

"You'd best tell her to leave them biscuits alone," Harley commented. "She's hefty enough already. She gets any bigger and she'll get too big to throw a saddle on her."

They chuckled over Harley's remark, but Tom was still more concerned about the two lawmen that just happened to show up right after they hit town. "That one feller was lookin' real hard at us before they walked out the door. I don't know, Harley, maybe it ain't such a good idea to hole up here. Might be we oughta ride on outta here, head a little farther west, maybe over to the Arbuckle Mountains."

When Harley looked as if considering that possibility, Tiny was quick to respond. "You wouldn't have no place to get a drink or a good meal, if you were holed up in that little patch of mountains," he reminded them. "And you sure wouldn't have a friendly gal like Baby to take care of your needs." He paused to let that sink in, then continued. "It ain't nothin' but a stroke of bad luck that brought them lawmen in here to hassle me. I'm thinkin' it would be a simple problem to fix, though. Now that I've thought about it a little, I know those two jaspers were bluffin'. There ain't no posse on their way over here from Fort Smith, and I doubt the Texas Rangers know where the hell you two went. I'll tell you what else I'm thinkin'. I'm thinkin' it would be worth a hundred dollars a head to me to have them two lawmen rubbed out. That would take care of any problems I might have with 'em, and I reckon it would take care of anything you boys were worried about, too, wouldn't it?" He could tell by their expressions that he had caused a spark. "The only trouble is, Stump Grissom and one of the Atkins brothers are in jail. If they weren't, I'd have 'em take care of them deputies. And as much as they enjoy killin' lawmen, they'da done it for nothin', especially since they killed one of the brothers." He scratched his chin whiskers thoughtfully and said, "What I need to figure out is how to spring 'em from jail."

Tom and Harley exchanged glances, then both nodded. "Might be you don't need to get them boys outta jail, if you weren't just blowin' smoke about that hundred dollars a head," Harley said. "It didn't bother me none to shoot that bank teller, and there ain't never been nothin' wrong about shootin' a lawman. Ain't that right, Tom?" Tom said that it definitely was. He was thinking that two hundred dollars was almost as much as they got from robbing the bank.

"I'm a man of my word," Tiny responded. "Like I said, it would be worth one hundred a head to get rid of those two lawmen. I reckon I didn't think about you boys wantin' the job."

"So it's a deal?" Tom asked.

"It's a deal," Tiny answered, "and the sooner, the better."

"Well, I reckon tomorrow is soon enough, then," Harley said. "We'll just take a little ride into town in the mornin' and see if we can find 'em." He hesitated a moment. "I reckon that's where they'll be. That's where the jail is, ain't it?"

"We'll find out where they are," Tom said. "They might not be together, so we'll try to see if we can catch 'em when they are. That way, we could get the job done quicker and get outta town before some citizen has time to take a shot at us."

"That's a fact," Tiny agreed. "You don't wanna get just one of 'em and have the other'n comin' after you." *And me, too,* he was thinking.

"Most likely they'll be comin' back here to check on you. Why don't we just shoot the dirty rats down when they walk in?" Harley proposed.

"No," Tiny responded at once. "We don't want 'em killed anywhere close to this place. That might bring a posse here. You've gotta catch 'em in town or someplace outside of town, anywhere but here."

The planning might have been simpler had they known of a decision being made in town that night.

• • •

"What did you fellers decide?" Horace Watson asked when he walked over to the fire where Will and Ed were discussing their plans for the next day. He poured a cup of coffee for himself and sat down.

Ed answered him. "Well, like I was tellin' Will, we can't keep those four prisoners here in that little jail. We need to get started back to Fort Smith with 'em. This business with Tiny McGee down at Boggy Town was something we didn't know about or come prepared to handle. At least we took care of the problem we were sent down here to handle, so we need to take 'em to trial. Hell, we even arrested the two that robbed the store in McAlester. Will don't wanna leave till we put McGee outta business."

"Ain't no tellin' how long that's gonna take," Horace speculated. "That's a long time to hold those four, ain't it?"

"How about you and Horace transportin' those four prisoners back to Fort Smith, and I'll stay here and work on the problem at Boggy Town?" Will proposed. "Would you have any trouble with that?"

Ed shrugged. "No, I got no problem with that. I've transported more than four before. I'm more concerned with what you might run into by yourself."

"I ain't takin' it lightly," Will said. "But if we

don't keep after that big jasper, he's gonna have more and more outlaws on the run showin' up in Boggy Town. And before you know it, you're gonna need the army to come in and clear 'em out. If we can, I'd rather try to stop him before it gets to that point. Look at those two we saw in the saloon tonight. No tellin' what they're on the run for. And, hell, he's sellin' whiskey to the Indians, too. That's what's got Jim Little Eagle so worked up."

"All right," Ed said. "I'll load 'em up in the mornin' and start back to Fort Smith with 'em. You watch yourself, Will. That's a dangerous man you're messin' with, and he's got a lot invested in that damn Boggy Town he's tryin' to start up. When I get to Fort Smith, I'll most likely turn around and come back, maybe with some more help."

"I'll be careful," Will promised. "What about you, Horace? You won't have a posseman with you on the trip back. You okay with that?"

"I'm okay with it," Horace answered. "I'll be Ed's posseman and do the cookin', too."

Ed was in a hurry to get started the next day, so he had Will and Horace up well before daylight that morning to break camp. After the horses were hitched up to the jail wagon, Ed rigged a lead line and tied the extra horses they had picked up to it. Will kept the horse Raymond Atkins had ridden to use as a packhorse—the others would be taken to Fort Smith with the prisoners. When he was ready, Will unlocked the jail and they paraded four disgruntled prisoners outside. With shackles on their feet and their hands cuffed together, they complained bitterly over the sleepless night just passed. It was obvious that Stump and Bob didn't get along with the Bowers brothers. "What about some breakfast?" Stump Grissom protested. "You gotta feed us."

"When we stop to rest the horses," Ed replied. "Then we'll feed you." That brought on a chorus of grumbling from all four prisoners that continued well after they were all loaded into the jail wagon. The extra supplies Horace had acquired while Will and Ed had gone down to Boggy Town were loaded on the extra horses. When all was ready, Will wished them an uneventful journey and stood beside the jail wagon as Horace climbed up in the driver's seat. Ed climbed on his gray gelding and gave Will a little salute with a touch to the brim of his hat with his forefinger.

He stood back when Horace started his team of horses, and as the wagon rolled by him, he saw Bob Atkins glaring at him through the bars. "I ain't gonna forget you, Tanner," Bob growled.

"Is that a fact?" Will responded. "I reckon I'll always remember you, too." With no real plan for how he was going to approach the Boggy

Town problem, he stood and watched the wagon rolling slowly out of town. He hoped Dan Stone wasn't going to raise hell with him for staying behind. *Hope to hell Ed and Horace don't have any trouble,* he thought as he locked the jail door. *First thing to do is take the horses to the stable, then have myself a good breakfast at Lottie Mabry's dinin' room,* he decided.

"Set yourself anywhere you want, long as somebody else ain't already settin' there," An unfamiliar face greeted him when he walked into the dining room. "You want coffee?"

"Yep, I sure do," Will replied, then out of habit, he sat down at a small table against a side wall, facing the front door, while she went to fetch the coffeepot.

Lottie Mabry came from the kitchen at that moment, and upon seeing him, walked over to greet him. "Will Tanner," she said, "it's been a little while since you've been in town. I heard you put a stop to those three hell-raisers last night. It's a wonder somebody hasn't gotten shot by now."

"How've you been, Lottie?" Will responded. "I see you've got some new help since the last time I was here." As he said it, the newcomer arrived with his coffee.

"Yeah, I guess that's right," Lottie said. "Lou-Bell, this is U.S. Deputy Marshal Will Tanner." Turning back to Will, she said, "Will, this is

Louise Bellone. We call her Lou-Bell for short. It just seems to fit." Back to Lou-Bell, she said, "Will usually likes his eggs scrambled, sausage, fried potatoes, and biscuits." To Will again, she asked, "Is that about right, or have you changed your taste?"

"You sure have some memory," Will answered her, then said, "I'm pleased to make your acquaintance, Lou-Bell, and I reckon we'll go with what Lottie said." Lottie smiled, pleased with her memory. He decided that was as good a breakfast as any, even though he had set his mind on pancakes before he walked in. And to have ordered differently would have taken some satisfaction from Lottie.

"Take good care of him," Lottie said to Lou-Bell. "He stopped those three crazy hell-raisers last night." When Lou-Bell went to the kitchen to place Will's order, Lottie said, "Ted Murdock just left here a couple of minutes ago. He said you had to shoot one of those men."

" 'Fraid so," Will replied. "Things don't always go the way you want 'em to." He was afraid she wanted more details, but he was spared when she was called to another table. In short order, his breakfast was delivered, and Lou-Bell filled his cup again. He was glad to see the quality was as good as he remembered. When he finished, he told Lottie it was the best in the territory, as was his usual habit everywhere he ate.

He left the dining room and walked down the street to the stable to get his horse. He figured he might as well start watching the comings and goings at Mama's Kitchen. Stanley Coons saw him coming and walked out of the barn door to meet him. "Good morning, Will. I just gave that buckskin of yours a portion of oats. You fixin' to saddle him up?"

"Yep," Will replied, "I think I'll take a little ride down the creek."

"I saw Ed Pine and the jail wagon leavin' town early this morning." Stanley was about to say more when he suddenly spun around and dropped to the ground when he was struck in the shoulder. A fraction of a second after, the sound of the rifle rang out. In the next few seconds, that shot was followed by others. Reacting immediately, Will hit the ground, grabbed Stanley's collar, and dragged him behind the open door of the barn as a hail of bullets flew all about them.

"Hang on, I gotcha!" Will grunted as he continued to drag the wounded man. "We gotta find more cover than this door!" Even as he said it, the door started taking rounds from what Will figured to be more than one rifle. Once he got Stanley all the way inside the barn, he took a quick look at the shoulder wound, pulled his bandanna off, and stuffed it over the wound. "Here, hold this tight against that wound," he said. Dazed and partially in shock, Stanley just stared up at him, but he held the bandanna on his shoulder. "You're gonna be all right," Will assured him. "You just lie here and hold that wound while I try to see who's shootin' at us."

Up the street, at the back corner of the jailhouse, the two snipers hurriedly reloaded their rifles. "We got one of 'em!" Harley exclaimed. "I don't know if we got the other one or not. They both went down, but I don't know if that one that dragged the first one was hit."

"Damn it," Tom swore. "We shoulda got closer while they was standin' outside talkin'. Now what are we gonna do?"

"I don't know," Harley answered, "but I ain't plannin' on goin' in that barn lookin' for 'em." He walked over to the opposite corner to take a look up the street, concerned now about the possibility of gunfire from some of the merchants. "Ain't nobody stuck their nose out yet. I'm thinkin' we'd best make ourselves scarce before somebody decides to take a shot at us."

Still staring at the barn beside the stables, Tom said, "I don't see no sign of anybody comin' outta there. There's a heap of holes in that door. You reckon we mighta hit somethin'?"

"I don't know," Harley said. "Why don't you go down there and see? I'm gonna jump on my horse and get the hell outta here. We had a perfect chance and we messed it up. Let's go on back to Boggy Town. If that other one wasn't hit, he'll most likely come lookin' for us. We'll just shoot him down when he shows up."

"Tiny said he didn't want those deputies shot at his place," Tom reminded him.

"Yeah, well, things have changed, and we've got a better chance of gettin' that lawman if he shows up down there." He suddenly jumped backward when a chunk of siding next to his head suddenly flew up in the air and the report of a rifle sang out. "Damn!" he exclaimed. "I'm gettin' outta here!" He took off at a sprint for the horses in the trees forty yards behind the jail. Tom was right behind him.

Kneeling in the hayloft of Stanley's barn, Will swore under his breath for taking the shot when he really didn't have one. He took one more shot when he got a glimpse of a flying coat tail heading toward the creek behind the jail. Although anxious to get after them right away, he knew he had to take care of Stanley, so he went back down the ladder as quickly as he could. He found Stanley where he had left him, but he was sitting up now. "Did you see him?" he asked. "Why did he shoot at us?"

Will was glad to see that the wound was not that serious. "There was more than one," he said. "And I'm thinkin' you got hit because they thought you were either Ed Pine or me. We gotta get you to the doctor to take care of that shoulder. You think you can walk?"

"Yeah, I think I can," he replied, and started to struggle to get on his feet. Will took hold of his good arm and helped him up. When Stanley saw that he was steady on his feet, he looked at Will with a look of awe and stated, "I ain't ever been shot before. It's kinda like gettin' kicked by a horse."

"I reckon it is," Will agreed. "Can you make it to Doc's, or do I need to hitch up your buckboard?"

"I think I can make it," Stanley said.

Will gave him another looking-over and decided it best not to leave him to make it alone. "I'll tell you what, I'm gonna saddle Buster, anyway. I'll let him tote you up to Doc's."

"If you think so," Stanley said. "This is the first time I've ever been shot," he repeated, as if it was a rite of passage.

"Yep," Will responded. "This must be your lucky day." He went into the stable to fetch Buster. Working as fast as he could, he saddled the buckskin and helped Stanley up into the saddle. Then he led the horse up the street to Dr. Lowell's office.

Like most of the other residents of Atoka, Doc was standing out in front of his office to see what the trouble was, now that the shooting was over. "I should have expected you to show up here when I heard all that shooting. Business always picks up when you're in town." He cocked his head to give Stanley a sideways glance. "Didn't expect to see you mixed up in it, Coons."

In no mood to deal with Doc's cynicism at the moment, Will helped Stanley down off Buster. "He happened to get caught with some lead that was meant for me." He had a trail to follow that was getting colder by the minute, so he asked Stanley if he thought he could get back to the stable without help.

"Well, if he can't, I'll see that he gets home," Doc said, surprising them both. "You look like you're itching to go after whoever that was that did all the shooting, and I'd just as soon have you catch 'em."

" 'Preciate it, Doc," Will said. "I'll pay your bill when I get back." He stepped up in the stirrup and turned to Stanley. "I'm awful sorry you got in the way of those bullets."

"I ain't blamin' you, Will. Only thing is, you're gonna have to take care of your horses yourself when you get back," Stanley replied. Will threw his leg over and settled in the saddle, and Buster started out at a fast walk, heading for the last place Will got a glimpse of a flying coat tail. As he rode away, he heard Stanley telling Doc that this was the first time he had ever been shot.

Will paused briefly at the back corner of the jail to notice a great many empty shell casings scattered on the ground. They told him what he already knew, that this was where the snipers had set up to ambush him. In their haste to retreat, they had taken no pains to disguise their route of flight. Aided by an early-morning light rain, the tracks of two men running toward the trees by the creek were easy to see. Will didn't bother to dismount until halfway to the trees. He pulled Buster to a sudden stop and jumped down to examine the ground where the impressions on the wet ground looked to have been left by one of the men falling. Near the center of the marks, he saw several drops of blood and one blood smear. *Could be that second shot found meat,* he thought. But if it did, it must not have been serious because the impressions in the ground told him that the man had gotten on his feet again.

He looked now toward the creek. The tracks told him that both men continued on toward the trees. He stopped to make sure before following, but he could have easily seen their horses if they were hiding in the cottonwoods, waiting for him in ambush. Since they were not, he rode Buster into the trees. Although he was 99 percent sure where the two had fled, he climbed down from the saddle to search for a trail to follow, just to be totally certain. The tracks were not so easily seen once he reached the trees until he came upon a spot where their horses were tied. To make doubly sure he found the right spot, the horses had been thoughtful enough to leave fresh droppings for him to find. There was no mystery to solve. He felt pretty confident he was following the two men he had seen in Mama's Kitchen, and his purpose in scouting their trail was to make sure they were heading back there. Once he was satisfied they were not running in a different direction, he stopped looking for tracks and headed straight toward Boggy Town and Mama's Kitchen.

CHAPTER 5

Tiny McGee walked out on the front porch of Mama's Kitchen when he heard the sound of fast-approaching horses. He was surprised to see Harley and Tom back so soon. From the lathered appearance of their horses, he guessed that they had galloped them all the way back from town. "Did you get 'em?" he asked.

"Got one of 'em, for sure," Harley answered as he climbed down from the saddle. "The other one, maybe. They both went down."

"If you got both of 'em, why'd you have to wear those horses out to get back here?" Tiny wanted to know. "You ain't got a posse on your tail, have you?" Harley walked around to the other side of Tom's horse to give him a hand to get down. "What the hell?" Tiny exclaimed when he saw the blood on Tom's leg. "You've got a posse on your tail, and you're leadin' 'em right to my door," he quickly surmised. Immediately irate, he fumed, "I told you to keep this business away from my door!"

"Keep your shirt on, Tiny," Harley responded. "There ain't no posse chasin' us, and there ain't nobody saw us. There was somebody else up in the hayloft at the stables, and they started shootin' at the corner of the jailhouse where we was hidin'. So we decided to get outta there before somebody did see us." He looked at Tom, who was poking around the bullet hole in his lower leg. "And Tom was hit by a stray shot. Just plain bad luck, that's all that it was, but ain't nobody after us. Nobody saw us."

Tiny considered what Harley was saying and decided to believe him, so he calmed down a little. "Well, if you're sure, come on inside and Etta can take a look at that leg. It won't be the first bullet she's dug outta somebody's hide." He took another look at Tom, standing there holding on to his saddle horn in an effort not to put much weight on his left leg. "You look like you've been crawling in the mud."

Tom shook his head and grimaced. "I took a dive when we was runnin' for the horses. That bullet tripped me when it hit my leg, sent me for a tumble, I wanna tell ya. I landed flat on my belly." He unconsciously took a few swipes across his chest with his hand in an effort to brush some of the wet dirt off.

"Well, come on," Tiny said, and turned to go back inside. As soon as he was inside the door, he yelled, "Etta! We got a patient for you. Tom went out and got hisself shot in the leg."

In a few seconds, the scrawny little woman came into the saloon and stood, hands on hips, watching Tom limp into the room. "Must not be too bad if he can walk on it," she decided. "Bring him on in the kitchen." Without waiting to see if they did or not, she spun around and went back into the kitchen, where Ida Simpson sat at the table, drinking a cup of coffee with Teddy Green, who took care of the barn and stable, and Bud the bartender. "Set down on that chair," Etta directed Tom when he limped in behind her. She pointed to a chair in the corner close to the stove. "He got shot," she said to Ida, who was just before asking the question, as Etta opened the pantry door. She came out of the pantry carrying a bottle of whiskey.

"Good," Tom said when he saw it. "I could use a drink right now."

"It ain't for drinkin'," Etta replied. When he responded with such a pitiful expression, she shrugged and said, "Might help, at that." She picked up a glass and poured him a stiff drink. She proceeded to remove his boot and sock. That wasn't enough to give her access to the wound, since she couldn't pull his trouser leg up far enough. So she told him to drop his trousers and pull his wounded leg out of them. When Ida asked if she could help, Etta told her to fill the large dishpan with hot water from the kettle on the stove. Bud got up from the table and returned to the bar before Etta found something for him to do. "You were mighty lucky," she told Tom when she examined the wound. "There ain't no bullet in there. It went clear through. A little bit higher and it mighta broke your knee, but it didn't hit bone a-tall. Went in the back of your calf and out the front. Just dug a tunnel. I'll clean it up and wrap a bandage around it, and you'll be ready to go to the square dance."

"Maybe that's just what I'll do," Tom boasted, and tossed the rest of his drink back, "if I knew where there was a square dance. Maybe I'd take you with . . . Yow!" He yelled before he could finish, when she cleaned around the wound with the hot water. Before he could catch his breath again, she splashed whiskey all over the raw area. He let out another bellow, this one louder than the first.

"I'll bandage it up now and it'll heal up if you don't get it dirty," she said, and handed the bottle to Ida, who poured some in her coffee before setting it on the table.

With his leg bandaged and back in his trouser leg, Tom hobbled back into the saloon, carrying his boot and sock. "What was all that hollerin'?" Tiny asked, and winked at Harley.

"She poured whiskey on that wound," Tom answered, "and didn't give me no warnin' a-tall, just poured it on. It burnt like fire."

"What a waste of good likker," Harley commented. "You didn't holler that loud when the bullet hit you."

"That oughta tell you my whiskey ain't watered down none," Tiny said, and poured another drink for them. Getting back to a more serious issue, he said, "I know what the deal was, and I intend to pay you what I promised, but you can understand that I ain't payin' until I know for sure they're dead."

"Sure, Tiny," Harley said. "We ain't askin' you to. Might be best to wait a day or two, then ride into town to see if they're still there."

"I can save you the trouble." The statement came from the front door. They turned as one to see Will Tanner standing there, his rifle trained on them. All three bolted upright immediately, with Tom the first to reach for his six-gun. The front sight hadn't cleared his holster when the .44 slug from Will's rifle struck his chest. Harley, his eyes wide, as if seeing a ghost, started to go for his gun. But he threw his hands up when he saw that Will had already cranked the next round into the chamber and was gazing at him as if inviting him to try it. "Get on your feet," Will ordered. When Harley did so, Will ordered him to walk over away from the table before telling him to unbuckle his gun belt and let it drop to the floor. He did so as a precaution against Tiny making a move to go for Harley's gun. "Now kick it over this way." When he did, Will bent down, picked it up, and stuck it in his belt. "You're under arrest for the attempted murder of a U.S. Deputy Marshal and a citizen of Atoka." Aware that Bud was gradually working his way down the bar, and assuming there was a shotgun down at that end, Will warned him. "You, behind the bar, you can keep on inchin' down there to that shotgun. When you reach it, I want you to grab it by the barrel and lay it on the bar. If it comes up from under there with the barrel lookin' at me, I won't wait. I'll cut you down. You understand?" Bud nodded rapidly and reached under the bar and pulled out a double-barreled shotgun, carefully holding it by the barrel.

Since he was not wearing a gun, and Tom was sprawled on the floor on top of his, Tiny had no choice but to sit there and watch his bartender surrender the shotgun. When Will took a couple of steps over and picked up the shotgun from the bar, Tiny complained. "You got no right comin' into my place of business and shootin' people," he protested. "Harley's been here all the time."

"That's right," Harley spoke up. "I don't know what you're talkin' about. You just shot Tom for no reason a-tall. We ain't gone nowhere since you was in here last night."

"Is that a fact, Harley?" Will asked. "Is Harley your first name or your last name?" When Harley replied that it was none of his business, Will shrugged. "Well, in my way of thinkin', there's plenty of reasons to shoot somebody who's drawn a weapon and is fixin' to shoot me. And you say you ain't been anywhere? Well, somebody's been ridin' the hell out of your horses, and I'm wonderin' what caused that bloody leg on your late friend's body. I'm pretty sure I shot him in the chest just now." He motioned toward the door with the barrel of his rifle. "Now, start walkin' to that door, you're wastin' my time." Glancing at Tiny again, he warned, "You just stay right where you are till I tell you to move, and we'll be out of your way in a minute or two."

Feeling helpless to do anything about the invasion of his saloon, Tiny sat at the table as he had been ordered to do. He couldn't help wondering why Will was alone. He expected Ed Pine to come in from the back door at any minute. When he didn't, he finally asked, "Where's that other deputy?"

"He's takin' care of some other business," Will answered. "I expect you're wonderin' about the man who got shot at the stable. That was Stanley Coons, the owner, and that's one of the charges your friend, here, will stand trial for." Upon hearing that, Tiny shot an accusing glance in Harley's direction. It was returned with a shrug and a look of chagrin from Harley. When Harley started toward the door, Will motioned for Tiny to get on his feet. "I expect you'd best walk out with us."

"What for?" Tiny asked. "I sure as hell ain't had nothin' to do with whatever these two did in town."

"It would just be the sociable thing to do, since

he's one of your customers," Will answered. In fact, he was not willing to leave Tiny inside, unguarded, while he tried to get Harley on a horse and make his departure.

With thoughts along a similar line, Tiny remained seated. "I'll just set here till you're gone. Ain't no use for me to walk outside with you."

"I'm afraid I'm gonna have to insist," Will said, and brought his rifle around to aim it directly at him. "It's either that, or I'm gonna put a bullet in you to slow you down, so make up your mind."

Tiny did not react immediately, his dark, hairy features reflecting the anger he felt, believing that the stoic lawman would do exactly that. After a long moment when he locked his gaze with that of the lawman, he mumbled, "You weasel," and got up from the chair. Will marched the two disgruntled men out the door.

When they were outside, he directed Tiny to have a seat on the porch steps. Then he broke Bud's shotgun open, removed the two shells, and put them in his pocket. He threw the empty shotgun out in the yard while Harley climbed on one of the weary horses at the rail. To Harley's disappointment, the saddle sling that usually held his rifle was empty, causing him to curse.

When Harley was seated on his horse, Will reached in his saddlebag and pulled his handcuffs out. "Behind your back," he ordered with a tap on one of Harley's arms. Understanding, Harley put his hands behind his back. Still not trusting Tiny for even a minute, Will cocked his Winchester and leaned it against the post of the hitching rail, where he could snatch it up in a hurry. Keeping a watchful eye on the door, in case Bud found another weapon, he quickly clamped the cuffs around Harley's wrists. His precautions brought only a snort of contempt from the massive man seated on the steps. With Harley in the saddle, his hands behind his back, Will untied Harley's reins from the rail and held on to them while he picked up his rifle and stepped up on Buster. "I expect you'll be packin' up your belongin's and movin' outta here pretty quick now," he said to Tiny.

"Yeah," Tiny responded sarcastically, calling Will's bluff. "I expect I'd better, before that posse and all them Texas Rangers come ridin' in here." When Will started to leave, Tiny blurted, "What about the money them two owe me for stayin' here?"

"That fellow lyin' in there on the floor is the one to see about that," Will answered.

"What if he ain't got no money on him?" Tiny asked.

"Send your bill to the U.S. Marshals' office in Fort Smith."

"Yeah, and you can go to hell, too," Tiny responded. He figured he was going to get more than what the two of them owed him, because he would gain Tom Freeman's horse, saddle, and anything he had of value in his saddlebags.

"I'll be checkin' on you," Will promised. "Pack up your stuff and no more sales of whiskey to white or Indian." He wheeled Buster away from the rail and led Harley's horse toward the path that led to the creek trail. To McGee's disappointment, Tom's horse followed along behind Harley's. Will had saved himself a little time when he first arrived by tying one of the horses' reins behind the saddle of the other one. He had figured he was there to arrest two men and he might find himself a little busy while trying to get away without trouble from Tiny. He had no way of knowing which horse belonged to which outlaw. It just happened that Harley's turned out to be the lead horse. Once he reached the path, he urged Buster into a lope in case one of Tiny's people ran out right away with a rifle for him. Looking back, however, he could still see him seated on the steps, like an angry boulder. Will knew now that Tiny McGee was going to be difficult to shut down, and as hard to move out of the Nations as the boulder he resembled.

The problem facing him now, was what to do with his prisoner. The small converted storeroom that served as the jail had no office, no additional room of any kind. He couldn't transport his prisoner back to Fort Smith, a trip of more than two and a half days. That would be the normal procedure, but even if he returned to Atoka immediately, he would be away for at least five days. And he couldn't afford to let this business with McGee go on that long.

Behind him, an enraged Tiny McGee got up from the steps and walked out in the yard to retrieve the shotgun—fuming over the realization that one lone man had walked into his bar and overpowered the four of them.

Once Will was on the trail that followed the creek back to town, he eased Buster back to a walk. The two horses behind him had already been run pretty hard, so he thought it best not to push them. He still had the key to the jail, so he took Harley there right away and locked him up. Like everyone else he had locked in the small storeroom, Harley at once complained that it was not a real jail. He could still hear him complaining as he locked the door and took the horses down to the stable. Much to his surprise, Stanley Coons was at the barn. "Didn't expect to find you here," Will said when he led the three horses in. Jim Little Eagle was with him. "Thought you'd be home restin' your wound," Will said to Stanley.

"It ain't near as bad as I thought it would be," Stanley said. "I just ain't mucked out no stalls. I got Jimmy Barnet to do that for me for twenty-five cents a day. He's back in the stables now." He reached up and rubbed his shoulder. "I don't think it'll be any time at all before I get my arm outta this sling, so I won't need him that long."

"Barnet," Will asked. "Is that the railroad stationmaster's son?" He was familiar with Sam Barnet.

"That's right," Stanley replied, then turned his attention to the horses Will brought in. "I see you got a couple extra horses. Do they belong to the men who shot me? Have you got 'em in jail?"

"One of 'em," Will answered. "The other one didn't wanna be arrested, so he ended up dead." He went on to tell Stanley and Jim about the problem with the temporary jail. "It wouldn't be near the problem if it was two rooms, so I could stay there at night to guard my prisoner." He decided he was going to have to do what Jim Little Eagle did. Jim just locked up his Indian prisoners and went home at night.

"I see them plenty enough when I lock 'em up," Jim said. "I don't wanna spend the night with 'em."

Young Jimmy Barnet walked in from the stable then to tell Stanley he was finished. As Stanley dug in his pocket for a quarter, the sight of the stationmaster's son gave him an idea. "Say, Jimmy, did your daddy ever put anything in those empty storerooms behind the train station?"

"No, sir, not that I know of," Jimmy replied.

Stanley turned back to Will. "That might be the answer to your problem with the jail. Solid building with two rooms. That's right, ain't it, Jimmy?" He asked to check his memory, and when Jimmy said that was true, he continued. "That would give you a room to hold your prisoner and another room to use as your office."

That captured Will's interest at once. "You might be right," he said. "I'll go over to the station right now and talk to Sam about it. You wanna go with me, Jim?"

"No," Jim replied, "I gotta ride over to Switchback Creek. Leon Coyote Killer sent word that some young bucks have been causin' trouble there. He thinks they got themselves some firewater somewhere."

"I expect that would likely be from Mama's Kitchen," Will said. "I'm gonna pay Tiny McGee a little visit after I get my prisoner taken care of." He left Buster and the other two horses in Stanley's care after Stanley assured him he could take care of them with just his good arm. "I'd best pull the saddles off and put 'em in the tack room for ya. I don't want you strainin' your wound," Will said.

After the horses were turned out in the corral, Will walked to the other end of town to find Sam Barnet sweeping his office floor. "Be with you in a minute," Sam called out when he heard Will come in the door. "Will Tanner!" Sam greeted him when he turned around and came to the ticket window. "How you doin'? I heard you were in town." He laughed, then added, "A fellow would have to be deef and dumb not to know you were in town. What can I do for you?"

"Well, I'm hopin' you can help the U.S. Marshals Service," Will answered. Then he went on to explain what he had in mind.

Barnet heard him out, then turned a serious face to him. "You know I'm always ready to help you out, Will. But, dang it, turn that storeroom into a jailhouse? You know that's the railroad's property, and I ain't got any say-so a-tall about what it's used for. I don't know what the folks at the MKT would say about that."

"I understand your position, Sam," Will said. "But it would just be for a little while, until I can get a jail wagon over here to transport the prisoner to Fort Smith. And I would be sleepin' in one of the rooms to guard the prisoner."

"Dang it, Will, I wish I could help you," he said. "I just don't know what would happen if my bosses found out I done it."

It didn't appear that Sam was going to be persuaded, so Will tried one more thing. "I thought it would be in the railroad's interest to have this man captured. Him and his partner were plannin' to rob the train right here in this station. I expect they'd be mighty glad to see he goes to Fort Smith for trial." He shook his head as if concerned. "I ain't seen anything but the outside of that storeroom we're talkin' about, but from the looks of it, I'd say it's a lot more likely to hold this outlaw than Jim Little Eagle's smokehouse jail."

As Will had hoped, Sam was caused to reconsider his position after hearing Will's elaborate lie. "Now, you've really got me confused," he confessed. "If it's in the railroad's interest, I reckon that makes a difference." Still he was reluctant to give his permission.

"That's a fact," Will prodded. "It would definitely be in the railroad's best interest." He paused, watching Sam's wrinkled brow as he wrestled with it. "But you're the one who makes the decision," Will continued. "And if you say you don't want . . ." That was as far as he got before Sam stopped him.

"Hellfire," he blurted. "You can use it. Let me get my keys and I'll open it for you." He reached over his desk and got a ring of keys, then Will waited while he closed the ticket window and came out the office door. Locking that door, he said, "Follow me."

The storerooms were a good thirty yards from Sam's office. Upon closer inspection, Will found it to be even more solid than Stanley had described. And as Stanley had said, there were two rooms, connected by a sturdy door. The front room was smaller, which, in Will's mind, made it just right for an office and living area. There was even a small stove in that room and it looked to still be brand-new, having never been used before. Both the outside door and the door between the two rooms had large padlocks. Sam unlocked them both, then removed the keys from his ring and gave them to Will. He stood back while Will gave the two rooms a thorough going-over. Looking at the small windows, each one fitted with iron bars, Will was moved to say, "Hell, Sam, this *is* a jail."

His statement brought a smile and a look of pride to Sam's face. "They built this place near the end of the Civil War after the Union army struck the munitions depot in McAlester. This place was built to store weapons and ammunition, but they never got to put the first gun in here."

"I'll take good care of it," Will promised. "I'll transfer my prisoner over here today and move all my gear into the front room. Then I'll sleep here tonight, so you'll know I've got my eye on things." He extended his hand. "Sam, the Marshals Service appreciates your help on this. And I know you were a little uneasy about it, so I guarantee you I won't say anything to anybody about a train robber in here."

"Right," Sam said. "It's best to keep it quiet, even from my bosses."

"All right, Harley, pick up your blanket and anything else you've got layin' around, it's time to move you outta here."

Harley immediately looked alarmed. "Move me outta here? You just put me in this stinkin' smokehouse. Where am I goin'?"

"You're goin' to a better place," Will answered. "You'll be better off than you are here."

Jumping whole hog to the wrong conclusion, Harley backed away from the door. "Hold on, now," he pleaded. "You can't just hang a man without givin' him a trial. I ain't had no trial! You're supposed to be an officer of the law, it's your job to see I get to Fort Smith all right." When Will said nothing right away, instead staring at him in disbelief, Harley wailed. "Me and Tom Freeman never had no grudge against you. It was only for the money, two hundred dollars to shoot you and the other deputy." Then realizing that was a foolish thing to admit to, he tried to soften it with a lie. "Me and Tom had us an agreement. Neither one of us was gonna shoot to kill. We was just gonna wound you and see if Tiny would pay us for that."

Will continued to say nothing, content to let the frightened man rattle on. He was amazed to hear this outright confession that named McGee as the instigator of the attempted dry-gulch. It confirmed what Will thought he had heard when he walked in on them that morning at Mama's Kitchen. When Harley finally ended his plea and stood against the back wall of the small room, his chin on his chest, resolved that this was his immediate end, Will spoke. "Whatever gave you the idea I was fixin' to hang you? I never said anything about hangin' you. I'm just movin' you to a bigger place where I think you'll be a little more comfortable."

"Oh."

"Now, pick up your blanket and that straw tick," Will ordered, and pointed to one of the two pallets that served for beds. Harley was quick to obey his commands, even showing a spark of enthusiasm for the job now that he realized he wasn't on his way to a rope over a limb. Will marched him over to the new jail and locked him inside the back room. "I'll get you a bucket of water and an empty bucket from the other place. Then I'll see about gettin' you set up with Lottie Mabry to furnish your meals while you're in here."

" 'Bout time for one now, ain't it?" Harley asked as Will was leaving.

His question created a problem Will hadn't thought about till then. The new jail was working out nicely but for one thing. He would have to be there to unlock the door every time Harley had to be fed. "It'll be a while yet," he answered. "You'll get two meals a day, breakfast and supper, and it ain't quite time for supper." He didn't wait to hear Harley's complaints about that.

CHAPTER 6

By the time he got to Lottie's dining room, Will realized that Harley had not been far off when he said it was time to eat. So after he made arrangements with Lottie to feed his prisoner, he waited there while Harley's supper was prepared. While he waited, he sat down and drank a cup of coffee Lou-Bell brought him. By the time the food was ready, he had already decided he would wait until the next day to pay Tiny McGee a visit, and finish moving into his new quarters tonight. It was a happy turn of events for Harley, and Will was surprised to find a stack of wood and kindling outside the door when he returned with the food. He could crank up the little stove and make his and Harley's coffee.

While Will was spending the evening making his prisoner comfortable, two riders arrived at Mama's Kitchen, down in Boggy Town. When they walked into the saloon, they paused just inside the front door to look the room over— not so much in caution—more like admiration. "Howdy, Ward," Bud Tilton sang out, then yelled, "Tiny, come up front!"

"Bud," Ward Hawkins acknowledged, then turned toward the kitchen door to await Tiny's appearance. It was no more than a few seconds before Tiny came in, responding to the urgency in Bud's voice. "Howdy, partner," he said to Tiny. "The place looks pretty good, considerin' how quick it went up. You remember Bill Todd—rode with us in Kansas."

"I sure do. It's been a while since then," Tiny said, offering his hand. He remembered Bill Todd from their cattle rustling days as a man quick to draw his weapon with little provocation. Todd shook his hand but said nothing.

"Bill's come back to ride with us and he came along on this trip to take care of me," Hawkins joked. "We sold that big herd of cattle in Houston two weeks ago, so you'll have a wagon up here any day now with a good supply of whiskey. Luke Cobb and the rest of the boys oughta show up here in a few days. They moved another small herd of cows over to Houston, then they'll be along. They didn't need me and Bill to help 'em, so we came ahead. I wanted to be here when that shipment of whiskey got here." He paused to ask, "How's business?" He looked at the empty saloon and commented, "I hope this ain't one of your busy days."

"Don't go by this," Tiny quickly reassured him. "We're doin' all right, considerin' we ain't been open no longer'n we have. It's just like we figured, there's enough white men in the territory now, and when a man likes a drink of likker, he'll find a way to get it. And right now, Boggy Town is the place to get it. We just need to get the word out." He let Hawkins grin over that for a minute before giving him the bad news. "A little problem's come up in the last couple of days, though." He went on to tell him about the recent visit by the two deputies from the marshals' office in Fort Smith.

"Damn," Hawkins swore. One of the main reasons they had built this place was because the Texas Rangers were beginning to close in on them in Texas. "Marshals, that is sorry news. How'd they get onto you?"

"There's one of them Choctaw policemen that lives a couple of miles on the other side of Atoka. He called a pair of deputies in here because some of the Injuns we were sellin' whiskey to have been givin' him problems. I told him we don't sell whiskey to Injuns, but he called the deputies in."

"Maybe them deputies need a little bit of money to look the other way," Todd suggested.

"Done tried that," Tiny replied. "There ain't nothin' worse than an honest lawman, and I had two of 'em in here. They ain't been in town but two days and they've already killed two of my customers and hauled three more off to jail." He let Hawkins and Todd digest that, then continued. "And that ain't all. He knows we're sellin' whiskey and he's ordered me to shut this place down. I tried to tell him this ain't nothin' but an eatin' place—ain't no saloon—but he knows damn well what I'm sellin'."

Hawkins shook his head, clearly irritated. This was not what he had ridden up from Texas to hear. "Damn it all," he swore. His business partnership with Tiny McGee was important to Hawkins, but Tiny was not a partner in everything Hawkins was involved in. This place on Muddy Boggy Creek was planned to be his safe refuge from the Texas Rangers, while providing him with income at the same time. He considered himself a businessman, although it was a business outside of the law. He and Bill Todd had visited a new bank opening up in Sherman, Texas, on their way up to Atoka. He made it a point to meet the president of the bank, and in conversation with him, learned that there were also plans in the not-too-distant future to build a sister bank in Gainesville. He had planned to make sure Boggy Town was operating smoothly before hitting the Sherman bank, it being a short ride from the Oklahoma border. Then when the Gainesville bank was established, he would strike it, with an even shorter ride of only eight miles to the border. He shook his head and asked, "You say there was two of 'em?"

"There was the first time they came in here," Tiny said. "But this mornin', the one that came here and killed Tom Freeman, then arrested Dave Harley, was by himself. They told me there was a big posse of deputies and a company of Texas Rangers already on their way to make sure I was closed up. But I saw right through that, and it looks like I was right, because they woulda been here by now. I'm thinkin' the marshals are spread so thin, they can't cover all they're supposed to. Hell, this one's partner has already gone from here. This hotshot deputy that was here this mornin' is all by his lonesome."

"Then it looks like to me we can take care of this problem with no trouble a-tall," Hawkins decided, and looked at Todd, who nodded in agreement. "All we got to do is wait for his next visit."

"While we're waitin'," Tiny said, "you and Bill can move your possibles in one of the rooms in the bunkhouse on the back of the buildin'. I'll call Teddy up from the barn to take care of your horses."

Tiny expected another visit from the deputy marshal that night, so he told Teddy to be alert in case the lawman showed up. Overhearing him, Hawkins told him there was no need to worry about getting ready to receive this one lone lawman. "We'll set right here in the saloon and drink a little whiskey, maybe play some cards. When he comes ridin' in here, we'll just shoot him, and Teddy, there, can dig a hole back of the barn. That'll take care of our problem with your deputy marshal." So, after supper, that's what they did, but it turned out to be a peaceful night, with no visit from the law. Hawkins found it to be downright disappointing, but no more so than Bill Todd did. They played cards until late that night with no business for the saloon other than two cowhands from a ranch down on Clear Boggy Creek. They didn't stay long, since they had a long ride back. And the main purpose of their visit was to spend some time with *Baby*. Ida tried to persuade them to buy more whiskey, but their funds were meager at best and soon ran out. It was not the kind of evening Tiny would have liked to have for Ward Hawkins's first trip to the saloon since it was finished. "No need to worry," Hawkins said. "The word will get around pretty fast and then we'll see some business." He didn't have to tell Tiny that the problem with the deputy marshal had to be resolved first.

Unaware of the reception committee hopefully awaiting him in Boggy Town, Will spent the first night in his new jail. There were improvements that would have made it a little easier to work with, like a pass-through window in the door to Harley's cell room. But it definitely beat Jim Little Eagle's tiny jail. He went to Lottie's for breakfast the next morning and returned with breakfast for Harley, who seemed to be none the worse after his first night in his new lodgings. With his *jailer* duties done for the morning, he could now get back to the business of enforcing the law. He was down at the stable when Jim Little Eagle found him.

"How you like your new jailhouse?" Jim asked as Will threw his saddle on Buster. Will gave him a positive report on the railroad storeroom and suggested that it might be a good idea to approach the railroad for permanent use of the building. "What you gonna do about that Boggy Town business?" Jim asked.

"Well, I gave McGee a warnin', and I reckon if I don't see any sign that he's packin' up to close down, then I'll arrest him and take him to Fort Smith for trial."

"What about the other people who work for him?" Jim wondered. "He's got two men working there and two women, too."

"It's a problem, all right," Will answered, not certain, himself, how effective he could be in shutting the place down. Jim was asking the same questions that he had been turning over in his mind. "I thought about just runnin' 'em outta town, burn the damn place down if I have to. It depends on whether or not they put up any resistance when I go to arrest McGee. If they do, I expect I'll have to arrest all of 'em."

Jim heard him out, but when Will finished, Jim had to say, "I don't think that's a good plan. You gonna get yourself killed."

"You might be right," Will responded, "but I

can't just let 'em go on sellin' whiskey until Dan Stone can muster a posse to come down here and close him up."

"I think I go with you," Jim said. "You gonna need another man."

"Well, I can sure use your help, if you're sure you wanna do it. You might be takin' a chance on makin' Mary a widow," Will said. "That McGee fellow's got a wide streak of mean in him."

"You and me together," Jim said, "we catch 'em."

Will had to smile. "Right, we catch 'em." He had worked with Jim Little Eagle more than any of the other Indian policemen in the Nations, and he appreciated his volunteering his services. "All right, let's take a little ride down Boggy Creek and see what's goin' on at Mama's Kitchen."

After checking his weapons to make sure they were loaded and his cartridge belt was fully loaded as well, Will climbed aboard Buster, and he and Jim crossed over the railroad tracks and started down the trail beside Muddy Boggy Creek. When they reached the grove of trees where Will had stopped to look the place over on his first visit to Mama's Kitchen, he pulled up again to see if anything was going on. There were no horses at the hitching rail, but Jim pointed out some extra horses in the corral. "They not here last time I was," he said. "I think maybe McGee's got some customers in the bunkhouse."

"I think you're right," Will said. He hadn't checked the horses in the corral the last time he was there, but he didn't question Jim's opinion. "I'd like to ride in kinda quiet-like, so they don't get up a reception for me. You wanna come in from the back?"

"That's as good as any plan," Jim answered. "Maybe I see who's using those rooms in back." He pulled his horse back. "Give me a little while to get around behind." He wheeled the paint gelding and rode back along the creek for a little way. Will sat there on Buster, watching him until he saw him cut back down to the creek bank to come up through the trees behind the saloon. Then, instead of riding down to the path that led to the front door, Will guided Buster through the trees and laurel bushes to come up from the side of the front porch. He figured it would be unlikely that anyone around the barn or corral could see him on that side of the saloon.

Hearing no shouts of warning as he approached, he rode up to the porch. He pulled his rifle from the saddle sling and dismounted, dropping Buster's reins to the ground. Thinking Jim should have had enough time to get to the back of the building, he cranked a cartridge into the chamber and stepped up on the porch. When he opened the door, he let it swing wide, so he could see the whole room. But he was careful to stand to the side of the opening just in case he was greeted with a barrage of bullets. When he wasn't, he stepped inside, his rifle held ready to fire, to confront four startled men seated around one of the tables. From the dishes on the table, it was obvious that they had just finished breakfast, even though the hour was late for that meal. It was also plain to see they were now enjoying a cigar with an after-breakfast drink from the whiskey bottle in the center of the table. Upon sighting Will, the two men facing him immediately jerked to attention. One of them, a face Will had not seen before, started to reach for his weapon, causing Will to warn him. "I wouldn't, if I were you."

Already confused by Bud Tilton and Bill Todd's sudden reaction, Tiny and Ward Hawkins looked behind them to see what had caused it. Startled at first sight of the deputy, Tiny hesitated a few moments to calm himself before speaking. "Well, well, look what just blew in the door. Gentlemen, this here is an official U.S. Deputy Marshal, come to call on us this mornin'."

"That looks like a whiskey bottle in the middle of the table," Will said.

"That's what it is, all right," Tiny answered without hesitation. "We was just havin' a little drink after breakfast. It's the best thing to settle greasy bacon in your belly. It's an old family remedy. These two boys are cousins of mine. They brought the whiskey with 'em, 'cause they knew I couldn't sell 'em any."

McGee was having himself too good a time with his sarcasm to suit Will. So, he said, "That bottle looks just like the bottles you sell whiskey in. I reckon maybe you didn't think I was serious when I said you have to shut this place down." Tiny and Ward both turned their chairs around to face him. Will pointed his rifle at Hawkins. "What's your name? How long do you plan to stay here?"

Hawkins formed an insolent smile for him and took his time answering. "Until I feel like ridin' on," he said, ignoring the first question.

It didn't take but a second to determine the caliber of man Hawkins was. Of the two strangers, he was no doubt the one calling the shots. In contrast, the other one continued to sit motionless, saying nothing. He stared at Will under half-closed eyelids as if there was no one home behind the heavy eyebrows. Will decided he would be the first one to make a move in the event this face-off came to a violent end. Shifting his gaze back to Hawkins, he asked a question. "Are you aware of the law prohibiting the sale of alcoholic beverages in Oklahoma Territory?"

Hawkins favored him with a tired smile. "Yes, I am, Deputy. But like my friend, here, said, I brought this whiskey with me for my own personal use. Just outta curiosity, let me ask you a question. Is it true what they say about the MKT Railroad bein' the deadline, and it's open season on any lawman caught west of that line?"

Will answered his smile with one of his own. "Yeah, I have heard that old wives tale, but you're settin' east of that line where it's open season on outlaws."

No one else said anything for a long moment, waiting to see if this boil was going to come to a head. Hawkins finally smiled again and said, "You've got a helluva lot of guts to come walkin' in here like this, talkin' about closin' this place down. What are you gonna do if Tiny says *To hell with you?*"

"Then I expect I'll shut this place down and take Tiny to Fort Smith for trial," Will answered.

His answer brought a chuckle from Hawkins. He seemed to find enjoyment in the situation, considering the odds against the one lone lawman. "I swear, I'd like to know your name, Deputy, so I can remember you when anybody talks about damn fool moves, I can tell 'em about you."

"My name's Will Tanner," he said. "What's yours? Or are you ridin' under another name these days?"

"Hell, no," he said at once. "My name's Ward Hawkins, and I've enjoyed this little chat with you, Will Tanner. But I wanna know what you're gonna do now. Are you thinkin' about arrestin' me for takin' a drink of whiskey with an old friend?"

"No," Will answered. "Like I reminded Tiny

yesterday, he's got till tomorrow to move outta here, and if he doesn't, I will close this place down and take him to jail. As for you, I've got no reason to hold you and your talkative friend, there, since you're just passin' through this part of the territory. And in case you didn't know it, you *are* just passin' through."

Hawkins found the conversation downright entertaining, especially with what he had in mind to end it. Aware now that Tiny and Bill Todd were becoming antsy, wondering when he would have had his fun and would bring the discussion to a close, Hawkins finally asked a final question. "Tell me, Deputy Will Tanner, how are you gonna back outta here without gettin' killed? There's four of us. You'll be lucky if you get off one shot, and I'm bettin' you don't get that one off before Bill Todd guns you down. I ain't got no idea how fast you are with that rifle, but I know how fast Todd is." The insolent smile returned to his face, this one even wider than before.

"Well, since you asked," Will calmly replied, "My rifle is cocked and loaded, so I feel like I can beat Mr. Todd, if he starts to draw. And I expect the fellow behind you will most likely pick you to shoot first. I'm willin' to bet on myself to be fast enough to get a second shot off before I go down. And that leaves Jim behind you to finish it up. I like our odds." Thinking he was bluffing, all four turned at once to find Jim Little Eagle standing with his rifle in one hand, his revolver in the other, both aimed at their backs.

"What the hell?" Tiny McGee blurted. "How did you . . . ?" He could not understand how the Choctaw policeman could have gotten past the women in the kitchen without their raising an alarm.

"All right," Will said. "Now that everybody's got the picture of what's gonna happen if one of you makes the wrong move, I'm gonna say it again. This place is out of business. Sellin' whiskey is against the law. When I come back here tomorrow, if you're still open, you're goin' to jail." He turned to address Hawkins. "And I expect you'll be gone. If you're not, I'll consider it a refusal to obey the law and you'll go to jail, too." He paused a moment to judge their reaction to his orders. It was as he expected, so he said, "Damn it, man, I'm tryin' to cut you some slack. You ain't gonna like it if you don't take advantage of it and get out of Indian Territory."

"You're makin' one helluva mistake, Tanner," Hawkins said. "Me and Todd ain't broke no laws in this territory, so you can't tell us to move on. And as far as you threatenin' Tiny, I expect it'll be different the next time you show up here, now that we know what you're gonna try to do. I'm thinkin' it's you that ain't gonna like it."

"I'm sorry to hear you say that, Hawkins. I'm doin' my best to give you lawbreakers the chance to clear out. And I'll still give you that chance. Jim and I are gonna let you think it over, just like I said I would, but I'm gonna need to have you take those weapons outta your holsters real easy-like, two fingers on the handle, like they were red-hot. Lay 'em on the table. Jim'll pick 'em up, and we'll leave 'em out by the porch when we leave." With Will's rifle staring them in the face, and the Indian behind them, Hawkins saw that he had no choice, so he pulled his .44, holding it with only his thumb and forefinger, as ordered. He laid it carefully on the table, his smile transformed into a smirk of defiance. Tiny, as was usually the case, was wearing no sidearm. Neither was Bud. They weren't accustomed to wearing gun belts while they were working in the saloon. Bill Todd, however, was not inclined to go along, and he sensed a distraction when Hawkins surrendered his weapon. He slowly reached for his six-gun, but instead of pulling it with two fingers, he suddenly whipped it out of his holster to fire. He died with a stark expression of surprise on his face as Will's .44 slug hit him square in his chest.

Tiny and Hawkins jumped in response to the sudden firing of the weapon, both men expecting the killing to continue. They settled down when it was apparent that Will was not going to go back on his word and simply finish them off as well. A violent man, himself, Hawkins took it as a sign of weakness, and it encouraged him to regain his sarcastic manner. "Is that your penalty for takin' a drink of whiskey? That's the only crime he committed in your territory."

"You sayin' I shoulda let him shoot me?" Will asked. "He thought he saw a chance and he took it. It was a stupid move, tryin' to draw on a cocked rifle, and sittin' in a chair at the time. Now, Jim, if you'd pick up Mr. Todd's six-gun, I'll get Mr. Hawkins's gun and we'll let these gentlemen get to work packin' up to leave."

"You mighta just bit off a chew you ain't big enough to swallow," Tiny warned. "You're all by yourself, you and that Injun. I'm waitin' to see all them deputies and Texas Rangers you said were on their way here. You ain't big enough to keep outlaws from comin' here."

"You've got till tomorrow," Will responded. "That's my last word on the matter. Come on, Jim." The Choctaw policeman walked around the table to stand beside Will, and the two of them backed slowly toward the door. "We'll leave your weapons on the porch," Will reminded them. Once Will and Jim were outside, they hustled quickly off the side of the porch where Will had left his horse. To give themselves a little more time, they pitched the two pistols under the porch. Will stepped up into the saddle and Jim jumped up behind him to direct him down along the creek bank to the spot where his horse was tied. Once they got there, they felt they were safe from any shots from the saloon.

"Sometimes I think you a little bit crazy," Jim felt the need to remark.

"I can't disagree with you," Will said. "But we got outta there alive."

"When you shoot that man when he tried to shoot you, why you don't go ahead and shoot the other three?" Jim asked. "They all outlaws. They all say they gonna stay. We shoot 'em and no more problem."

"Well, I can't say that wouldn't solve the problem," Will said after a moment's thought. "But I reckon I didn't just go ahead and shoot all four of 'em because, as a deputy marshal, it's my job to arrest those breaking the law if I can. That way, they go before a judge and get the kind of sentence that fits the crime." Thinking back on it, he asked, "You were a long time comin' in there. You run into trouble?"

"I was busy," Jim said, then shook his head. "White man law, crazy law. Better you shoot them because later on, they shoot you, if they get the chance." He climbed up on the paint gelding. "What you gonna do now?" He was convinced that McGee and Hawkins had no intention of packing up and running.

"Well," Will replied, "we tried a little white-man's law today. I'm gonna give 'em till tomorrow night, then I'll try a little Indian law."

That captured Jim's interest. "If you do that, maybe you need an Indian to help you again."

"That's up to you, but you might wind up with a better chance of gettin' shot than you did today. I ain't anxious to make Mary a widow." He turned Buster toward town and rode off up the bank to hit the trail back to Atoka.

Behind them, two angry men and one shaken bartender were trying to make sense of what had just happened. Wondering why neither Etta nor Ida had given them warning about Jim Little Eagle coming in the back door, Tiny stormed into the kitchen. Finding no one there, he opened the pantry and found both women tied up together, hand and foot, and gagged with dish towels. "How the hell did you let him do this, without makin' a sound?" Tiny demanded.

"He caught me comin' outta the outhouse," Etta explained. "He said he'd kill me if I made a sound. He looked like he meant it, so I did what he said. He had a big coil of rope and he tied me up. Then he went to the back door and tapped on it till Ida got up from the table to see what was the matter. When she opened the door, he grabbed her and pulled her out the door. She let out a little squeak, but he told her, if she made another sound, he was gonna kill her. We was both scared to death."

"How did you get in the pantry?" Hawkins asked.

"He walked us in there, then tied us up together."

"And you still didn't make a sound?" Tiny asked. "You coulda gave out a yell or somethin', and everything woulda turned out a helluva lot different."

"I reckon you're right about that," Etta responded sarcastically. "Me and Ida woulda had our throats cut."

Ward Hawkins stood there, staring in disbelief at the two shaken women. "Will Tanner," he said, as if committing it to memory. "He's a problem that needs fixin'. He got the jump on us this time, but he's gonna pay hell when he tries it again."

"I ain't worried about takin' care of Tanner," Tiny said. "What I'm worried about is him telegraphin' Fort Smith to send a bunch of lawmen down here to help him. We might have to get outta here in a hurry."

"I ain't ready to lose everything we've put into this place," Hawkins stated. "I think that deputy ain't got nobody but that damn Injun to help him. If he had a posse on the way, he wouldn't be comin' in here givin' us warnin's, like he did today. It just don't make sense. He wouldn'ta showed his hand. He woulda waited till his posse got here, and they would have come down on us without any warnin' a-tall. The fact is, he can't close us down by himself, him and that Injun. He's just tryin' to bluff us into pullin' up stakes and movin' on outta his hair."

Hawkins's argument began to make sense to Tiny. "You might be right about that 'cause he did take a damn fool chance comin' in here today like he did. If it wasn't for these two women too scared to yell, we'da shot him down and his Injun, too. And we'da been done with him." He paused to consider that for a moment before confessing. "I shouldn'ta built this place here, so damn close to that town and the railroad. But I thought it would be a good spot, easier for men on the run to get to."

"I thought at the time you shoulda gone farther west, to the Arbuckles or beyond," Hawkins said. "But there ain't nothin' we can do about that now." He gave a shake of his head to emphasize his next statement. "We'll be ready for him next time he shows his face in that door—just cut him down where he stands. Everybody knows those deputies outta Fort Smith are already spread too thin to send a bunch of 'em down here in Injun Territory." He paused to consider another thought. "It's a damn shame Bill Todd tried to make a move on Tanner. I'da sent him into town to do the job there." That reminded him of another job. "Come on, we might as well drag Bill outta the saloon." He didn't confess to them that the loss of Bill Todd would mean he had to find another gunman he could trust to work with him in his "banking business."

When they went back in the saloon, Bud was

already trying to sop up some of the blood that had gotten on the floor. When Tiny and Hawkins came from the kitchen, he said, "He's done some bleedin', but most of it's on him. I went outside to fetch your guns. The fool threw 'em under the porch. I had to crawl under there to get 'em."

Hawkins picked his gun up from the table and returned it to his holster before asking Bud if he had searched Todd's pockets. When Bud said he had not, Hawkins checked them, himself, finding some money in one of them. He unbuckled Todd's gun belt and pulled it out from under the body. "Anything else you want, help yourself," he said to Bud and Teddy Green, who had heard the shot and came from the barn. "Then you can drag him outta here."

"Dig a hole for him," Tiny told them, "somewhere out back of the barn."

CHAPTER 7

When they returned to town, Will and Jim Little Eagle rode down to the stable and Will turned Buster out in the corral. Jim left him after hearing what plans Will had in mind to follow up that morning's visit to Boggy Town. "Count me in," Jim told him. "I'll be ready after I take care of anything I've got to do in my job."

Will told him there was no need to come back until after supper. "I won't need you till tonight, if I need you at all. I know you've got your own business to take care of. And I'm just goin' to spend most of the afternoon keepin' an eye on Mama's Kitchen to see if there's any chance they're movin' outta there, like I told 'em to."

Saying he'd be back to help him, Jim rode to his cabin west of town to see if anyone had come looking for him while he was away. After talking to Stanley Coons for a while, Will went to the jail to check on his prisoner. "I wish to hell you'd arrest somebody else," Harley complained. "I need somebody to talk to. I'm goin' crazy in here by myself."

While he could sympathize with him for the solitary confinement–like conditions, Will could offer nothing beyond advice. "Look at it like it's a good opportunity to meditate and think about how you need to change your life to something more useful."

"Damn," Harley muttered in disgust.

There was nothing for him to do at the jail by the railroad tracks, and he soon grew tired of listening to Harley's constant conversation with himself. It was close to the time when Lottie would be opening her doors for the noon meal, so he decided he might as well have some coffee, maybe a piece of pie to go with it, before he rode out to Boggy Town. Lottie was in the process of turning her OPEN sign over when he walked up. "Well, hello again," Lottie said, and held the door open for him. "You must be hungry. I thought I might not see you again till suppertime."

"I reckon I just had a cravin' for a cup of coffee and maybe a piece of pie, if you've got any."

"Will apple do?" Lottie asked, knowing that it would. "Brant's store got in a big barrel of dried apples yesterday, so I made sure I got me some. Lou-Bell made the pie. She bakes a pretty good apple pie. You sure you don't want me to cook you a steak before you eat your pie?"

It didn't take much persuasion on her part. He hesitated for only about thirty seconds before he said, "You talked me into it."

She laughed. "You're awful easy. I'll get you some coffee." She turned and went to the kitchen.

Will was finding it more and more inconvenient

to perform his secondary job as a jailer for Harley. Primary among these duties was the feeding chores. He had made arrangements with Lottie to prepare Harley's meals. But he had to be there every time they were delivered to unlock the door and keep an eye on Harley, lest he decided to make a try for freedom. There was no one in town to take a temporary job as jailer, and no one Will was willing to ask to risk their lives.

In a matter of minutes, Lou-Bell came from the kitchen with his coffee. "Lottie said we had a special customer come to eat," she joked. "How ya doin', Will? Things have quieted down quite a bit since you came to town. I hope it'll last for a while."

"I hope so, too," he replied. Further conversation was interrupted when a couple of customers came in to eat. When Lou-Bell went to their table to greet them, he heard her welcome them as strangers. At this particular time, Will was interested in strangers in town, so he made it a point to take a good look and try to listen to their conversation. They were not loud in their talk, but catching a word here and there, he decided they might be freighters of some kind and were just passing through town.

While he was eating his steak, he told Lottie to fix a plate for his prisoner, deciding that he might still be watching Mama's Kitchen when suppertime rolled around and might not get back in time to feed Harley. So, when it was ready for him, he took the plate and complimented Lou-Bell on the pie. When he got outside, he saw a heavy freight wagon parked at the side of the dining room, so he was right about the two men in Lottie's. It would have held no further interest to him, had it not been so obviously heavy-loaded. And the load was tied down tight under a canvas cover. It was enough to trigger his curiosity, so he decided to take a peek under that tarp to see what they were hauling. He walked around the wagon until he found a loose tuck in the canvas right behind the driver's seat. Holding Harley's dinner carefully in one hand, he pulled the canvas up enough to see with the other. The wagon was loaded with barrels, stacked one upon another. Painted on the barrels was the simple word MOLASSES. *Now who in hell would be buying all that molasses in this part of Indian Territory?* he asked himself, but he didn't take long in making an assumption. He was willing to bet that wagonload of molasses was on its way to Boggy Town. Thinking he'd best make sure, he hurried down to the jail to deliver Harley's meal. As he unlocked the door to the outer room that he was using as an office and bedroom, he could hear Harley in the other room carrying on a conversation with some imaginary person. *Maybe he was right, and he is going crazy,* Will thought.

Harley was happy to get the plate of food, however, and said as much. "You ain't as big a hardcase as I thought you was," Harley said, then yelled, "You goin' again?" when Will went out the door, in a hurry to get to the stable.

As he led Buster out of the stable, he looked up toward the end of the street and was glad to see the freight wagon still sitting where it was before. There were some things he needed at Brant's General Merchandise if everything went the way he anticipated that night, so he rode Buster up to the store. Since the wagon had not moved, he took his time making his purchases at Brant's. He was loading them on his horse when the two men finally left Lottie's. One of them, a man toting a tremendous belly before him, was still rubbing that belly and talking away the whole time he was climbing up on the wagon seat. His partner, in contrast, just listened and grinned as he hoisted his skinny frame up beside him. *Probably talking about the apple pie,* Will thought. He stood beside his horse and watched the big-bellied man drive his horses around the building and start out toward the creek.

When he saw the wagon appear on the other side of the rooming house, he climbed up into the saddle, but held Buster there until he saw the wagon turn onto the road to McAlester. Then he gave Buster a gentle nudge and the buckskin started walking slowly after the wagon.

Maintaining a distance far behind, he kept pace with the wagon until it came to the bridge across Muddy Boggy Creek, a short distance north of town. When the wagon left the main road and began following the trail along Muddy Boggy, there was no doubt where they were heading. And there was little chance those barrels were filled with molasses. Certain where they were going now, Will held Buster back, not willing to risk being seen by the two he followed. He was not thinking to take any action right away. Instead, he planned to watch the activity around Mama's Kitchen while it was still daylight, just in the wild chance Tiny and Hawkins had decided to heed his warnings and pull out. He was still bound to keep his word when he told them they had until tomorrow night to leave, even though he expected them to deny him. When he thought he had given the wagon enough time to remain out of his sight, he started up again.

When he reached the grove of trees from which he had watched the saloon before, he pulled Buster into the thickest part of it and rode down next to the water. He dismounted and left him there near some laurel bushes, where he could drink from the creek if he wanted. Then with his rifle in hand, he made his way back up the bank to the same spot where he had watched Mama's Kitchen before. The first thing that registered in his mind was the big freight wagon just pulling up behind the barn. While he watched, Tiny and Hawkins came from the main building to greet the drivers. Bud Tilton was not far behind them. It looked to be a joyful event as the two men who delivered the load untied the canvas and rolled it back to show the barrels. Will counted nine of them. Teddy Green came from the barn then, carrying two large boards to be used as a ramp. When they were fixed in place, Teddy helped the two wagon drivers roll the barrels off the wagon. Bud jumped in to help Teddy roll the barrels into the back door of the barn. *Just like happy little ants getting ready for the winter,* Will thought. Thinking of something Tiny McGee had said, Will declared, "Looks like Tiny's callin' my bluff." As soon as all the barrels were unloaded, everyone went into the saloon to settle up.

There was no need to continue watching the activity around Mama's Kitchen. The acceptance of the "molasses" delivery was confirmation enough for Will to determine Tiny and Hawkins's intention to stay put and continue their establishment of Boggy Town. He would wait until dark to take the next step in dealing with them. For now, he needed to go back to town and prepare to take care of another piece of business, so he went to get his horse. In the saddle again, he rode the trail back to Atoka, where he had things to do.

As soon as he got to town, he went straight to the telegraph office and sent a wire to Marshal

Dan Stone requesting another deputy and a jail wagon as soon as possible. He also asked for an advance of expense money to feed four additional prisoners. When that was done, he rode out to the McAlester road, where it crossed Muddy Boggy Creek, to wait for the appearance of the empty freight wagon.

Close to suppertime now, he waited until the wagon appeared, coming up the narrow trail, but he made no move on it. Playing a hunch, he remained there on the side of the road and watched as the wagon turned back toward town. Both men nodded to him as they passed by and he returned the gesture, then pulled Buster in behind the wagon, but not so close as to cause suspicion. He figured they had just gotten paid for the "molasses" they delivered and were feeling in a mood to celebrate. In all likelihood, they had a drink of whiskey before they left Boggy Town. There being no saloon in Atoka, the next best thing would be a good supper before starting back to wherever they had come from. Will felt confident the man with the big belly would be so inclined. That left Lottie's, a place they had already discovered to have a good meal. Of course, Will allowed, they might have brought a bottle from Mama's Kitchen, but that's not the same as going someplace where a couple of women would wait on them. If his hunch proved correct, it would make it a little easier to make the arrest.

His guess proved to be a good one. The wagon pulled in beside Lottie's as before, so he followed them in, after giving them a minute or two to get themselves settled. He paused at the door to see them pick a table, then he went in to be greeted by Lou-Bell. "Howdy, Will," she said with a friendly smile. "You're gettin' to be a regular."

"Always am when I'm in town," Will replied. "I'll just sit over here near the door." He answered "Yes" when she asked if he wanted coffee. There were a couple of reasons he was being so casual about arresting the two men for bringing whiskey into the Nations. It would be much easier to make the arrest when they least expected it. But he also decided he might as well let them enjoy their supper. It would save him the cost of providing one for them. Dan Stone should appreciate that, he thought.

He finished his supper rather quickly, even though the two men he watched seemed to be in no hurry to be on their way. When Lottie came to visit with him, he told her he would need a plate for his prisoner as usual, even though it was of some concern to him as to whether or not he could make an arrest while carrying a plate of food. His problem was solved when Jim Little Eagle walked in. "You said come back after supper," Jim said as he sat down at the table with him. "I see your horse outside."

"You came at just the right time," Will said with a chuckle. "I'm gonna need an extra hand here in a minute or two. Have a seat and I'll buy you a cup of coffee while we wait."

Jim shrugged and sat down, then asked, "What are we waiting for?"

"See those two men at the table back there? They came offa that wagon parked beside the buildin'. They just hauled a load of whiskey to Boggy Town, so I'm gonna arrest 'em as soon as they finish eating."

Confused, Jim took another look at the two men, casually finishing up their supper. "Do they know that?"

"Not yet," Will answered. "I thought I'd let 'em pay for their supper, save the government a little money. And we'll wait till they go outside, so we don't make a fuss in Lottie's dinin' room." Lou-Bell arrived at the table then, carrying Harley's supper. Will asked her to bring Jim Little Eagle a cup of coffee.

Seeing the plate of food, Jim grunted, "Now I see why you needed me."

"Or I can carry the food and you make the arrest," Will said.

"I got no authority," Jim replied, also joking.

Jim still had half a cup of his coffee left when Will said it was time to go. The two men showed signs of leaving and Will wanted to wait for them outside, so he stood up. Jim took the rest of his coffee in two big gulps, then followed suit. "Don't forget Harley's supper," Will said.

Outside, Will walked over near a corner of the front of the building, and he and Jim waited there, as if having a casual conversation. In less than a minute, the two freighters came out of the dining room and passed by them on the way to their wagon. Engrossed in their own conversation, they were unaware of the two lawmen following close behind them until the big-bellied one started to step up on the wagon seat. "Just hold it right there," Will ordered. "Don't move and you won't get shot."

They did as they were told, both men with their hands up and facing the wagon. "Listen, mister," Pete Jessup responded at once, "we ain't got nothin' but an empty wagon and I just spent the last penny I had in that eatin' place."

"He's tellin' you the honest truth," his skinny partner volunteered.

"You sayin' you just gave that wagonload of whiskey to Tiny McGee for nothin'?" Will asked. "I was willin' to give you fellows credit for more brains than that. We'll do a recount after we get to the jail."

"Jail?" Ernie Pratt exclaimed. "Are you a lawman? I thought you was fixin' to hold us up. Hell, we can cut you in for a share of our money. Can't we, Pete?"

"Long as it ain't too big a share," Pete replied.

"Always take care of the law. It'd be worth it to us to let us be on our way, and we'll get on outta town right away."

"That's a fact," Ernie declared. "We was plannin' to leave right now. We ain't broke no laws or raised hell a-tall. When you get right down to it, you ain't got nothin' to arrest us for."

"Sorry to disappoint you boys," Will said. "I'm arresting you for sellin' whiskey in Indian Territory. I think you know that's against the law, so put your hands behind you."

Still hoping for mercy, Ernie argued their case further as he stuck his hands behind his back. "Me and Pete ain't sellin' no whiskey in Indian Territory. We're just a couple of wagon drivers, deliverin' the freight. We ain't got nothin' to do with what that freight might be. Besides, them barrels said they was full of molasses. Nobody said anything to us about whiskey."

Will almost caught himself feeling sorry for the two men. And had he truly believed they had not knowingly participated in the selling of whiskey in Indian Territory, he might have been inclined to let them go with a warning not to come back. But that would set a bad example for other "innocent men" involved in the supplying of whiskey to the Nations. Besides that, he felt pretty confident that he would find a considerable amount of money when he ordered them to empty their pockets before locking them up. "Well, I reckon somebody is sayin' something to you now," he replied. "You can turn around now and we'll take a little walk over to the railroad track. After we get you comfortable for the night, I'll take your mules and wagon down to the stable."

"That wagon and team don't belong to us," Pete said. Making one last appeal then, he asked, "How 'bout it, Sheriff? What would it take to let us go? We could afford a tidy little sum, just for the chance to leave this town behind for good and never come back."

"I ain't the sheriff," Will answered, "and now you're also guilty of tryin' to bribe a U.S. Deputy Marshal, so start walkin'." He prodded Pete in the back with the muzzle of his rifle to get him started in the right direction. Then, taking a blind shot at a chance to get some more incriminating information, he said, "Don't worry about those four mules and the freight wagon. We'll take good care of 'em. Who do I get in touch with to come and get 'em?"

"They belong to Ward Hawkins," Pete blurted without thinking and before Ernie could bump him with his shoulder to stop him. "I don't know where he is right now," he quickly added.

"I'll try to get in touch with him," Will said.

Darkness was approaching when they marched the two prisoners up to the jail. When they went inside Will's office, Harley called out from his jail room, "Is that you, Will? You bring me any supper?" He had already decided that he wouldn't get another meal today, since Will brought him one close after noon.

"Yeah, Harley," Will called back. "Jim Little Eagle took pity on you and brought you a plate of food. But you've been complainin' so much about needin' some company, so I brought you some." That gave Harley something to wonder about and served to keep him quiet for a bit while Will and Jim searched the new prisoners. As Will suspected, each man was carrying more than one hundred dollars, which was pretty hefty pay for the average mule skinner to drive a team from somewhere in Texas—which was Will's guess. After he counted it out to the penny, he gave each man five dollars back. "Just so you don't go around broke," he told them. Then he got a tablet out of a canvas bag that held some of his other belongings and wrote the sum down with an explanation as to what the money represented. Then he asked Jim to sign it as a witness to the amount. "I'll turn this money in to Dan Stone when I get back to Fort Smith." He went through that formality for Jim's sake. He just thought it would keep the Choctaw policeman from wondering. But he also intended to keep an account of the money because he knew he was going to spend some of it for his new jail. He needed things like a coffeepot bigger than the small pot he carried with him and extra cups,

127

blankets, and other things he hadn't even thought of yet. He also thought it a good idea to let Pete and Ernie know their money was going to the court in Fort Smith, and not in his pocket.

Jim shrugged indifferently. "No need, they take your word for it. But I sign if you want."

Will unlocked the cell room and removed the cuffs from his new prisoners. The three of them all squinted in the faint light now entering the small barred windows in an effort to judge their cellmates. Harley quickly took his supper from Jim Little Eagle, fearful he might be asked to share it. Will assured him that Pete and Ernie had already had their supper. "I bought some blankets and a couple of candles for you. They're on my horse. I'll bring 'em to you after I take care of Ward Hawkins's mules. I expect you'll need some matches, too. And I'll give you some, if you'll promise me you won't set the jail on fire. 'Cause, if you do, locked up tight as this building is, you'd all cook like pigs in an oven."

He and Jim left them to get acquainted with one another and went to get their horses. On Buster, Will took hold of the bridle of the lead mule and led the wagon down to the stable. Jim Little Eagle stood by, patiently waiting for Will to tell Stanley Coons who the mules belonged to and what he should do with them. When that was taken care of, Jim wanted to know the purpose of his presence. "This afternoon, you said you need me tonight after supper. Did you need me just to carry a plate of supper to your prisoner? I could have sent Mary to do that."

Will laughed. "No, but you did do a good job of it—didn't look to me like you spilled a crumb." Jim grunted in response. Will continued. "No, from what I saw down there this afternoon, Hawkins and McGee don't have any plans to pack up and leave. To the contrary, I followed these two jaspers we just locked up to Boggy Town with a wagon carryin' barrels of whiskey, which they unloaded into the barn. And now, one of those fellows said the wagon and the mules belong to Ward Hawkins. That sorta brings it all back on Hawkins, doesn't it? All that, to me, is enough to know for sure they are defyin' the law and have every intention of sellin' whiskey to white and Indian, no matter what the law says. So I'm plannin' to make a little Indian raid down there tonight, and if you'd like to be part of it, you're welcome to come along. I expect you're more qualified to make an Indian raid than I am. But that ain't to say I'd think badly of you if you didn't want to get too involved with what should be the business of the Marshals Service."

"It ain't all white-man's business," Jim was quick to respond. "That coyote is poisoning my people with his rotgut firewater. This is my fight, too. I go with you."

"Good, I knew you would. I'll tell you what I had in mind." After he told Jim what he was planning to do, Jim said that he'd like to be a part of it.

CHAPTER 8

Will and Jim waited until the moon was high overhead before riding down the trail to Boggy Town. When they approached the structure called Mama's Kitchen, they swung off the trail and rode down through the trees along the edge of the creek. Coming up behind the saloon, they dismounted and tied their horses about twenty-five yards from the rear of the barn, where they could get to them in a hurry, if need be. The next thing to find out was where everybody was, so, leaving his rifle on his horse, Will carried a crowbar instead, as they carefully made their way up from the creek and along the side of the main building. There were a couple of horses tied at the hitching rail, evidence that Tiny had a couple of customers. That was a good sign on this night. It would contribute to the distraction Will intended. Moving up beside the front window, he peeked inside to see if he could account for everyone. Luck seemed to be in his favor, for he saw Teddy Green sitting at one of the tables with two men Will had not seen before and assumed were the riders of the horses out front. So, it appeared that no one was in the barn or stable, which was his primary concern. He turned to signal Jim.

They went at once to the rear of the barn,

where Will had seen them storing the whiskey barrels. The door was latched shut with a padlock protecting it. Will went to work on the latch, but soon found out they were fixed solid with bolts that ran through the door. Not to be discouraged, he went to the hinges of one of the doors and went to work again with his crowbar. The hinges proved less formidable, having been held in place by nails, and the crowbar soon backed the hinges off the side of the door. Then he and Jim lifted the door and swung it open from the hinged side. With the little light that found its way through the open door, they could see the whiskey barrels seated on a cushion of hay, the bungholes up. All in a row, he counted eleven barrels, which told him Tiny already had a couple of barrels before this shipment arrived. He and Jim went to work to determine how hard it was going to be to lift the bungs from the barrels, and found it to be easier than they had expected. So, Jim left Will to lift the bungs from the rest of the barrels and roll each barrel upside down while he went to the stable and opened all of the stalls.

Abandoning his crowbar, Will ran to his horse to get his rifle. While the horses in the stalls began to wander out into the barnyard, Jim went to the corral and opened it. Then he hurried back to the front of the saloon and untied the horses belonging to the two customers. By the time he returned to the back of the barn, Will had turned all the barrels upside down and their contents were slowly emptying. The fumes that began to fill the small storeroom were definitely not those of molasses. "I reckon we're ready," Will said, and Jim nodded, then let out an earsplitting Indian war cry that pierced the peaceful night. At the same time, both of them started firing their rifles—Jim, up into the sky, stampeding the horses in the corral—Will, standing in the doorway of the storeroom, firing at the barrels of whiskey. He was not really sure what the result of his next trick would be, but he thought it would do the job he envisioned. He had hoped his rifle fire into each barrel would ignite the fumes from the whiskey, but they had failed to this point. So he picked up a handful of hay, struck a match, and set it on fire. He started to take it over to the row of barrels, but halfway there, the fumes caught it and he was almost engulfed in the sudden fireball that resulted. In the meantime, Jim was still firing shot after shot into the air, accompanied by his piercing war cries, stampeding the horses across the yard and up toward the creek trail.

"Damn, Will," Jim blurted when he saw the ball of fire that followed Will out the door. "Are you all right?"

"Yeah," Will answered, "but I thought I blew myself up for a moment there." He looked back in the door and saw that the whiskey-soaked hay under the barrels had provided a perfect bed of kindling for the fire that was now catching the walls of the storeroom. In a matter of minutes, the entire barn would be ablaze. "I expect we'd best back away from here now and watch the show."

Inside the saloon, there was an immediate reaction to the sudden scream of a savage Indian, causing several of the occupants to jump to their feet at the same time, knocking a whiskey bottle over on the table. The volley of rifle shots that followed, and the frightened squeals of the horses, brought Etta in from the kitchen to scream with Ida, while everyone else ran to the door. "Indians!" Tiny yelled when he saw the horses stampeding toward the trail above the creek. "They're stealin' the horses!"

"Head 'em off!" Hawkins bellowed at the two cowhands struck dumb by the sudden interruption in their evening of drinking.

"Oh hell," one of the cowhands blurted, "they run ours off, too. We can't head 'em off."

In pure distress, Hawkins glared at Tiny. "We've got to do somethin'," he wailed. "They've run off all the horses! Get after them, damn it! We can't lose those horses."

Every bit as shocked and confused as Hawkins, and everybody else in the room, Tiny could only stand in the middle of the room, blinking his eyes in response to Hawkins's ranting. Finally, he brought himself back to his senses. "There can't be many of 'em, and they ain't shot at us yet, so they're just after horses. We need to get out there and stop 'em before they get too far ahead with 'em! Bud, Teddy, grab your guns." He turned to Ida then and barked, "Shut up that damn noise."

Only after the men ran out on the porch did they realize that the barn was ablaze. Thinking to see renegade Indians riding after the horses, they were confused to see not a single rider going after them. No one was struck harder than Hawkins when he saw that the fire had started in the room where the whiskey was stored. The whole storeroom resembled a blazing furnace, and there was no hope of salvaging a drop of Tiny's entire stock of whiskey. It represented the loss of the stolen cattle to buy the whiskey and the loss of the revenue expected in the sale of the whiskey. Hawkins was furious. He stood at the edge of the porch, staring at the blazing barn while Tiny, Bud, and Teddy ran around in frantic confusion, knowing the fire was already too far ahead of them for any hope of saving the barn or stable. Then it occurred to him. "Renegade Indians, my ass," Hawkins roared. He turned to Tiny when his outburst caused the bewildered man to look his way. "U.S. Deputy Marshal Will Tanner," Hawkins pronounced solemnly. "That's who this little visit is from. It ain't from nobody else. And it's gonna cost him his life. He found out he couldn't run us out, so he decided to burn us out. All right, he hurt us bad this time, but the fight's just beginnin'."

"He did more than hurt us," Tiny complained. "He damn nigh wiped us out. We sure as hell can't hang on here servin' nothin' but Etta's meat loaf. Our main business was gonna be from outlaws on the run, that and the sale of whiskey to the locals, includin' the damn Injuns." Helpless to save the barn and stables, Hawkins walked back inside. Tiny followed him, still complaining bitterly. "Where we gonna get the money to rebuild the barn and get more whiskey?" He looked at the bottle on its side on the table, half of the whiskey spilled out on the table. In a fit of rage, he suddenly kicked the table over, sending the bottle flying.

"The same place we got the money for the whiskey we just lost," Hawkins calmly answered the question. "Rustlin' cattle. But first, we need to take care of Will Tanner."

On the far side of the creek, their horses standing in a willow thicket, Will and Jim Little Eagle watched the results of their raid from a sandy bank. "I don't know if we finally run them outta here for good, or if we just open a big can of trouble," Jim commented. "Maybe they think it was Indians stealing horses, I don't know."

"I don't know, either," Will answered. "One

thing for sure, though, they're sure as hell not gonna sell that whiskey to anybody. Maybe Tiny and Hawkins will think it ain't worth it to try to stay here. If they don't, then I expect I'll arrest 'em. We didn't know about Tiny and Hawkins when Dan Stone sent Ed and me down here. If he'd known how big a problem this was, he'd most likely have called in some other deputies to go with us."

"You told me you wire Stone to send a jail wagon," Jim said. "You gonna take those prisoners you got back to Fort Smith when that wagon comes?"

Will knew what Jim's concern was. "No, I expect I'll send them back with whoever comes with the wagon. After the hornet's nest we stirred up tonight, I intend to stay around to try to handle any trouble that comes because of that 'Indian' raid."

"I think that Tiny fellow got no brains, but Hawkins, maybe I think he might be smart enough to know who did that," Jim said as they saw Teddy and Bud walking around the burning buildings, helpless to do anything about the fire.

"I expect you may be right," was all Will could say. "Now, we'll have to wait and see what he's gonna do about it—pack up and leave, I hope. If not, I'm gonna have to arrest him."

"I think you'd best be mighty careful," Jim said. "I think maybe we put a target on your back tonight, you and me."

"You keep a careful eye from now on, too," Will replied. They watched the healthy fire for a little while longer before Will said, "I reckon the show's over for tonight. You'd best get along home before Mary finds out what I've put you up to tonight."

It was late when Will returned to his office in the temporary jail. There were no sounds coming from the room where his prisoners slept except for some snoring. *Sounds like they're getting along pretty well,* he thought, and decided he wouldn't bother checking on them until morning. He unrolled his bedroll and was asleep within minutes.

He was awakened the next morning by Harley, yelling to see if he was there. "Yeah, I'm here," Will answered. "Whaddaya want, Harley?"

"It stinks like hell in here," Harley replied. "This slop bucket needs emptyin', and we need some fresh water. There's three of us now, you know."

"All right, just hold your nose for a minute," Will said while he got up and strapped on his gun belt. "Back away from the door," he ordered, then unlocked the door and opened it wide so he could see all three prisoners before he stood in the doorway. He decided right away that Harley's complaint was legitimate. "Pick up the buckets, both of 'em," he said to Harley, "and bring 'em on outside." He drew his Colt and stepped back to give him room.

"Hey, don't get them buckets mixed up," Pete Jessup called after Harley as he went out the door.

"You don't have to worry 'bout that," Harley called back as Will closed the door, locked it, and picked up his coffeepot as he followed Harley out the door. Harley started walking toward a clump of bushes about thirty yards from the back of the jail when Will pointed them out. "You don't have to walk all the way down there with me," Harley said. "I ain't likely to try to run."

"I don't mind it at all," Will replied. "It's just that I need to keep in pistol range 'cause I ain't gonna hesitate to shoot you, if you do take a notion to run." He couldn't hear Harley's muffled response. After Harley emptied the slop bucket and rinsed it with water left in the fresh water bucket, Will walked him to the pump by the railroad depot to get fresh water and filled his coffeepot as well.

"Whaddaya plannin' to do about Tiny and Boggy Town?" Harley asked on the way back to the jail.

"What do you wanna know that for?" Will replied. "You worried about Tiny?"

"You know you ain't gonna stop outlaws from comin' down here," Harley said. "The word's done got out about Boggy Town bein' the place to hole up. That's the reason me and Tom Freeman showed up here. And they're gonna be mad as hell when they get here and find out Tiny's been shut down. You ain't but one man, Deputy. You'd do well to clear outta this town while you still can."

"I swear, I appreciate your concern for my health," Will responded. "I didn't know you cared what happened to me. Move along now, if you wanna get any breakfast this mornin'." He was already weary of the job of jailer, and he was very much aware that the job wasn't going to end anytime soon. He marched Harley back to jail and locked him in again. "I'm goin' to get it now," he said, in answer to Pete's question, asking when they would get breakfast.

There were only a couple of people in Lottie's when Will walked in the door and Lottie came to greet him when she saw him. "Mornin', Will," she said cheerfully. "You want your usual?" He said that he did, then she asked, "We feedin' prisoners this mornin'?"

"Yep," he replied, "breakfasts for three. If things go the way I'm hopin', you might need to cook for a couple more. And I expect I'll need you to feed 'em for maybe a week. Is that any problem?"

"No, I can feed 'em, but we need to work out some kind of arrangement for paying me," she said.

"How 'bout if I pay you a lump sum in advance? Then we won't have to keep track of it every day. You just figure out what it'll cost for these three, say, for a week, all right? If I add a couple more prisoners, I'll make up the difference."

"That'll work," she said, happy to hear she was sure to be compensated for her service. "It'll be a little trouble for you to carry three plates over to your new jail. I'll let Lou-Bell help you carry them when you're ready to go." Lou-Bell approached the table just then with a cup of coffee for him. Turning to her, Lottie joked, "That would be all right, wouldn't it, Lou-Bell, if I sent you to jail with Will?"

"Be all right with me," she replied. "I wouldn't mind bein' locked up with Will."

"You'd be locked up with my three prisoners," Will said.

"Now, that might be more'n I'd wanna handle," Lou-Bell stated.

He laughed with the two women, then Lou-Bell left to wait on another table, and Lottie returned to the kitchen. It occurred to him that the playful conversation just passed with them caused him to think of Sophie Bennett. And that thought reminded him that he had not thought of her for a couple of days. He pictured her now, still planning and preparing with her mother for the wedding to take place on Christmas. He had denied it for weeks, but truth be known, he dreaded it almost as much as he dreaded having to arrest Hawkins and Tiny. He hadn't even bought her a ring, and he knew his heart should be filled with excitement at the thought of the ceremony. *I wish to hell we could just jump over a broom together and be done with it.* His thoughts were then returned to Indian Territory with the arrival of Lottie and his breakfast.

His breakfast finished, he and Lou-Bell walked over to the railroad tracks to deliver the prisoners' breakfasts. "Now, that's what I call a first-class jail, when you serve women with your breakfast," Harley remarked when he saw Lou-Bell.

"Watch your mouth, Harley," Will warned, "or I'll tell this lady to throw yours out the door."

"That's right, Harley," Pete Jessup said, recognizing Lou-Bell from the dining room. "That ain't no way to talk in front of a lady."

Will handed the plates to them one by one, then locked the door again, after telling them he would boil some coffee as soon as he got the fire stirred up again in the stove. "I hope you weren't offended by that impolite talk," he said to Lou-Bell.

"Shucks, no," she replied. "That's the first time anybody's called me a lady in a helluva long time—even if it was by a common outlaw." She gave him a big smile and walked out the door, heading back to Lottie's.

He had more important things to think about then, so while he waited for the prisoners to finish their breakfast, he walked over to Brant's store. He needed more .44 cartridges. He had used up quite a few the night before. After returning the prisoners' plates, he walked down to the stable and saddled Buster, checked his Winchester for the third time, then slid it into the saddle sling and climbed up on the patient buckskin. Once more, he set out to strike the trail leading east along Muddy Boggy Creek.

As before, he was not comfortable in riding boldly down the path to Mama's Kitchen. This time, he felt even more likely to be the target of a rifle shot, after last night's raid. When within a couple hundred yards of the path, he reined Buster back to a halt while he looked at the thin wisps of smoke floating up from the clearing ahead. After a moment, he nudged Buster and crossed over the creek to come up behind the main building where he and Jim Little Eagle had surveyed the damage the night before. It was even more devastating in the light of day, for there was nothing remaining of the barn and stable but a low pile of smoking timbers. He waited there for a while, watching the main building and the sleeping quarters behind. There was no activity outside the buildings at all. The horses had been recovered and were all in the corral, which had survived the fire, showing evidence of it in its scorched rails and gate. He had hoped to get a chance to isolate one of the two men he came for, but there appeared to be little chance for that. Everyone was evidently inside the main barroom.

He nudged Buster again and the big buckskin walked slowly across the creek, then along the side of the building until he reached the front porch. He was glad to see no horses tied at the hitching rail. What he was going to attempt to do might have been that much more difficult if he had to contend with customers. Piled on the far side of the porch, Will saw what appeared to be saddles and other tack that had been saved from the fire. Stepping out of the saddle and onto the porch, he grabbed the two sets of hand irons from his saddle horn and hung them on the back of his belt. Then he moved cautiously up to the same window he and Ed Pine had approached the first time they came. The thought crossed his mind that he might be about to make a foolish move, but there was no turning back at this point. Through the window, he could account for all four of the men. Tiny and Hawkins were sitting at a table drinking coffee. Over at the bar, Bud was talking to Teddy. With a live round already cranked in the chamber of his Winchester, he slid quickly past the window and grasped the handle of the front door. He paused there to listen for any sound from inside. There was none that suggested he had been spotted through the window. Slowly, he turned the door handle and eased the door open only a few inches at a time, continuing as long as there was no reaction from those inside. Finally, the door was open just wide enough for him to see all four men.

Ida Simpson came into the barroom from the kitchen, but stopped suddenly in the doorway, dropping the cup and saucer she had been holding, frozen by the sight of the man at the front door. The sound of the cup and saucer crashing to the floor caused all four men to jump, startled, as they jerked their heads around toward the sound. "What in the hell's the matter with you?" Tiny barked when she said nothing, but continued to stare straight ahead, her eyes opened wide. "What?" Tiny asked again, then turned to see what she was staring at. He immediately reached for the handgun he was now wearing, only to cry out in pain when struck in the shoulder by the .44 slug from the Winchester. Hawkins had the same reaction but thought better of it when he realized Will had already cranked in another round, anticipating his move.

Bud and Teddy remained frozen in place, neither wearing a gun. "You two," Will commanded, "get over there next to the table. Take a wide turn around the end of that bar," he said, knowing there was a shotgun propped under it. Bud did as he was told and took an exaggerated turn around the end of the bar. "That's close enough," Will said when they were within a couple feet of the table. "Now, mister," he said to Teddy, "I want you to show me how slowly you can lift those six-shooters outta both their holsters and bring 'em to me—one at a time, if you please." With no recourse other than to obey, Teddy lifted the weapon out of Tiny's holster, holding it by the handle as if it was hot. Tiny groaned in pain, even as he scowled menacingly in Will's direction. Will took the weapon from Teddy and stuck it in his belt. "That's fine. Now do the same for Hawkins, there."

Teddy repeated his cautious retrieval on Hawkins's weapon, causing the furious outlaw to threaten Will, "You've gone too damn far for your own good. You're signin' your death warrant right now."

Will took the weapon from Teddy and stuck it in his belt as well. "I gave you fair warnin', Hawkins. I gave you and Tiny the chance to get your stuff together and get outta Indian Territory. But you were too damn dumb to take that opportunity, so now you're under arrest and you're goin' to trial." He looked at Bud, standing wide-eyed, scarcely able to believe what was going on. "Now, I've got a job for you. Will reached behind his back and pulled the handcuffs from his cartridge belt. "Pull Tiny's hands behind his back and put these on his wrists. I wanna hear those irons click into place." Tiny uttered an oath as Bud pulled his wrists back, causing Bud to apologize and say he couldn't help himself. After Bud repeated the routine on Hawkins's wrists, Will said, "Now, we're all of us gonna walk out on the porch. You, too," he said to Ida and Etta, who were standing, watching in amazement. He didn't trust either one of them not to grab that shotgun behind the bar when he went out on the porch.

He waited, but neither Tiny nor Hawkins made a move to get up, both determined to defy him, knowing he couldn't physically move them himself. "I can't walk," Tiny said. "You shot me."

"I didn't tell you to walk on your hands," Will said. "Get your big ass outta that chair." Tiny made no move to get up.

Certain now they had him stymied, Hawkins sneered at him and said, "And I ain't got no intention of gettin' up, either."

"You're sure that's the way you wanna play it?" Will asked.

"That's the way, you mangy cuss," Hawkins answered. "We ain't goin' nowhere."

"Have it your way," Will said. "It sure makes my job a whole lot easier." He cleared his throat and started to recite, as if addressing a high court. "By the powers vested in me by the Federal Court for the Western District of Arkansas, I judge these two defendants to be guilty of selling whiskey in these territories designated as Indian Territory, and further hiring assassins to attempt murder of a federal deputy marshal, and resistin' arrest. The penalty for these crimes is death by Winchester, sentences to be carried out immediately." He brought his Winchester up in the position of port arms, then pulled it up to firing position and took dead aim at Hawkins's head.

"Hold it! Damn you!" Hawkins cried out, not at all certain that Will was bluffing. "You can't just shoot us down!"

"The hell I can't," Will responded. "And believe me, I'd rather do it than have to mess with transportin' you all the way to Fort Smith." He brought the rifle to bear on Hawkins's forehead again.

"I give up!" Tiny blurted, and stood up, knocking his chair over in the process. He was convinced the deputy meant to do exactly as he threatened.

"Damn," Will sighed as if really disappointed. "Are you sure? Might be a better idea to just get it over with and be done with it."

When Tiny just shook his head and repeated his surrender, Will looked at Hawkins again. "Well, one will be a lot less trouble and cost to the government than if I had to bother with both of you." He took dead aim at Hawkins again.

"All right, damn you," Hawkins said, deciding Will was just crazy enough to do it. He got to his feet, and when Will lowered his rifle a little and motioned toward the door with it, the two prisoners started walking. There would be opportunities to escape. Fort Smith was a long ride from Atoka.

Convinced that Will wouldn't hesitate to shoot, everybody went out on the porch as instructed. Pointing his finger at Teddy, Will said, "Get a couple of bridles off that pile and go to the corral and bring two horses up here." Teddy did as he was told and picked up two bridles. When he paused to ask if he should bring any particular two horses, Will replied, "I don't give a damn which two. Just bring two horses." When Teddy returned with the horses, Will had him and Bud saddle them and lead them up beside the porch to make it easy for Hawkins and Tiny to step into the saddle with their hands behind their backs. Since he knew which saddle belonged to each man, Teddy placed them on the proper horse. There were no saddlebags. Hawkins's were in the bunkhouse wing of the building.

"What are you gonna do about this bullet you put in my shoulder?" Tiny asked as he was sitting on his horse, waiting for Hawkins to climb in the saddle. "That thing is startin' to hurt."

"I'll take care of it when we get to town," Will told him. "Maybe it'll remind you on the way there that it ain't a good idea to draw on a deputy marshal." He stepped onto Buster then and took the reins of both the other two horses. To the four people standing to watch the event, he said, "The rest of you go on about your business now. You ladies can try to make a go of it as an eatin' place, but there won't be any sale of whiskey. I'll be checkin' on you." He nudged Buster then and headed up the path to the creek trail. Behind him, he left the two men and the two women standing speechless, staring at one another in astonishment, scarcely able to believe what had just happened.

"Well, I'll be . . ." Harley started when the cell room door was opened and Ward Hawkins stood in the doorway while Will removed his hand irons, then gave him a little push to start him into the room. In the brief few moments the door was open, Harley got a glimpse of Tiny McGee through the outside door, sitting on a horse tied to the door handle. Harley stepped back to give him room while exclaiming in disbelief, "Ward Hawkins . . . and Tiny! How the hell did he . . . ?" Pete and Ernie backed away to give Hawkins room, equally astonished to see him. Answering with no more than an angry scowl, Hawkins looked around him at the room that served as a jail. "I saw Tiny outside," Harley went on. "Where's he takin' him?"

"To the doctor," Hawkins finally answered him, after a long pause to calm down. "He's got a bullet in his shoulder."

"Tanner?" Harley asked.

"Well, who the hell else would it be?" Hawkins shot back. He was in no mood for Harley's stupid questions. He looked around again in disgust at his new lodgings. "This ain't no jail. This is a smokehouse."

"This ain't a smokehouse," Harley promptly informed him. "This here's a railroad storeroom. That first place he put me in was a smokehouse. This is a hotel compared to that." He nodded toward Pete and Ernie. "That's what I've been tellin' these boys."

"Yeah?" Hawkins responded. "Well, we need to find a way to bust outta this hotel." He immediately went to the windows to test their strength.

"I done tested ever'one of them little windows," Harley told him. "Them bars are solid as can be. Even if they weren't, Tiny couldn't get his big self through one." He looked at Hawkins and figured, "You'd have a pretty hard time, yourself." He watched Hawkins start to fume again and tried to ease his mood. "It ain't so bad in here. Tanner don't bother you much. He's gone most of the time. And the chuck is damn good. They bring it from the dinin' room at the boardin'house."

"Shut up, Harley," Hawkins ordered, thinking he had run on long enough with his role as senior resident.

"Right!" Harley responded at once.

At the upper end of the street, Dr. Franklyn Lowell's housekeeper and nurse opened the door for Will and his prisoner. "Doctor be with you in a minute," the Choctaw woman said, openly eyeing Tiny.

"Back in with another gunshot prisoner, I see," Doc Lowell greeted Will when he came into the room. He paused to study Tiny carefully, glancing at the bullet hole in his shoulder, but giving more scrutiny to his handcuffed wrists.

Noticing, Will asked, "You want me to take the cuffs off him?"

Sizing Tiny up very quickly, Doc replied, "Hell no, I believe I'd rather have him in handcuffs. He looks like he might be like bringing a bull in here."

"Well, at least it ain't suppertime," Will said, remembering the last time he brought in a gunshot wound and the doctor's complaining.

Doc smiled. "That's a fact. I reckon I oughta thank you for that, for a change." He took another long look at the huge man and was inspired to comment, "You mighta been better off taking him to a veterinarian." He laughed in appreciation for his humor. He didn't spend much time removing the bullet from Tiny's shoulder, performing his work with the big man's hands still locked behind his back. When it was done, Will escorted the patient back to the jail, which was rapidly getting crowded.

When he released Tiny into the room, there was a new wave of protests from his prisoners. "I reckon that's the price you have to pay for ridin' the wrong side of the law," Will told them when they complained about the cramped quarters. While Will was at the doctor's office with Tiny, Ward Hawkins wasted no time in establishing his superiority in the crowded cell room. He routed Harley out of the corner under the west window, since it seemed to be the warmest spot in the otherwise chilly room. Harley was not happy about it, but was afraid to protest and made a show of moving willingly. Hawkins informed them that Tiny would be beside him when he came back from the doctor.

Will watched Tiny till he sat down against the back wall next to Hawkins. It was not lost on him that he had collected a dangerous group of men, all working for Ward Hawkins in one way or another. The thought prompted him to wonder if he had given the room a close-enough inspection before deciding to use it as a jail. If Dan Stone acted immediately upon his request for a jail wagon and didn't wait for Ed Pine to get to Fort Smith, a wagon might arrive in five days. With that in mind, he informed his prisoners that their stay there might be about five days. So it would be in their best interest to take it easy. He figured it could well be a longer stay, but there was no sense in aggravating them even more. "We'll water you and feed you and make it as easy as we can, if you behave yourselves."

Hawkins could not resist answering him. "You've made a couple of mistakes since you came ridin' into town, Tanner, but this one is the one that's gonna cost you the most. You're just foolin' yourself if you think you're gonna take me to jail in Fort Smith. If you'da been smart, you could have made a tidy sum of money with a little cooperation. But it's too late for that now. Your number's up. Damned if I know how you've lasted this long."

"Thanks for the warnin', Hawkins," Will answered. "The rest of you," he addressed them, "the man runnin' his mouth just then ain't no better than any of the others of you. You're all prisoners of the Western District of Arkansas, so it might be time to think for yourselves. And the easier you make it on me, the easier I'll make it on you. I'll bring you some dinner when it's time." With that, he locked the door, thinking it was going to be one hell of a week coming up.

CHAPTER 9

The situation in the converted railroad storehouse had a rocky beginning, wrought with arguments and near-fights for the first twenty-four hours. But into the second day, things inside the cell room settled down due to plain boredom and a feeling of hopelessness—that is, except for Ward Hawkins. "He's gonna slip up sometime," he said. "The five of us are too much for him to handle. And when he does, all of us have to be ready to jump him. I don't care how tight this building is, we'll get our chance to break out. Just be ready when it comes."

In spite of his attempt to encourage them, not all of them were willing to sacrifice their lives for the good of the others. There was naturally talk of simply rushing Will the next time he opened the door. As Hawkins pointed out, he couldn't shoot all of them. They couldn't deny that, but some, like Harley, and in particular, Pete Jessup and Ernie Pratt, were not enthusiastic about getting shot down to effect Hawkins and Tiny's freedom. Pete and Ernie were paid to deliver a wagonload of whiskey and that was really the only ties they had to Ward Hawkins's gang of outlaws. Harley was subject to a more serious charge, having attempted to murder the deputy. But he had seen

Will in action, and he could readily imagine that he would manage to kill at least two of them if they tried to rush him. To say the least, Hawkins was not pleased by their lack of commitment. He still had hope beyond his fellow prisoners, however, and that hope was making its way to Mama's Kitchen even then.

"What the hell?" Luke Cobb muttered to Jace Palmer as the group of five riders pulled up to a stop on the trail above Mama's Kitchen. All five paused to stare at the charred remains of what had once been a barn and stable.

"This don't look good," Jace replied, having been told by Ward Hawkins that Tiny had built a complex of barn and stables to support a saloon and bunkhouse. "Reckon we oughta be careful 'bout ridin' down there?"

Marley White pulled up beside them in time to hear Cobb's answer to Jace's question. "Don't see any reason to be very careful," Cobb said. "There ain't no sign of anybody around the place. If there's anybody here, they're inside that main house." With that, he gave his horse a kick and rode down the path to the saloon.

Hearing the horses ride up out front, Bud Tilton walked out on the porch to meet them. They were strangers to him, since he had been hired by Tiny and had never ridden with the gang. Before he could say anything, Cobb blurted, "Where's Hawkins?"

"He's in jail," Bud answered as the riders stepped down.

"In jail?" Cobb asked. "What the hell are you talkin' about? Where's Tiny?"

"He's in jail, too," Bud answered.

"What the hell happened here?" Cobb demanded. "Marshals? Army? Who did this?"

"Far as we know, it was just one deputy done it all," Bud replied. "He mighta had some Injuns helpin' him when he burned down the barn. But he was by hisself when he took Hawkins and Tiny to jail."

"What about Bill Todd?" Archie Todd asked. "Did they take him to jail, too?"

"No," Bud answered. "He's dead. He tried to draw on that deputy and the deputy shot him." Seeing the sudden flare of anger in Archie's face, Bud quickly offered, "I dug him a nice grave out behind the barn."

Archie threw his head back and howled like a wolf. "Where is he, that deputy?" he demanded, ready to ride after him at once.

"Take it easy, Archie," Cobb said. "That's sorry news, all right, and we're sure as hell gonna take care of it. But first, we've gotta see what's what before we go off half-cocked." He turned back to Bud. "Who else is here?" When Bud told him there was Teddy Green and the two women, Cobb said, "All right, we'll go inside and get a drink, and your cook can get us up somethin' to eat."

"There ain't a helluva lot of whiskey left," Bud was quick to inform him, "just what was under the counter."

"What the hell are you talkin' about?" Cobb demanded. "You just got a wagonload of whiskey shipped up here. Where's that whiskey?" Bud told him that it had been in the barn and had gone up in smoke, whereupon Cobb was inspired to issue a long string of swear words. He, like Hawkins, appreciated the moneymaking potential for that amount of whiskey in a territory where whiskey was unlawful. That was in addition to the cost in rustled cattle to pay for it. After a few minutes, when he calmed down a bit, Cobb said, "All right, then, we'll take care of our horses and that'll give your cook time to scare up some grub." He paused to consider then. "You have got food to cook, ain't you?"

"Yes, sir," Bud answered. "We've got food. It's just whiskey we're short of." He stood there for a few seconds to watch them lead their horses off toward the corral before going back inside to tell the three watching through the window who they were.

"Hawkins didn't say nothin' about them fellers showin' up here, did he?" Teddy Green asked.

"Not to me, he didn't," Bud answered. "He mighta told Tiny, but he didn't say squat about it to me."

"I knew about it," Etta spoke up. "Tiny told me

I was probably gonna have to do some cookin'
for five extra mouths. He didn't say how soon,
though. I reckon they'll be movin' their stuff into
the bunkhouse."

After their horses were corralled, the five
outlaws carried their personal belongings into
the bunkhouse before entering the back door of
the saloon. Ida was in the kitchen helping Etta
prepare a meal for their guests, while Bud and
Teddy did their best to welcome them. After
asking them what their jobs were, Cobb wanted
to know how one man was able to come into
their saloon and take two men like Hawkins and
Tiny out under arrest. He was not satisfied with
Bud and Teddy's explanation and told them so.
"It's hard enough to understand how this feller—
Tanner, was that his name?—could walk in here
and arrest them. But why in hell didn't one of
you just shoot the son of a gun down?" They both
tried to explain how it happened, that by surprise
and carefulness, he pulled it off. "Well, we're
damn sure gonna take care of Deputy Tanner
right quick. Where have they got Hawkins and
Tiny in jail?"

"In town," Teddy answered, "in a railroad
storage room, I heard."

Cobb thought about that for a moment. "I
think before I'll take the boys into town to bust
'em out, I'll go in this afternoon by myself to
look it over." He had never been to Atoka, so he

thought it a good idea to see what he might have to contend with.

"I think I wanna go in with you," Archie said. "I wanna see the sidewinder that killed my brother. If there's any chance to shoot the varmint, it oughta be my right to do it."

Cobb nodded, then said, "I reckon you're right, Archie." He glanced at the others sitting around the table. "But I don't want no more to come. We go ridin' in there, all five of us, it might tip him off. Like I said, I wanna see what's what before we go get 'em outta there."

The discussion continued after Etta and Ida brought the food to the table. Bud and Teddy told them about the night of the raid and how the barrels of whiskey went up with the barn and the stables. "We thought for sure it was Injuns stealin' the horses. It sure sounded like Injuns, but they let the horses out just so we'd go chase 'em 'stead of puttin' the fire out."

"But you think it weren't no Injuns a-tall?" Marley White asked. "You say it was just that one lawman?"

"Well, we never laid eyes on him, but we're pretty sure that's who it was. He mighta had that Choctaw policeman helpin' him," Teddy replied. "And when we went after the horses, we didn't see hide nor hair of the first Injun. There weren't nobody chasin' the horses but us."

"Sounds to me like it's the lawman that burned

that barn down, all right," Cobb said. "Maybe we'll run into him this afternoon. I'd buy him a drink, but there ain't no saloon in town."

Luke Cobb and Archie Todd rode the length of the short main street before turning around to ride back again. There was not much activity to see in the middle of the day to indicate the town was thriving. To the contrary, it was almost sleepy. Cobb nodded toward Brant's General Merchandise and they stopped their horses there and stepped down from the saddle. "Quiet little town you got here," Cobb said to the man behind the counter, who was staring at him quite curiously.

"I guess you could say that," Tom Brant replied. "First time in Atoka?"

"Yep," Cobb answered cheerfully. "First time we've been up this way."

"Just passing through, or are you planning to be here awhile?" Tom asked.

"We're just passin' through. Thought maybe I could buy some smokin' tobacco from you." He glanced in Archie's direction. "You need anything, Archie?" His sullen partner merely shook his head. He needed only one thing at the moment and that was to catch the image of Will Tanner lined up with his front sight. Cobb turned back to Tom. "Don't mind my quiet friend, here. He ain't been in the best of spirits for the last

161

couple of days." When Tom returned with his tobacco, Cobb said, "Heard you had some outlaw trouble here a few days ago."

"Nothin' real bad," Tom said, not wishing to paint an unattractive picture of the town. "The real trouble was with a place about three miles from town, but a deputy marshal came down to take care of it. And he took care of it right quick—got 'em locked up in jail."

"Is that a fact?" Cobb responded. "Got 'em in jail, huh? I just rode up the street and I didn't even see a jail. Didn't even see the sheriff's office."

"We don't have a sheriff yet—don't have a jail, either. That's the reason we needed a deputy marshal to come take care of our problem." He walked over to the door and pointed toward the railroad tracks. "Yonder's the jail. At least that's what he's using for a jail."

Cobb walked over to the door and stared in the direction pointed out. "That's some kinda railroad shack, ain't it?"

"Yes, sir," Tom replied. "That's what it is, and I'll be glad to see him empty it, too. He's supposed to have a jail wagon on the way here from Fort Smith and I'll be glad to see it roll outta town."

"On the way, huh?" Cobb reacted. It prompted a look of urgency in Archie's eyes as well. "I'd like to meet this deputy. Have you seen him in town today?"

"Will Tanner's his name," Tom volunteered. "I haven't seen him so far today, but he'll be around. He might be in the dining room by the boardinghouse."

"Maybe we'll bump into him before we leave town." He paid Tom for the tobacco and they walked outside. Looking up and down the street, they saw no one that might be Will Tanner.

"Let's go to the boardin'house dinin' room," Archie said as they climbed up into the saddle. "That feller said he might be there."

"All right," Cobb agreed, "but let's go take a look at that jailhouse. If that lawman ain't around, maybe we can talk to Hawkins and Tiny. I wanna get a good look at that place, especially the door." He started off toward the railroad tracks and the storage house Tom had pointed out.

With five prisoners in his makeshift jailhouse now, Will had needed help at feeding time. So he had borrowed a four-wheel railroad handcart from Sam Barnet and enlisted the help of his son, Jimmy, to haul the meals from Lottie Mabry's kitchen to the jail. With thoughts of the same possibility Hawkins had talked up to his fellow prisoners, Will was concerned about the possibility of getting jumped by all five of them when he brought them their meals. To offset that possibility, he got a small table from Jim Little Eagle's jail and placed it next to the door into the cell room. The table was almost as wide as the door opening, so it fit almost perfectly inside it. At meal times then, he could pull the table into the opening when he opened the door. Then he put the plates on the table and had the prisoners line up single file, to step forward, pick up a plate, then step back to eat. Will figured it must be pretty effective, since the first time he tried it, it clearly seemed to displease Hawkins. He imagined Hawkins might find it difficult to convince one of the others to sacrifice his life so that he might escape.

It would be a good while before time to feed his prisoners, so Will decided to walk down to the stable to see how Buster was doing, since he had not been ridden lately. Stanley Coons walked out to the corral when he saw Will approaching, carrying his Winchester rifle as usual. "I believe that buckskin gets downright homesick for you if you don't ride him every mornin'," Stanley said when he saw Buster go immediately to the rail to meet Will.

"Yeah," Will japed. "He always comes to let me know whether you're treatin' him right or not." He let the big gelding rub his muzzle up and down on his chest as he stroked his neck.

"Whaddaya gonna do about that jail full of prisoners?" Stanley asked. "Tom Brant was askin' me if I knew. I think he and one or two others are a little uneasy about that railroad shack bein' the only thing holdin' some pretty rough outlaws."

"Oh, is that right?" Will responded. "I thought I told everybody I have to hold 'em there till I get a jail wagon from Fort Smith. Then I'll haul 'em outta here. That place is more than a shack, though. It's about as secure as most jails, so there ain't nothin' to worry about unless I forget to lock the door."

"Right," Stanley said. "That's what I told Tom."

Will doubted that. "Maybe I'll go by the store and talk to Tom about the strength of that storeroom. I ain't worried about it, and I'm sleepin' in the room right next to it." He talked to Stanley for a few minutes longer before giving Buster a little scratching behind his ears, then turning to leave. "Hopefully, I'll get a jail wagon in here in a day or two." He didn't express it, but it couldn't come a day too soon for him. He was not cut out to be a jailer and he had things he needed to do in Fort Smith. He confessed to himself that he didn't particularly look forward to those things, either. They had to do with the fancy wedding Sophie and her mother were planning.

When he walked into the store, Tom Brant was standing in front of the counter. "Howdy, Will," he said. "Two fellows were just in here and said they'd like to meet you. And they asked me where the jail was. I told them we don't have a jail, but if he was talkin' about the temporary jail, it's over by the railroad tracks."

That grabbed Will's attention right away. "Did you know 'em?" he asked. And when told they were strangers, he asked, "Where'd they go?"

"They went over yonder to your jail." He walked to the front door and pointed to the storeroom. Will looked that way just in time to see two men disappear from view as they rode around the back of the cell room.

Cobb pulled his horse up under the small window at the back corner of the building. "Hawkins, you in there?"

"Yeah," the voice came back right away. "Is that you, Cobb?" Hawkins asked, certain that it had to be him.

"Yeah, it's me," Cobb answered. "How the hell did you ever let yourself get in a fix like this? Is Tiny in there with you?"

"Yep," Tiny answered for himself, "I'm in here, too."

"He caught us when we weren't expectin' it," Hawkins answered Cobb's question. "He got the drop on us before we even knew he was in the place." Finished with small talk, Hawkins got right to the point. "Never mind that, you gotta get us outta this damn jail. There's five of us in here and I've already stayed longer than I intended to."

"All right," Cobb replied. "Tell me what I'm up against. All I've heard so far is there ain't but one man that's doin' the arrestin'. Is that right?"

"That's a fact, I'm sorry to say," Hawkins answered.

"He's got some help from a Choctaw lawman," Tiny said.

"That's right," Hawkins said, "but most of the time it's just that one damn deputy. He's all you've got to worry about. He ain't gettin' no help from anybody else in town. Ain't nobody gonna get in the way, even if you shoot him down in the street, so the sooner you find him, the sooner we'll get outta here."

"I got Archie Todd with me," Cobb said. "Understand this Tanner fellow killed his brother."

"That's a fact," Hawkins replied. "Bill tried a dumb-fool move, thought he could draw and shoot a man standin' there with a rifle already cocked and ready to fire."

"That don't make no difference," Archie declared, more than a little angered over Hawkins's comment that his brother had made a dumb move. "He's gonna pay for it, and I'm gonna be the one to do it."

"If it works out that way," Cobb was quick to comment. "Ain't none of us gonna pass up a shot at him."

"Somethin' I can help you fellows with?" The voice came from behind them, startling both riders. They turned to see Will Tanner standing there, his rifle held ready to fire. Reacting immediately, Archie yanked his horse around to face him, only to hear Jim Little Eagle cranking a cartridge into his rifle as he walked around from the front of the jail. It was enough to discourage Archie from following through with his intention.

Cobb had no choice but to play the game. "You the sheriff?" Will told him that he was a deputy marshal. "I was just passin' through and the fellow over at the store told me a friend of mine was locked up over here, so we thought we'd try to say hello to him before we left town."

"Is that a fact?" Will responded. "Who might that be?"

"Ward Hawkins," Cobb answered. "I've bought cattle from him before, and I was just wonderin' what he could have done to get thrown in jail."

"Mister, you need to be more careful about who you pick as friends," Will said. "I don't wanna hold you up, since you're just passin' through. And visitin' hours are over now, anyway, but I'm glad you got the chance to say hello to your friend."

"Right, Sheriff, I mean, Deputy," Cobb replied. "I guess we'd best be gettin' along." He turned his horse back toward the back of the building. "Come on, Archie." Archie hesitated, reluctant to ride away without taking action, his angry glare never leaving Will. Finally, he followed when Cobb rode around the back of the jail.

Will started toward the front to meet Jim. "Howdy, Jim," he greeted him. "You sure came at the right time. Stand back here by the corner." Puzzled by the request, Jim nevertheless did as Will suggested. Then Will pulled his rifle up to his shoulder as if aiming at a target and stepped around the corner to the front in time to meet Archie Todd galloping toward him with pistol in hand. Archie reeled backward when Will's shot struck him in the chest, causing him to stand straight up in the stirrups as he galloped past Will to slide out of the saddle some ten or twelve yards away. Knowing Archie was dead, Will immediately turned his attention to Cobb and ran around the front of the jail, his rifle cocked and ready to fire again. But Cobb had no intention of joining the assassination attempt triggered by Archie. He was already at full gallop in the other direction.

"How you know he was gonna do that?" Jim Little Eagle asked when he ran to catch up with Will.

"I just had a feelin'," Will replied. "When his friend left, that one looked like he didn't wanna leave without takin' a shot at somebody." He turned to look back at the body lying on the other side of the railroad tracks. "Looks like we've got some more business for Ted Murdock. Hope that fellow has enough money on him to pay Ted to bury him." His comment may have been casual, but his thoughts had taken a more serious direction. These two strangers showing up was not a good sign at all. They were obviously connected to the men he had in jail, and now he had to wonder how many more had arrived. Whatever the number, now there was one less, and that was the only positive he could come up with. He had to be on the alert whenever a stranger showed up in town. The only difference between him and a deer was the fact that he knew it was open season on him. The next question that came to mind, in addition to how many he might be facing, was, Would they be bold enough to assault the jail?

Watching him, Jim Little Eagle sensed Will was turning something over in his mind. "Whatcha gonna do now?" Jim asked. "You think those men come to keep that saloon open?"

"I don't know," Will answered him. "I was just thinkin' about that." He was torn between guarding the jail and riding out to scout Boggy Town. "I reckon I need to ride down to that saloon to try to see what they're up to, and how many there are." Jim volunteered to scout the place for him, but Will said that he wanted to do it himself, so that he might become familiar with the faces. "I wanna recognize any of 'em that show up in town. I'd appreciate it if you could keep an eye on the jail while I'm gone." Jim agreed to do that, and Will emphasized that he didn't want him to get in a gunfight with a gang of outlaws, should that happen. "Just let me know where they went," he said. "I don't wanna get you killed." Jim promised he'd be careful.

CHAPTER 10

He rode down a trail that had become very familiar to him in the last couple of weeks, and as before, he left Buster in the same place next to the water while he walked to a closer spot in the trees. The only horse at the hitching rail in front of Mama's Kitchen was the red roan he had seen Luke Cobb riding. The small corral next to the burnt ruins of the stable had more horses in it, but he didn't know how many were riding horses and how many were packhorses. With his back against a large cottonwood, he sat down to watch the place for a while, hoping to get some idea of the number of new arrivals. His wait turned out to be one of almost two hours with very little learned about his opposition. He recognized Teddy Green when he came out of the saloon to fetch more wood for the fire, and Etta Grise when she threw some dirty dishwater out the back door. The only one of the new arrivals he got a look at was a tall, thin man wearing a derby hat who came outside to visit the outhouse. Since it appeared that his scouting wasn't going to provide much information beyond recognition of two of the new arrivals, he decided to return to town. It would soon be time to feed his prisoners. *If I'm lucky,* he thought, *maybe there were only three, and now that number has been reduced to two.*

Inside Mama's Kitchen, Ben Cassady leaned back in his chair and spit a stream of tobacco juice toward the fireplace and paused to hear it sizzle when it struck a burning stick of firewood. Satisfied then, he returned his attention to the discussion under way at the table. "I swear, that sure is sorry news about Archie. Can't blame him, though, he was pretty worked up when he heard about Bill. I reckon I woulda been, too, if it hadda been my brother."

"It was a damn fool thing to do," Cobb said. "He went chargin' around that buildin' and that lawman was just standin' there waitin' for him, like he knew Archie was gonna come after him."

"Did you say there was five of 'em in that jail?" Marley White asked. "If Hawkins and Tiny was in there, who was the other three?"

"I don't know for sure," Cobb answered. "I didn't get the chance to ask about 'em. If I had to guess, though, I wouldn't be surprised if two of 'em is the fellers I paid to drive that load of likker up here. There was a freight wagon parked beside the stable that looked a helluva lot like the one we loaded them barrels on. I don't know who the other 'un coulda been, maybe somebody Tiny knows."

"What you thinkin' about doin'?" Jace Palmer

asked. "Just bust in that place and get 'em out?"

"Somethin' like that, I reckon." Cobb was still thinking it over. "That place he's usin' for his jail is a pretty stout buildin'. That feller in the store said the railroad built it while the war was goin' on, and they built it to hold guns and ammunition. So they made sure it wouldn't be easy to break into. I'd say we could set it on fire, but we might cook Hawkins and Tiny if we tried that. Whatever we do, we'd best get about it, though, 'cause that feller in the store said there's a jail wagon and some more deputies on the way from Fort Smith."

"Damn," Jace swore. "Why can't we just break the door down? Is it made outta iron or somethin'?"

"No," Cobb replied. "It looks like solid oak, and it's heavy and it's got a heavy padlock on it."

Jace shook his head and cursed. "If that door is made outta wood, I guarantee you we can break it down." He looked around at Teddy Green. "Have you got a heavy hammer or an ax?" Teddy said he could use the ax he split firewood with. "There you go." Jace turned back to Cobb. "We'll chop the damn door down. Course, we oughta take care of that lawman first."

His three partners thought that over and no one could think of a better plan, so it was decided that was to be their best bet. Being a somewhat sensible man, Marley pointed out that it would be a mite safer if they took care of the deputy first, like Jace said, instead of assaulting the door while he was inside with a rifle. "And all that would take is to catch him outside the jail and shoot the devil."

"What about the rest of the people in that town?" Ben asked. "Anybody likely to help the deputy? Somebody that might take a potshot at us?"

"It'd sure surprise me if they did," Cobb answered. "I didn't see anybody that looked like they'd likely stick their necks out to stop us."

"What about the Injun you said was there with him?" Jace asked.

In the heat of the discussion, Cobb had forgotten about Jim Little Eagle. When he had talked with Tom Brant in the store, it seemed that Tom always talked about the deputy marshal acting alone. "Well, he was there when Archie got shot. That's a fact. But he didn't have no part in the shootin', and I don't think he's with him all the time." He shrugged indifferently. "But, hell, if he shows up, we'll shoot him, too."

Marley reached up to push his derby back a little from his forehead. "You know, ain't nobody said nothin' about what we're gonna do after we get Hawkins and Tiny outta that jail. I don't know 'bout the rest of you boys, but I'm thinkin' Boggy Town is stone-cold dead. We ain't gonna be able to run no saloon here after this. There'll be a company of soldiers down here, lookin' to take all of us to the gallows. Who the hell picked this spot to build this place, anyway?"

"I reckon it was mostly Tiny's idea," Cobb said, "but it don't seem like the best place right now, does it?" Afraid that talk like that might encourage thinking toward simply getting on their horses and riding farther west, to the Arbuckle Mountains or beyond, he was quick to remind, "What we gotta do right away is get Ward and Tiny outta that jail, then we might decide to put this place behind us."

Off to the side, Bud and Teddy leaned on the bar, while Etta and Ida stood by the kitchen door. All four were listening with close attention to the conversation taking place among the four men. Not one of them believed that Hawkins nor Tiny, and certainly not Cobb, would feel any need to take them with them if they decided to leave. In whispered speculation, the two women wondered if they might stay on at Mama's Kitchen when the outlaws left. Maybe, they thought, they could run it as a real kitchen, at least well enough to survive, if Bud and Teddy would stay on to help them. "We'll talk to 'em later," Ida whispered, " 'cause Hawkins ain't gonna want either one of 'em. And we ain't likely to find a place anywhere else we could just move into."

"Wonder if we could turn that bunkhouse into a kind of hotel," Etta said. Ida answered with a shrug. It was enough to set both minds to speculate.

"All right," Cobb said. "I reckon we've all agreed that the best thing to do is to break into that jail and get them outta there. The thing we gotta decide now is when to do it. We don't know when those extra deputies are gonna get here, so we can't wait too long."

"Why don't we go tonight when the town's closed up?" Jace suggested.

"That'd be all right, but what about that deputy?" Ben asked. "You said it looked like that place had two rooms. What if he's sleepin' in there? We go to work on that door and as soon as we break it down, we're liable to get a dose of what Archie and Bill got."

That gave them something to think about, but after a few moments, Cobb said, "For Pete's sake, we're talkin' about one man. The four of us oughta give *him* the same dose Archie and Bill Todd got." The discussion continued for another thirty minutes before it was finally decided to ride into town the next day, find the lawman, and attack the jail in broad daylight. The general consensus was that the citizens of the town would be helpless to do anything about it. There was also a unanimous decision that when it was done, it was best to abandon Tiny's idea that Atoka was the best place to build an outlaws' refuge.

"Hawkins might not like that," Ben said. "He's put a lotta money in this place."

"That don't make no difference," Cobb responded. "If he wants to stay, then, hell, he can stay, but I guarantee ya, Mrs. Cobb's little boy ain't gonna stay with him." He shrugged and added, "Hell, he's gonna have to build another barn and stables, anyway. He might as well build 'em someplace that ain't on a railroad that'll bring soldiers and lawmen down here." It was not lost on Cobb that this might be his opportunity to take charge of the gang, if Hawkins insisted on staying there. "Yes, sir," he declared further, "sometimes it pays to know what's best in the long run. If it'd been me callin' the shots, we'da never built this place to start with. I ain't sayin' nothin' against Ward or Tiny. They had their reasons, I reckon. I'm just sayin' I woulda done somethin' different."

"Well, I reckon that about decides it," Marley commented. He looked over at the two women standing by the kitchen door. "I hope to hell you women have got somethin' started for supper." That prompted them to retreat to the kitchen at once. Marley spoke out to Bud then. "You might as well break out another bottle of that likker you got under the counter. We might as well drink it till it runs out."

"You know, Cobb, I'm thinkin' we're gonna need supplies and money when we leave here," Jace commented. "And with that lawman dead, there won't be nobody to stop us from cleanin' that town out. There's four of us here, and you said there's five in that jail. I don't see how the people in town can do anything about it."

"Yeah," Cobb said, "that's the same thing I was thinkin'," even though it hadn't crossed his mind.

With no knowledge of how great the odds might be stacking up against him, Will Tanner carried on with his assumed obligations to his prisoners. Using his method of dispensing meals by using the table in the doorway, the prisoners were fed. Lou-Bell came with Jimmy and the cart. She would deal the plates one at a time while Will stood by with his rifle. He was well aware of an attitude change in Ward Hawkins and Tiny McGee. Still belligerent, their demeanor had turned almost casual. He could only conclude it was because of the appearance of the two visitors to the jail that afternoon. His senses told him that he now had a target on his back, and it prompted him to take more precautions than he normally would have. He was also of the opinion that he had best stay close to the jail, with a sharp eye for any strangers who showed up in town. Still with no idea how many of Hawkins's friends had come to Boggy Town, he could identify only two—the man he had faced at the jail, and the thin man wearing the derby hat. It was not the best situation to be in.

Not surprising, Jim Little Eagle was ready to help him, and Will felt obligated to caution him about the chances of getting shot in the back. Jim told him he was well aware of that, but he would stand with him nevertheless. Will sent Jim home for his supper while he remained in the front room of the jail. When darkness began to gather, he locked the padlock on the front door, and with his rifle and plenty of ammunition, he retreated to a position on the railroad platform against the back of the telegraph office. There were two large barrels sitting on the platform, so he used them for cover. He was convinced that an attempt to break his prisoners out was sure to come that night. It figured that it was the sole reason for the two who showed up at the jail that afternoon, to get a good look at their target. With a blanket against the cold, he sat with his back against the telegraph office, planning to stay awake all night. He figured he had a better chance of defeating the break-in attempt from outside the jail. He had been at his post no more than an hour when Jim showed up, after leaving his horse with Stanley Coons.

With the arrival of morning, Will had to confess that his conviction that there would be an attempt to free his prisoners during the night had been wrong. The first rays of the dawn left him to wonder if they knew he and Jim were lying in wait for them. "Looks like I just cost us both a good night's sleep," he told the Choctaw policeman. "I sure had this one figured wrong."

"I go home and sleep a little bit after I eat," Jim said.

With prisoners to feed, Will was going to have to go to Lottie's dining room for breakfast, so he said, "I oughta at least feed you some breakfast. Come on and go to Lottie's with me."

"I think maybe I better go home," Jim said. "Mary be worried. I'll be back."

"All right," Will replied. "But tell Stanley Coons I'll pay him for takin' care of your horse."

"I tell him," Jim said, and started toward the stable. Will unlocked the jail and went in only long enough to leave his blanket.

Hearing him come into the office, Harley called out, "Hey, Tanner, is that you? It's gettin' along toward breakfast time, ain't it?"

"Yeah, Tanner." Will recognized the voice as Hawkins's. "Go get us some breakfast." He still sounded cocky. "And we need you to change these buckets."

"In due time," Will answered, aware of Hawkins's tendency to needle him, as if he was cocksure his jail time would be short-lived. "Just relax and enjoy your time together."

"You're a little bit early," Lou-Bell greeted him at the door. "The biscuits ain't quite ready, but the coffee's done. So set yourself down and I'll get you some while you wait."

"Much obliged," he said, and went to one of the little tables by a window where he could see the jail. He was still wondering about the night just passed and speculating on the possibility that Hawkins's friends might try in broad daylight. It occurred to him that maybe they outthought him and figured he would be set up and waiting for them to strike at night. He looked up and smiled at Lou-Bell when she brought his coffee.

"Reckon you want the regular five plates of breakfast for your prisoners," she said, just to be sure. "Didn't none of 'em die during the night, did they?"

He gave her half a chuckle, thinking it more a concern than she thought. "Nope," he answered, "still need five." By the time he finished his first cup of coffee, she came back with a breakfast of ham and eggs to go with his biscuits. A few early risers from the boardinghouse next door came in and Will was careful to notice each one. They were strangers to him, but not to Lottie and Lou-Bell, so he didn't concern himself with them. He had to tell himself that anybody he was worried about would hardly come for breakfast. When he had finished, he paid Lottie for his breakfast as well as any extra he owed for the meals she had prepared for the additional prisoners. She was always happy to be paid promptly, unaware that the two men who drove the freight wagon were paying for the prisoners' food. As he walked out the door, he told Lou-Bell, "I'll send Jimmy back here with the cart."

He walked along the board walkway on his way back to the jail, past the shops and the undertaker, past the blacksmith. As he approached Brant's store, a man riding a bay horse pulled up to the rail in front and dismounted. He looked once toward the railroad track before walking in the store. Immediately alert, Will stepped up to the door and pushed it open far enough to hear Tom Brant say, "Good morning, Willard, what brings you into town so early?"

"Cornmeal," Willard answered. "Genevieve wants to make corn bread for her pappy, so I had to ride five miles in here to get some cornmeal. I sure hope you ain't sold out."

Will laughed at himself for his caution. He eased the door closed and continued on his way to the jail, where he found Jimmy Barnet waiting with the four-wheel handcart. Will sent him promptly on his way to Lottie's to get the breakfasts. "It's all paid for," Will said. "Tell Lou-Bell I said to give you a hot biscuit with some jelly on it." He stood and watched the boy pull the handcart all the way up to Lottie's before he unlocked the jailhouse door and went inside. The prisoners' breakfast was managed without a hitch, the dirty dishes taken back on the cart, and it appeared to be just another day of waiting for a jail wagon from Fort Smith to show up.

• • •

It was a little before noon when the four outlaws slow-walked their horses four abreast past Stanley Coons's stables at the north end of the street. Seeing them pass, Stanley walked out to the door to watch them as they continued on toward the railroad depot. He thought about the shooting the day before at the jail and worried that Will Tanner might be in trouble, but not to the point where he might pick up his shotgun and run to help him. Instead, he hurried back inside to make sure his money box was closed and out of sight under a loose board with hay scattered over it.

On the other side of the blacksmith's forge, Ted Murdock peered out the window of his barbershop as the four rode slowly past his place. With faces of lethal determination, seeming to be searching for something, they immediately made Murdock think of the body still lying in his mortuary behind his barbershop. Thinking now that he should have buried it yesterday, he hurried back there to cover it with a sheet of canvas. He breathed a sigh of relief when he came back in the barbershop and saw that the four horsemen had walked on past his establishment. He decided it best not to open until later.

The four outlaws rode past him and went directly to the jail by the railroad tracks. The deputy was not there, since it was obvious that the building was locked up from the outside. So Cobb led his partners around to the window where he had talked to Hawkins before. "Ward, you still in there?"

Hawkins answered immediately. "Cobb? Hell, yes, I'm still in here." Feeling confident that he wouldn't be for long, now that Cobb and the others had arrived, he joked, "I thought about leavin', but it's so comfortable in this railroad hotel, and the grub is so good, I decided to hang around a little longer."

"Is that a fact?" Cobb returned in kind. "Well, if you ain't made up your mind, me and the boys can come back later on in the week." Getting serious then, he asked, "You got any idea where Tanner is? I'd like to take care of that jasper first before we start bustin' this place apart."

"No, I don't," Hawkins answered. "He ain't been back here since he fed us breakfast, but I think you're thinkin' straight to take care of him first. The town ain't that big. He's gotta be around somewhere. Somebody might be hidin' him in one of those stores."

"All right, we'll go from store to store. If he's in town, we'll find him, then we'll get you outta there."

"Tom!" Ellie Brant exclaimed. "Come look at this!"

Tom rushed from the storeroom where he

had been sifting weevils from a barrel of flour. "What is it?" he asked when he saw her standing by the window, but he saw at once what had caused her distress. Looking past her at the four riders stopped in front of his store, he had a sinking feeling that they had come to cause trouble. "Don't let 'em see you staring at 'em," he said. No sooner had he said it when two of the men turned their horses toward the store and proceeded to dismount. "Go back to the storeroom and shut the door!" Tom said as he went behind the counter to stand by the shotgun he kept propped there.

Luke Cobb pushed the door open wide, looking right and left to make sure there was no one in the store but the man behind the counter. When he saw no one else, he walked in, followed by Ben Cassady. Making an effort to present a casual greeting, Tom said, "Good morning, can I help you?" Neither Cobb nor Ben responded to his greeting. Cobb walked past the counter, opened the storeroom door, and looked in. Seeing no one but Ellie standing wide-eyed beside the back shelves, he closed the door again. "Is there something in particular you're looking for?" Tom asked. "Maybe I can help you find it."

Cobb looked at the obviously nervous man, smirked, and said, "Yeah, I'm lookin' for somethin' in particular. Will Tanner, have you seen him?"

There was little doubt left in Tom's mind now. The four men had come into town to do evil. He tried his best not to show his fear. "Will Tanner," he echoed. "No, at least not since I saw him go to the dining room for breakfast early this morning."

Convinced that the town might hide the lawman, Cobb walked past the storeroom door to another leading outside. "What's that out back? Is that where you live?"

"Yes," Tom answered. "That's my house."

"If I was to look in your house, I wouldn't find Tanner settin' around there somewhere, would I?"

"No, sir," Tom insisted. "That's my house," he repeated. "We don't have anything to do with Will Tanner. He's a U.S. Deputy Marshal, sent down here from Fort Smith. He ain't got nothing to do with us."

"Is that a fact?" Cobb replied. "Then you won't mind if we take a look in your house, will you?" While Tom sputtered for an answer, Cobb asked, "What's your name, mister?"

"Tom Brant," he answered.

"Just like it says on the sign," Cobb said. "Ben, open that door there and ask Mrs. Brant to take you for a look in that house out back."

Ben opened the door, almost hitting Ellie with it, since she had crept up to it in an attempt to hear what was being said in the store. "Come on outta there, sweetie," Ben chortled. "Let's go see what you got in that house." With one hand on her shoulder and the other holding his handgun, he walked behind her as she led him out the door and across a boardwalk to a tidy cabin behind the store. Cobb waited inside the store, leaning against the counter, watching Tom, a knowing grin on his face. At the door of the cabin, Ben continued to hold Ellie by her shoulder as she opened the door, using her to protect against a gun waiting inside. It was apparent that there was no one there as soon as they walked inside. Ben took a quick look around before returning to the store to report that Tanner wasn't there.

"Well, that didn't take long," Cobb said to Tom Brant. "Here's your wife back safe and sound and no harm done. You didn't even need that shotgun you're standin' over." He laughed then and said, "Hold on, Ben, I think I wanna try out one of those." He pointed to a rack of heavy axes standing near the front door. "That looks more like it might do the work on that door—better than the one I got from Teddy." He walked over and picked up one of the heavier models. "This was made for work on thick oak doors." He glanced in Brant's direction. "I'm gonna try this one out, and if I like it, I'll buy it." Leaving Brant to gape speechless, he walked out the door with the ax to continue their search for Will Tanner.

When Ellie Brant complained to her husband that Cobb took the ax without paying for it, he told her he was satisfied they had gotten off that cheap. "If we don't see those outlaws again, it was well worth the price."

It was the same for the four searchers at each place they stopped. There was no sign of Will Tanner and no one could tell them where he might have gone. Ted Murdock continued to watch their progress from the window of his barbershop, alarmed to see they were coming back his way. He had hoped they would not call on him, but it looked like he was not going to avoid their visit. All four walked in. "You the barber?" Jace demanded.

"Yes, sir," Murdock replied, his voice cracking with apprehension. "What can I do for you gentlemen? Haircuts, shaves?"

"Where's Will Tanner?" Jace blurted, with no patience for beating around the bush.

"Deputy Tanner?" Murdock fumbled. "Why, I have no idea. He hasn't been in here. Did you try over at the jail?"

"What's in that building behind this place?" Cobb asked, ignoring the question.

"Why, nothin' much," Murdock stammered. "It's my livin' quarters and a place where I do a little extra business sometimes."

"Let's have a look at it," Cobb said. "Whaddaya mean by 'a little extra business'? What kinda business?" Murdock could feel his throat going dry, unable to mask his fear, and Cobb sensed it. Whatever the reason, he knew the barber didn't want them to see inside that building. He fixed Murdock with a steely gaze. "What kinda business?" he repeated, this time with a threat in his tone.

"Mortuary," Murdock forced out. "I'm a mortician."

"He's a what?" Ben Cassady asked. "What the hell is that?"

"He's the undertaker," Marley White explained with a chuckle. "He cuts their throats in the barbershop, then buries 'em."

And the perfect place to hide a lawman who didn't want to be found, Cobb thought at once. "Let's go see your place," he said to Murdock.

"If you've got some kinda idea that Will Tanner is hidin' in my shop out back, I can assure you he's certainly not there."

His reluctance was enough to make Cobb feel he had hit upon a real possibility of finding the missing lawman. He dropped his hand to rest on his .44 and ordered, "We'll take a look in that place right now."

With no way out, Murdock said, "Yes, sir," and led them out the back door of the barbershop. He unlocked the door of his morgue and stood aside while they cautiously went inside.

"Ain't nobody in here," Jace called out, standing in the middle of the room, looking around him at the stove and cot in the front of the

190

room. Then he noticed the table in the rear of the room and what looked to be a body on it. It was covered with a white canvas sheet. "On the other hand," he called out again, "maybe there is." It occurred to him that it was a possibility the man they searched for might have hidden under the sheet, hoping they'd think it was a body. Alerted by his second statement, Cobb and the others came into the room, all with pistols drawn. Jace nodded toward the body on the table.

"That ain't Tanner on the table, there," Murdock was quick to assure them, fully alarmed now when they seemed intent upon seeing for themselves.

"Is that so?" Cobb responded. "Then there ain't nothin' to worry about, is there?" All four outlaws gathered around the table, their weapons cocked and aimed at the body. When Cobb nodded to him, Jace grabbed a corner of the canvas and jerked it off the table. All four stood, stunned and speechless, for a long moment, staring at the corpse of Archie Todd.

The silent void was broken then by Marley. "Well, I'll be a . . . it's Archie," he said, almost in a whisper. He and his partners turned at once toward Murdock, their guns pointed at the terrified barber-undertaker as if set to punish him for the death of their partner.

"Wait! Wait!" Murdock cried out, holding his hands up before him as if to protect himself from their guns. "It wasn't me that killed him. I'm just tryin' to prepare him for a decent burial. I swear, I had nothin' to do with his death. Will Tanner's the man you're lookin' for, and I don't have any idea where he is."

There was another silent impasse then as the four outlaws continued to stare at Archie's body. "Where's his stuff?" Cobb asked. "His money and his weapons, where are they?"

"The deputy's got 'em, I reckon," Murdock lied, hoping they didn't start to search for them, for they would not be hard to find.

Finally, Cobb decided they were just wasting their time there. "Cover him back up," he said, and Marley and Ben picked up the canvas sheet to spread over the corpse, much to Murdock's relief. When Archie was covered, Cobb turned his weapon upon the surprised undertaker and fired two shots into his midsection. The execution startled his fellow gang members as well as the unfortunate victim. "He's a lyin' lowlife," Cobb explained, turned, and walked out of the shop.

Jace looked at Marley and Ben, shrugged and said, "Reckon Cobb figures it's time somebody in this damn town started payin' for the trouble that deputy's started."

They followed him out of the shop to find him standing beside his horse, holding the ax he had taken from Brant's store. He looked at Jace and said, "I'm tired of searchin' this damn town for Will Tanner. It's plain to see he's cut and run, so I'm thinkin' to hell with him, I'm ready to bust Hawkins outta that jail."

CHAPTER 11

He heard the shots, but he was not sure where they had come from. Whatever the cause, it had come from one of the stores on the street. He had been in the telegraph office for about an hour now, first sending a telegram to Dan Stone in Fort Smith advising him of the situation in Atoka. With the arrival of new gang members, he had advised Stone of a need for additional deputies. After that wire was sent, the rest of the time was spent waiting for a reply from Stone, and for some reason, it was long in coming. Will could only imagine why. Probably, he figured, Stone was trying to call in the extra help. Jim Little Eagle had come to find him earlier to tell him he had been contacted by Sam Black Crow, who asked for his help in Muskogee. He said Sam's messenger, a young Creek boy, who was waiting outside, told him Sam needed help arresting a gang of Creek cattle rustlers. Will had told him to go ahead, everything seemed peaceful in town. Unaware of the arrival of Cobb and his men, since the railway station was about a hundred yards from the main street, he sat and passed the time talking to Sam Barnet.

Alert now, after hearing the shots, he ran out of the telegraph office in time to see the four riders pull up before the door of his jail. There was no mistaking their identity, for he easily recognized the one riding the red roan and the thin man wearing the derby hat. Without thinking, he cranked a cartridge into the chamber of his rifle as he made his way along the side of the telegraph office to the two barrels on the platform. Using them for cover, as he had the night before, he knelt on one knee and waited to see if they really planned to break into the jail.

"Let me take a lick at it," Ben said, and Cobb handed him the ax. Of the four, Ben was the biggest and proud of his strength. He walked up before the door, spit on his hands, and took a solid stance. Then he attacked the door with a mighty swing of the ax. The blade buried deeply in the solid oak, forcing him to strain hard to rock it back and forth in an effort to loosen it for a second blow. Winding up for another mighty swing, he landed another blow to the stubborn door. He grunted then, and to the other three's surprise, dropped to his knees and slowly keeled over on his side. Only then did Cobb notice the bullet hole in the back of Ben's coat. Realizing then what had just happened, Cobb yelled, "Get down!" It was too late for Marley, as a second shot from Will's rifle dropped him before he could react. He had not heard the first shot because the sound of it came at exactly the same time Ben's ax struck the door.

Realizing then where the shots were coming from, Cobb and Jace scrambled under the horses, trying to use them for protection. "Get behind the buildin'!" Cobb exclaimed, and grabbed the reins of all four horses. Using them for cover, he and Jace ran to the back of the jail, leading the horses. Once they reached the protection of the building, they pulled their rifles out of the saddle slings and prepared to defend themselves.

"Where the hell did that come from?" Jace blurted, still uncertain.

"The telegraph shack," Cobb replied. "The bushwhacker has been waitin' for us to show up here."

"Whadda we gonna do?" Jace exclaimed.

"We gotta see where he's shootin' from," Cobb told him. "Take your rifle and go to the other corner. I'll try to get a shot from this corner. Maybe he'll come outta his hidin' place."

Jace did as he was told and crawled up to the left-rear corner. He eased his rifle out past the back of the jail and jerked it back immediately when a shot from Will's rifle knocked a chunk of wood out of the corner post. "Damn!" Jace shouted. "I can't get out far enough to shoot without catchin' a bullet."

"Maybe I'll get a shot," Cobb said. Since he was at the right-rear corner, he didn't have to expose his body as much. So he eased his rifle around the corner, then slowly stuck his head around just enough to see with one eye beyond the front of the jail. He was immediately greeted with a rifle shot that struck the siding right beside his head. He jerked his head back and dragged his rifle back beside him, knowing he had escaped death by no more than a couple of inches. "Damn," he swore, realizing there was no way he and Jace could return fire without exposing themselves. The deputy was too accurate with that rifle. Aware now of noise coming from the inside of the jail, he let it register in his confusion. It was Hawkins and Tiny yelling from their cell room, trying to find out what was going on. "We can't do nothin' right now," he yelled back to them. "He's got us pinned down." He looked over at Jace, who was staring, wide-eyed, waiting to be told what to do. "We ain't got no choice," he said to him. "We've got to get outta here. We'll ride straight away from here. Keep the jail between us and that platform he's shootin' from. You take the reins of Marley's horse. I'll grab Ben's. Ride like hell."

"What about Ben and Marley?" Jace asked. "What if they ain't dead?"

"Ain't nothin' I can do about them," Cobb said. "If you wanna go back around the front of this buildin' to see, go right ahead." He got up from his position on the ground and stepped up into the saddle. He paused long enough to yell to those locked up inside, "He's got us treed, Ward.

Ain't no way we can get to you right now. We'll figure some way to get you later. We're gone!" He didn't wait for a reply and, giving the roan a kick, he was off at a gallop. Jace followed close behind him, lying low on his horse's neck, leading Marley's horse, unable to hear the cries of distress and frustration coming from inside the jail.

In his position behind the barrels on the railroad platform, Will could not see them leave until they were far enough away to come into view. By then, they were already nearing the reasonable limit of the Winchester's range. He took a couple of shots, anyway, but to no success. He stood up from behind the barrels and gazed at the rapidly disappearing horses as they galloped away to the south. He could not give chase for the simple reason he had no horse. He had not saddled Buster. The big buckskin was still in the stable and there was the matter of the shots he had heard when he was in the telegraph office. When that thought occurred, he looked toward the cluster of businesses that made up the main street. There were some people gathering in front of the barbershop, so he decided he should check on that before thinking of going after the two who escaped. They had run toward the south, but he figured they would ultimately circle back to return to Boggy Town, which was northeast of Atoka. Almost as an afterthought, he reminded himself that he had just shot two of the four outlaws, so he jumped down from the platform and moved quickly to the jail.

Both victims were lying, unmoving, in front of the jail. The heavy ax was still embedded in the middle of the oak door. A quick check told him that both men were dead, so he left them for the time being and ran to the barbershop. Tom Brant saw him coming and walked out to meet him. "It's Murdock," he said. "They shot him—twice, it looks like—he's dead. Then we heard all the shootin' at the jail and was afraid they'd killed you, too."

Will went in the barbershop to find the back door open, so he went on through to Murdock's room behind. There he found a couple of men looking over the scene of the shooting. One of them was Stanley Coons. Murdock's body was lying on the floor and the body of Archie Todd was on the table. Stanley looked at Will and said, "I reckon you're gonna need your horse. I'll help you saddle up."

" 'Preciate it," Will replied, and turned to follow Stanley outside.

"Wonder who we're supposed to call to take care of the bodies now?" Stanley asked. "Doc? Murdock ain't got no family."

"Maybe so," Will answered. "Maybe some of the other merchants can help out." There were two more in front of the jail to bury. They were his responsibility to take care of, since he had killed them. Murdock had already been paid to bury the one still lying on his table. Until the occasion of a new undertaker, Doc Lowell would seem the most qualified to perform that service. Will could well imagine the old grouch's response to the suggestion.

Back out on the street, Will was stopped by Tom Brant again. "That gang was in my store, and they walked out with an ax and never paid for it. Did you see it over there at the jail?"

"Yeah," Will answered, "I saw it. You can walk over and pick it up. You can't miss it." He started after Stanley again, who was already striding toward the stables, intent upon helping Will get after the two outlaws as soon as possible.

With all that had happened in less than an hour's time after Cobb and his men had called upon Ted Murdock, the one group of men who were left in the dark were the five prisoners in the jailhouse. Hearing the snap of bullets slapping the corners of the room that confined them, they could only speculate on what was happening. But when they heard the hurried declaration of retreat from Luke Cobb, seconds before he and Jace galloped away, it sent Hawkins into a rant of irate cursing. Confident to the point of smugness only hours before, he bellowed out his rage at the thought that he was now trapped in this jail. "It ain't lookin' too good for us right now, is it?"

Tiny McGee declared. Hawkins was too furious to answer him.

"He said they was gonna try to get us out later," Harley offered. Hawkins glared at him as if irate that he should even think it.

"I reckon that deputy will be goin' after 'em now," Pete Jessup offered. "I hope to hell he don't forget to get us our supper." His remark sent Hawkins into a deeper fit of anger, and the deep frown he aimed at him sent Pete to retreat to a corner beside Ernie Pratt. A cloud of silence hovered over the crowded cell room after that.

Once again, Will found himself on the trail along Muddy Boggy Creek. He realized that the two men he hunted now might not have returned to the outlaw hideout called Mama's Kitchen, but he felt strongly that they would. He would have appreciated Jim Little Eagle's help in an attempt to capture the two remaining outlaws. He was not sure, however, that there would be a possibility to arrest them. It was a lot more likely that this would be a kill-or-be-killed situation. These two were well aware that the crimes they had committed were hanging offenses, so there was not likely to be a surrender. It was time wasted even to think of that possibility, for he was convinced they would take any opportunity to shoot him. As he rode the three-plus miles to Boggy Town, he tried to decide the best plan to attack. The two he was after were proven killers, but he was uncertain about the others still at the hideout. What would be the reaction of the bartender and the hired hand who took care of the outside work and the horses? Then there were the two women, both hardened to life on the wrong side of the law. Would they join in the fight or stand aside to watch? The uncertainty was whether his fight was to be with two, four, or six. *Damn,* he thought, *I could sure use Jim Little Eagle.*

As he neared the hideout, he decided to cross the creek and approach it as he had done before, from the back. By the time he reached the place in the trail where he was to leave it and cross over to the other side, he had decided his mission was simply to take any shot he was presented with, playing the role of an assassin. Trying to make an arrest at all costs was a noble goal, but in this case was a foolish endeavor. He reminded himself that they had blatantly shot Ted Murdock down.

Inside Mama's Kitchen, Bud, Teddy, and the two women were once again interested bystanders watching another desperate drama unfold. Cobb and Jace had ridden into the yard only minutes before, leading the horses that Marley and Ben had ridden into town a few hours earlier. When Teddy asked what happened to the two missing men, Cobb replied in anger. "The piece of dirt was waitin' for us. That's what happened," he complained.

"Did he kill Ben and Marley?" Etta asked.

"Do you see Ben and Marley?" Cobb replied sarcastically as he checked his Colt to make sure it was fully loaded. "Teddy, get out there on the porch and keep your eyes peeled. Sing out if you see anybody."

"You think he's comin' after you?" Bud asked, thinking there might be the possibility Will Tanner might come to shoot the place to pieces.

"We ain't takin' no chances," Jace answered. "I expect he might." He turned to Cobb. "Whaddaya wanna do, Cobb? You think he's fool enough to come walkin' in here to arrest us?"

"I hope to hell he is," Cobb replied. "We gotta be ready for him, soon as he walks in that door."

"I don't think he's that dumb," Jace said. "I think he'll find himself a good spot above the path where he can watch anybody comin' in or out of the house. Try to pick us off like he did Marley and Ben at the jail." Cobb hesitated, giving that some thought. Jace continued, "I think we'd be better off hidin' in that burnt-down barn—somewhere we can watch the house and catch him if he comes sneakin' around in the yard."

Cobb wasn't sure what to do. He didn't feel confident that they could hole up in the saloon and guard against an attack by one man determined to find a way to get inside. "What about the horses?" Bud interrupted their planning. "The last time he pulled off that Injun raid, he run all the horses off the place, then set the barn on fire."

"That is somethin' to think about," Jace said. "Maybe we'd best watch the horses. We could do that if we hid in that burnt-out barn."

"Tanner's after us, he ain't after the horses," Cobb insisted, and when Jace started to interrupt, he cut him off. "I know what you're thinkin'— he'll stampede the horses to try to get us to come out to stop 'em. Well, I ain't plannin' to let him catch me out where he can get a shot at me. I say, let him come in here if he's fool enough, and I'll blow him to hell into next week. Teddy can watch the horses." He looked around the saloon until his gaze settled on the bar. "That's where I'll wait for him, right behind that fancy bar Tiny built. If you're smart, that's where you'll be. Go tell Teddy to take his rifle and go to the corral to watch the horses." Jace decided that was as good a plan as any, so he went out to tell Teddy.

"Watch the horses?" Teddy responded when Jace told him. He was already of a mind to saddle one of them and ride out of the mess Jace and Cobb had brought back to them. "What are you and Cobb gonna do?" When Jace said they were going to set up behind the bar and wait for

Tanner to come in after them, Teddy just stared in disbelief for a moment. "When he shoots me, then that'll be a signal for you and Cobb to know he's here, right?"

Jace didn't recognize the sarcasm at first, and answered, "Well, yeah, I reckon it would." Then realizing he was being japed, he got angry and said, "It's me and Cobb that deputy is comin' after. You ain't done nothin' to cause him to shoot you. So get on down to the corral, or I'm liable to shoot you."

Teddy knew what he wanted to tell him, but he didn't have the nerve to do it. So he said, "All right," and started walking toward the corral. As he did, he thought about the discussion he, Bud, Etta, and Ida had that afternoon after the four outlaws had left for town. Cobb was dead set on leaving Boggy Town, and Teddy and the other three had allowed themselves to think they could run the place inside the law. And even though the urge to saddle a horse and flee was strong at the moment, he knew he would stay, in hopes Cobb and Jace would be gone soon. Then, maybe there would be a chance the deputy would let the four of them remain to make it as best they could.

Inside the saloon, Cobb and Jace were preparing as if bracing for a military assault, using the bar as their fortification. They got their belongings from the bunkhouse section of the building and piled everything around behind their *fort*. There would be no need to leave the bar for anything. "Your job," Cobb told Etta and Ida, "is to make sure we've got plenty of food. Bud, you set yourself by that front window and keep an eye on the path down from the trail." He sent Ida to make sure the back door to the bunkhouse was barred. "If he wants a piece of us, he's gonna have to walk in that front door to get us," he said to Jace. "And after we take care of him, we'll go back and get Hawkins and the rest of the boys outta that jailhouse. There won't be nobody to stop us with him dead."

With an eye toward detail, and finding the preparations being made for their defense interesting, Etta was inspired to ask the two men a question. "After you've got everythin' fixed so you don't have to get out from behind that counter, whaddaya gonna do if you need to go to the outhouse?" There was no answer right away as the two men looked at each other with blank expressions. It was obvious they had made no provision for that possibility. " 'Cause I ain't about to clean up after two grown babies," she added.

"Go get us a couple of fruit jars," Jace finally said. "That oughta take care of it, if we have to pee," he said to Cobb. "Anything else, can wait."

Etta huffed scornfully. "If it comes to that, I'd pay a nickel to see you squattin' on a fruit jar." Without waiting for his response, she turned on her heel and went to the pantry to find a couple of empty fruit jars. When she returned, she handed one to each of them, along with a rag to clean up with. Turning to go to the kitchen just as Ida returned from the bunkhouse, she chuckled and muttered, "Fruit jars," as she passed Ida.

"You'd best watch your mouth, old woman," Cobb yelled after her. Curious, Ida followed her into the kitchen to find out what Etta meant. A few minutes later they could be heard laughing. Cobb was in no mood to be laughed at. "I swear, when we leave this place, I'm gonna shoot both of those witches," he said to Jace.

With no idea what defenses he might find in the saloon, Will walked his horse along the bank of the creek a couple of hundred yards away. He continued until he came to the thick growth of trees where he had left Buster on the night of the fire. Leaving the buckskin there again, he proceeded to move closer on foot. He was about to get even closer but stopped when he suddenly saw someone crouching by the corner of the corral. Carefully then, he moved to a position where he could get a better angle to identify him. It was the outside man they called Teddy, and he was apparently on guard to watch the horses. Will was not sure Teddy was guilty of anything beyond associating with outlaws. Consequently, he had no reason to harm him unless he chose to fight alongside Cobb and Jace. And that was an unknown he would have to deal with when the critical time came. At the present time, he could not chance causing Teddy to sound an alarm, so he backed away to think about his best option.

He knelt beside a large bush and took a look at the sun. It was already settling down closer to the hills he could see farther to the west. It would be getting dark before very much longer, the days being shorter this time of the year. He decided that darkness would be his friend. After a few more moments of thought, he also decided on a plan. It was a plan that might call for a great amount of patience, but it seemed to him to be his best option. With that in mind, he returned to the spot he had just left and paused to watch the huddled figure, trying to keep warm with a heavy coat pulled tight around him.

Shivering with the cold evening as the temperature began to drop, Teddy thought of where he would normally have been at that moment—sitting by the fire with his outside chores done for the day. He thought about the two outlaws inside the saloon, hiding behind the bar, like two rats in a rathole, and he truly wished they had been killed with the other two. He could see the smoke rising heavy out of the chimney and he could imagine them sitting warm inside the saloon. That picture was suddenly interrupted by the feel of the rifle against the back of his neck and the quiet voice close to his ear. "You make one sound and you're a dead man." He froze immediately. "If you do what I tell you, I have no reason to shoot you, but I promise you, if you don't, I will kill you. Now, get on your feet."

Shivering still, but now not so much from the cold, Teddy struggled to stand up, the rifle barrel still against his neck. Will reached over with one hand and picked up the rifle leaning against the corner of the corral. "You got another weapon on you?"

"No, sir," Teddy answered, knowing full well that it was Will Tanner. "I ain't wearin' no sidearm."

"All right," Will ordered. "We're gonna walk over there to that smokehouse on the other side of the outhouse. Remember what I told you about bein' quiet. I've got no interest in you, or anybody else inside that saloon but the two men who just killed a man in town and tried to break into the jail."

"Luke Cobb and Jace Palmer," Teddy blurted the names without being asked. "I ain't gonna make no noise."

Surprised to have their names, Will asked, "Anybody else in there besides the bartender and the two women?"

"No, sir," Teddy immediately supplied, "Bud Tilton, Etta Grise, and Ida Simpson. There ain't nobody else."

"Good," Will said, and walked him over to the

smokehouse he had checked a little while before. He opened the door and peered into the dark interior where a couple of hams were hanging. "I'm gonna let you stay in here for a while. If things work out, maybe I'll have some company for you." Teddy didn't hesitate but walked right in. Will couldn't help thinking he was happy to be captured. He closed the door and put the padlock in the hasp but didn't lock it. This was the way he had found it. "You just sit tight, I'll let you out directly," he said, and returned to the corner of the corral.

Inside the saloon, Etta announced that supper was ready. "You want me to set it on the table, or are you gonna set there and eat it behind the counter in your little fort?"

"Put it on the table," Cobb answered. "You keep on with that sassy mouth of yours and I might take a notion to close it for good."

"Yeah?" Etta came back. "Then who's gonna do the cookin' for you? Ida ain't much for cookin', and Bud don't know how to boil water."

"She's right," Ida said at once. "I ain't no cook." She went to help Etta put supper on the table and when it was set, Bud left the window and started toward the table.

"Whoa!" Cobb bellowed. "You just stay right there and keep watchin'. You can eat when we're done and back behind the bar."

Ida looked at Etta and shook her head, then she asked, "What about Teddy? Don't he get to eat?"

Cobb paused to consider that for a moment. "He needs to stay where he is and watch the horses." He thought a moment more. "If you're so worried about him, you can take him a plate—if you ain't worried about getting' shot."

"I ain't afraid of gettin' shot," she huffed. "Teddy's probably gettin' froze settin' out there in the cold." She picked up a plate and filled it, threw a blanket over her shoulders, and went out the kitchen door. "Damn!" she swore when she almost stumbled on the bottom step and came close to dropping the plate and the cup of coffee. "It's gettin' dark out here." Holding the plate of food carefully and trying to watch her step so as not to spill coffee out of the cup, she made her way toward the huddled figure at the corner of the corral. When within a few feet of him, she sang out, "You look like you're half-froze. I brought you some supper." He did not respond, causing her to think he'd gone to sleep. She placed the cup down next to him but jumped back, almost falling when he straightened up with his Colt .44 in his hand.

"Don't make a sound," he warned, "and you won't get hurt." Visibly terrified, she would have dropped the plate of food had he not taken it from her. She might have screamed, but she found herself incapable of making a sound.

211

Aware of it, he quickly tried to calm her. "You're all right, I'm not gonna harm you," he said in as soothing a tone as he could. "Just keep quiet and I'll take you to Teddy. He's safe, just like you'll be, if you do what I tell you." When she seemed to recover her wits, he handed the plate back to her, holstered his six-gun, and said, "Pick up the coffee and I'll take you to Teddy. I think he'll be glad to get it."

He led her across the backyard to the smokehouse and took the padlock out of the hasp. "You all right in there, Teddy?" When Teddy said that he was, Will said, "I brought you some company. She's got your supper."

Back in a corner of the smokehouse, Teddy pulled a match out of his pocket and struck it. Its brief light was enough to show Ida where he was, and she hurried toward him before it sputtered out. "Howdy, Ida," he said cheerfully. "I can surely use that." He took the cup and plate from her.

"Well, I'll be . . ." she started but was too surprised to finish. She turned to look at the silhouette standing in the open door. "I was afraid you'd killed him."

"I've got no quarrel with him," Will said. "You, either. You'll be in here a little while longer, till I see how this works out. Are Cobb and Jace still hunkered down behind the bar?"

She looked at once toward Teddy. He shrugged and said, "I told him."

She hesitated for just a moment, trying to decide where her loyalties should lie. In the next moment, she decided she owed none to Cobb and Jace. So she said, "That's where they are, and they're hopin' you come chargin' in the door."

"Much obliged," he said. "You two keep each other warm." He closed the door then and replaced the unlocked padlock. He returned to the corral then and prepared to wait again for a while to see if anyone else came to check on Teddy and Ida. He figured the more bystanders he got out of the saloon, the better, if it came down to a firefight in close quarters. And it could very well come to that.

Inside the saloon, Bud was finally allowed to eat his supper when Cobb and Jace retreated to their base behind the bar. Cobb changed his mind about permitting him to sit down at the table, however, and told Etta to dish up a plate for him and take it to him by the window. He was determined not to be surprised by the deputy. Bud was finishing up his supper before Jace suddenly asked, "How come Ida ain't back yet?"

Etta answered him. "Most likely she's waitin' for him to finish, so she can bring the dishes back."

That sounded reasonable, so it satisfied him for the moment. But as more time passed with still no sign of Ida, both Jace and Cobb became concerned. "Where the hell *is* she?" Cobb suddenly demanded. "He's damn sure had time to eat that plate of food by now."

Over by the front window, Bud offered what he considered a reasonable explanation. "You know what Baby does for a livin'," he said, calling Ida by her professional name. "Maybe ol' Teddy decided to take a little ride after supper. It wouldn't be the first time."

The thought of that served to infuriate Cobb, who was already getting more and more edgy waiting for Tanner to show up. "If he did, I swear, I'll shoot him. I sent him down there to watch the horses." He started to storm out the door but thought better of it, madder now to think that Teddy almost caused him to expose himself to a sniper waiting for him to come out. He turned about and pointed his finger at Bud. "Go down there and bring that whore back in here. And tell Teddy he's gonna answer to me!"

"Who's gonna watch for Will Tanner?" Bud asked, not particularly anxious to expose himself to whatever might be waiting outside the building.

"I will," Jace volunteered. "Go on and do what he said." He saw signs that Cobb was getting too edgy and he didn't trust him to keep his impatience in check. The thought crossed his mind that Teddy, and now Ida, had decided it was time to run. When Bud moved away from

214

the window, Jace stepped up to take his position. "Make sure Teddy's on the job down there. If he ain't there, you get back up here in a hurry and let me know." Bud nodded his understanding. "And bring Ida back here. We don't need her down there botherin' him."

With his shotgun in hand, Bud paused briefly at the back door and tried to scan the yard between the house and the corral before going down the steps. Full darkness had descended upon the clearing where Mama's Kitchen had been built and there was no sign of the moon as yet. It dawned on him that his vigil by the window was not of much value, because he couldn't see that much even now when he was outside. Not at all comfortable with the idea that someone might be watching him, now that he was outside, he hurried toward the burnt remains of the stable, even more eerie in the darkness. Halfway there, he was relieved to see the outline of Teddy's body by the corner of the corral. He hurried his step, anxious to impart his message and return to the relative safety of the saloon. "Hey, Teddy, Cobb ain't too happy with you. Where's Ida?"

"She's waitin' for you in the smokehouse," Will said, and straightened up to face him. Bud stepped back, startled, offering no resistance when Will reached out and took the shotgun out of his hand. "Don't make a sound. I'll tell you the same thing I told Teddy and Ida. You do what I tell you, and you won't get hurt. You understand?"

Bud nodded vigorously before answering, "Yes, sir, I understand."

"Good. We're goin' to the smokehouse where Teddy and Ida are waitin'." He turned Bud's shoulders toward the smokehouse and nudged him in the back to get him started. When he got to the smokehouse and opened the door, he asked, "Got room for one more?"

Teddy, who by this time was actually enjoying the drama being played out for the benefit of the two outlaws inside the saloon, was quick to answer. "Yes, sir! We're always glad to have one more for the party. Come on in, Bud."

No longer afraid for her safety, but not quite as joyful as Teddy, Ida wanted to ask a question. "Tell me, Will Tanner, what are you gonna do with us? Are we under arrest?" Her question caught the attention of Teddy and Bud.

"No," Will answered. "I've got no reason to arrest you. Let's just say you're in protective custody. When this is all over, whatever happens, you three, and the cook, too, are free to go your own way. I hope you won't have to stay in here much longer." He closed the door again and left them to discuss their situation.

As soon as they were sure he was gone, they all started talking at the same time, wondering what was going to happen next. There was concern about whether or not they were going to catch hell from Cobb and Jace, if the two outlaws came out on top. "I know who I'm hopin' is gonna win this fight," Teddy declared. Without asking him who, the other two quickly said they agreed with him.

"Wouldn't it be somethin' if Tanner could trick 'em into sending Etta out here with us?" Ida speculated.

CHAPTER 12

Inside the saloon it became strangely quiet. Etta Grise stood by the table, now empty of diners, baffled by the absence of the two people who had gone outside to contact Teddy. With no motivation to start cleaning up her kitchen, she remained in the saloon, watching the two obviously desperate men, aware of the mounting tension between them. Finally, after what seemed an inordinate amount of time since Bud went out the door, Jace spoke. "What in the hell is goin' on? He shoulda been back here by now."

"He's out there," Cobb declared solemnly. "Tanner, that's what's happened to 'em. He's out there and he's waitin' for us to come get him. But he's still a dead man if he tries to come in here to get us."

"I'm wastin' my time lookin' out this front window," Jace decided. "It's plain that he ain't in the front. He's back by the corral. That's where we sent everybody, and they ain't come back." To emphasize his belief, he returned to the bar. "The thing we ain't thought about is the fact that he's settin' down there at the corral with all our horses. We can't get outta here without walkin' into that rifle of his."

"We ain't wantin' to get outta here," Cobb

insisted. "We can sure as hell wait him out. We've got food and somebody to cook it. We'll wait him out till he gets hungry and tired of settin' down there by the corral. Then when he decides he's gonna try to come get us, we'll be waitin' for him."

"What if he decides to run our horses off?" Jace asked, still skeptical of their situation. "We was plannin' to leave here and go to the Arbuckles. I'd sure hate to have to walk there."

"He ain't gonna run the horses off," Cobb replied, not sure of it, since Jace brought it up, but reluctant to admit the possibility. "Stayin' right here where we can cut him down, if he finally does get up the guts to come in here after us, is the best thing to do." He glanced over at Etta, still standing, listening to the discussion. "Like I said, we've got food and somebody to cook it for us. We're in good shape. Ain't we, Etta?"

She didn't answer his question, making a statement instead. "I reckon I'd best get in there and clean up my kitchen," she said.

"And put on another pot of coffee," Cobb called after her as she disappeared through the door to the kitchen.

"Right!" Etta yelled back at him.

Back to Jace then, Cobb said, "We need to make sure we don't get sleepy till after we take care of Tanner. I swear, though, I've drunk so much coffee already that I might need to tell Etta to find me another fruit jar." He forced a chuckle in appreciation for his humor.

Jace made an effort to join in, but found nothing humorous about the situation the two of them found themselves in. He walked back to the front window, more as an effort to burn some of the nervous energy constantly building inside him, instead of watching for Tanner. The eerie disappearance of the three people they had sent to the corral was something he couldn't explain. And Jace needed to be able to see things plain as day. He was thinking now that he would have preferred to face Tanner while it was still daylight and take his chances in a face-to-face shoot-out. After another long interval of silence, he shrugged and walked back to the bar. "Etta!" he yelled. "Ain't that coffee ready yet?" He waited for a response, but there was none. "Etta!" he yelled again. When again there was no answer from the kitchen, he said, "Damned old woman, has she gone deaf?" He walked into the kitchen only to find it empty. Confused, because they would have seen her if she had come out of the kitchen to go to her room, he went to the pantry. When he didn't find her there, he moved quickly to the back door. It was unlocked! He quickly threw the bolt again, drawing his Colt at the same time and looking right and left in case Tanner was in the kitchen. Shaken now, he hurried back into the saloon to tell Cobb. "She's gone!" he blurted out, still with a drawn pistol.

"Whaddaya mean, 'She's gone'?" Cobb responded.

"I mean she's gone," Jace repeated. "She ain't in the kitchen. She didn't put no pot of coffee on the stove, and the back door was unlocked."

Cobb reacted in the same manner as his partner, drawing his weapon as well. Then it occurred to him. "Most likely she went to the outhouse. Did you lock the door?" Jace nodded, having never thought of that reasonable possibility. "Well, best leave it locked—make her knock to get back in. Then maybe she'll remember to use that thunder mug she's got under her bed next time."

Feeling irritated that he had not thought of that possibility, he said, "The old bag, she might as well have said, *Come on in, the door's open*." He swore, then said, "She coulda put the coffee on to boil before she went to the outhouse."

He would have been a lot madder at Etta had he known that she had been in the kitchen brief minutes before he had come to look for her. For as he and Cobb waited for her knock on the kitchen door, she was even then on her way to the corral, having made up her mind which side she was on. Equally mystified by the disappearance of Ida and Bud when they went to talk to Teddy, she did not believe any harm had come to them. In the brief time she had known Will Tanner, she

221

did not see him as a cruel and evil man. And at this particular stage in her sometimes-hard life, she feared very little of what might lie ahead in her future. Like Ida and Bud before her, she saw the dark image of someone crouching by the corner of the corral. Unlike them, she felt certain who the form actually was. "Hey, Will Tanner," she announced before getting within a dozen feet of him, "I'm comin' to join my friends. Where'd you put 'em?"

Will didn't answer right away, surprised by the greeting from the rambunctious woman, wearing a coat plus a blanket wrapped around her. "They're in the smokehouse, waitin' for you." He rose to his feet, still a little suspicious of her motives. "You ain't carryin' a weapon under that blanket, are you?"

"Nope," she replied, and opened the blanket wide so he could see.

"Don't get me wrong," he said, still cautious, lest she was up to some trick he couldn't see coming. "But you're my first volunteer for the smokehouse. The others had to be escorted at gunpoint." He said that, even though there had been no resistance from any of the three.

Not waiting for him, she made straight for the smokehouse. "I reckon I've got a feelin' that all three of 'em went to the smokehouse without givin' you any trouble a-tall," she called back over her shoulder. "I think all four of us are ready to see the last of that pair in the house. I'm bettin' that you ain't out to give us no trouble, since you know we ain't killed nobody, ain't rustled no cattle, or held up no banks. I don't know if Ida told you, but we've been talkin' about runnin' this place as a legitimate restaurant and stopover, with no whiskey sold. So, what I'm sayin' is, we're ready to bet on you to clean this place out, so don't let us down."

They had arrived at the smokehouse by the time Etta had said her piece, leaving Will somewhat astonished. He had in no way anticipated a desertion movement on the part of Tiny McGee's hired help, and he was still a little reluctant to accept it whole hog. From inside the smokehouse, Ida called out, "Etta, is that you?" She had evidently heard Etta chattering away as they approached.

"Yes, honey, it's me," Etta answered. "I decided to give up my evil ways and turn myself over to the law." Will opened the door and Etta stepped inside to be welcomed by Ida and the two men. "You all ran out on me and left me up there with those two jackasses."

"They still hidin' behind the bar?" Bud asked.

"That they are," Etta said. "When you never came back, I made up my mind that I weren't gonna be the only one left to wait on 'em. When Cobb hollered for me to make him some coffee, I walked into the kitchen and right on out the back door. I wanted to see what you were all up to, so I could join you."

"I reckon what's gonna happen to us now depends on what you're fixin' to do, Deputy," Bud said to Will. "You thinkin' about goin' in there to get 'em? 'Cause that's just what they're waitin' for you to try. Matter of fact, that's what they're hopin' you'll try. They're hunkered down behind that bar, like it was a fort." Will didn't answer right away, so Bud made another suggestion. "You might be thinkin' about settin' the place on fire and run 'em outta there." His idea caused a sudden silence among his three partners in mutiny.

"To tell you the truth," Will finally answered, "that's what I had in mind to do. I figured I'd probably have to." He could almost feel their silence at that point. "But if Etta is telling me the truth about what you plan to do with this place, I reckon I'll have to think of some other way to get them outta there. I ain't sure if this spot is a good one for the kind of place you're talkin' about, but I reckon you oughta have the chance to try it." His statement caused an immediate sigh of relief from all four.

"Dad-burn if that ain't damn decent of you," Teddy said.

"I swear, if you weren't a lawman, I'd give you a hug," Etta declared. "You'd be the first one I've ever hugged, though."

Will was trying to decide his next move while they were congratulating one another on their good fortune. He had not lied when he told them he had planned to burn Mama's Kitchen to the ground, to make sure no other outlaws tried to use it. It was a pretty secure building to break into. He had to give Tiny credit for that. Then an idea occurred to him and he asked Etta a question. "You said you came out the kitchen door. Did you lock it behind you?" He wasn't sure she could lock the door from the outside.

She verified that when she answered. "No, it ain't got no lock on the outside of that door. You have to latch it from the inside. I hate to disappoint you, but I heard one of 'em lock it when I was walkin' away from the house. Mighta been Jace. He was the one I heard hollerin' my name."

Will shook his head, disappointed. "Any other way to get in that saloon room? How 'bout from those rooms on the back?" Again he was disappointed when she said that Cobb and Jace had made sure all the other doors were barred. Then she suggested a plan that might work, but it would be dangerous.

"You know, I've been gone awhile, but it ain't been that long. I could go back and knock on the door, tell 'em I was usin' the outhouse. Then when they unlocked it, the rest would be up to you."

That was better than anything he could think of, but it might put her at risk. "Are you sure you wanna take a chance on that? You'd have to run like hell as soon as the bolt was thrown."

"You don't have to tell me that," she said. "I'll do it if you wanna try it."

"That's the only way I think I can get in there," he said. "The only problem is, I had planned to keep all four of you locked in this smokehouse in case I didn't make it. That way, they wouldn't know that you were helping me."

"Don't worry about that," Teddy said. "If they shoot you, Etta can tell 'em you forced her. Then she let us out when she ran away."

"If you're gonna do it, we'd best get to it," Etta said. "Much longer and he might not believe I was in the outhouse that long."

"All right, then, let's go," Will said. He and Etta hurried back toward the kitchen door, leaving three excited souls wishing him good luck. As they approached the steps to the kitchen, he couldn't help thinking of the possibility that this was all a planned trap. Etta might have been sent out to tell him this tale, and he was the one being set up for the big surprise. With that in mind, he held his Winchester ready with a thought of shooting her first, if this was a setup. He hoped to hell it wasn't.

When they got to the steps, Etta turned to him and whispered, "You ready?" He nodded, his rifle cocked and ready to fire. She stepped up and tried the handle. It was still locked, so she rapped hard on the door and yelled, "Unlock the damn door!"

In a matter of seconds, they heard the sound of boots running across the kitchen floor, and then a voice she identified as Jace's. "Is that you, Etta?"

"Well, who the hell do you think it is?" she came back at him. "Whadja lock the door for? I had to take a dump." She looked back at Will and nodded confidently.

There was a long moment of decision before they heard the bolt thrown open. Will grabbed her elbow, pulled her off the step and pointed toward the smokehouse. She needed no more encouragement and ran as fast as she could manage. Will stepped inside the screen door and braced himself to launch his body into whoever opened the door. He stood, poised for attack, his rifle ready until, finally, the handle turned slowly, so slowly that he realized the man on the other side of the door was not taking any chances. At last the door began to open, but for only a few inches, and Will could see just half of a face as Jace attempted to peek out to make sure Etta was alone. Before he could get a good look, Will threw his shoulder against the door and crashed into the kitchen, knocking Jace backward to stumble against the stove. He yelped in pain as he rolled across the hot surface, still holding on to his pistol when he hit the floor. In a panic, he fired a bullet that buried itself over the door, then cocked his weapon quickly, leaving Will no choice. He pumped one round into Jace's chest, quickly cranking another ready to fire but held up when Jace dropped back, finished. *I didn't have a choice,* Will told himself, his eyes fixed on the door to the saloon, expecting Cobb to come through it at any second.

There was no sound at all from the large room beyond the door for what seemed a long, long time. Will hurried to stand beside the open door, where he listened for sounds of movement that would indicate Cobb was advancing toward him. Finally, he heard Cobb call out, "Jace, you all right?"

"Jace is dead," Will answered him. "He made a mistake and paid for it. Now I'm givin' you a chance to surrender, so you don't get the same as he got." Standing beside the door, he could see the bar at the other side of the saloon. He drew his rifle up, steadied it against the doorjamb, and aimed at the oak counter. After a few long seconds with no response from behind the counter, he called out again. "What about it, Cobb? You ready to throw your gun out and walk away from here alive?"

"I'll tell you what, Tanner," Cobb answered. "Why don't you come on out here and arrest me?" Will saw the rifle suddenly appear on the top of the bar and jumped back just before a .44 slug embedded itself in the doorframe. Will popped back out long enough to throw a shot at the rifle but was not quick enough to hit it as it was jerked back behind the bar. In rapid succession, they repeated the exchange of shots, with neither man able to get a clean shot.

"We're just wastin' time and ammunition," Will said. "It's just a matter of time. You're either gonna walk outta here under arrest or get carried outta here to a shallow grave. You can't stay hunkered down behind that bar forever, and the only way out is by me. So whaddaya say, Cobb, you ready to play it smart?" He knew it would be a desperate chance, but he was not willing to carry on this standoff all night long. And as conditions stood at the moment, he could imagine it might go on that long, with the first one to run out of ammunition the loser. So he called out once more. "I'm gonna need you to throw out that rifle and your handgun, too. Make it easy on yourself." He was hoping to bait Cobb into talking, causing his own distraction.

"I gotta hand it to ya, Tanner, I'm damn surprised you was able to get past Jace. He was a good man. But now you're dealin' with somebody who eats lawmen for supper." Suddenly, he pushed his rifle up on the bar again and fired another round at the kitchen door, hoping to catch Will off guard. After the slug whistled through the open door, Will returned fire.

It's now or never, Will told himself then, when

he thought he could hear Cobb reloading. He pulled his boots off, and with his rifle aimed at the counter, he tiptoed out the door and across the room to drop quietly on one knee against the face of the bar. The sound of Cobb mumbling encouragement to himself as he finished reloading his rifle, told Will he had not been heard. At the sound of Cobb cranking in a new cartridge, Will laid his rifle on the floor, carefully, so as not to make a sound. With both hands free, he raised slightly to a crouch and waited for Cobb to pop up again to fire another round at the kitchen door. He had to be quick, so as soon as he heard the rifle hit the top of the bar, he sprang up and grabbed it by the barrel. Startled, Cobb's natural reaction was to pull the trigger, sending a shot across the room to strike the opposite wall. Then, fighting to hold on to his rifle, he tried to pull it away from Will until Will suddenly shoved the rifle back at Cobb, causing the butt to catch Cobb in the face, stunning him momentarily. It was long enough for Will to jerk the weapon free of Cobb's hands. Desperate now, Cobb lunged halfway across the counter at Will. But Will, still holding the rifle by the barrel, swung it like an ax, knocking the crazed outlaw to the floor. Will quickly looked over the counter to see Cobb lying apparently unconscious on the floor. Wasting no time, he moved around the end of the counter to make sure. Just as he rounded the end of the bar, Cobb suddenly rolled over with his revolver in his hand. There was no time to think—natural reaction took over. Will sent the bullet, already cocked and ready, into his chest. Cobb was dead when he pulled the trigger that sent a shot within inches of Will's ear.

Feeling suddenly exhausted, Will knelt down beside the body to make sure Cobb didn't spring up again. When it was obvious that he was dead, Will took a few moments to consider the course of attack he had just completed. It worked out in his favor, but he admitted to himself that he had been lucky. It could have just as easily worked out in Cobb's favor. *That might have canceled your wedding plans for sure, Sophie.* The thought sprang into his mind completely unexpected at a time like this. It caused him to pause a moment and decide that Sophie's mother was right when she said it was a mistake for her daughter to marry a deputy marshal. As before, when the subject popped into his mind, he found himself agreeing with Ruth Bennett. He had to wonder what he'd do if he found himself in a similar confrontation as this one after he was married. Would he have a tendency to play it safer—maybe even backing off? Then he remembered he had promised to leave the service after he and Sophie married. He was saved from further thoughts of it when he heard Teddy calling from the back door. "Cobb, are you all right?"

"He's dead," Will answered, his mind back to the business at hand. "You folks can come on back now."

In a few moments, Teddy appeared in the kitchen door, having stopped briefly to stare at Jace's body. "We heard all the shootin' and after it got quiet for a while, I thought I'd come see. I just hollered for Cobb before I came in," he started to explain, but Will interrupted.

"I figured," Will said. "No need to explain. Better to play it safe, in case Cobb was the one left standin', right?"

"Right," Teddy quickly agreed. "But I'm glad it was you," he was quick to add. He walked over to look at Cobb's body behind the bar. "You still mean what you said out there in the smokehouse—you ain't gonna arrest the rest of us?"

"That's right," Will said, then joked. "Besides, I ain't got any separate quarters for women in my little jailhouse."

Teddy laughed and said, "I'll go tell 'em to come back in and get warm. I expect they're about froze by now, especially Etta. She ain't much more'n skin and bones, anyway."

He was only gone for a couple of minutes when Will heard them come in the back door. "He left a mess on my kitchen floor," he heard Etta complain, and figured Jace had bled out on the floor. He had not taken the time to notice after he shot him. A few moments more, and the four of them came into the saloon. Etta was the first to go behind the counter to take a look at the late Luke Cobb. "I swear, I couldn't abide that man," she declared. "I have to say that's the best he's ever looked to me." She turned to face Will then. "Teddy said you're gonna keep your word about not arrestin' us. Is that a fact?"

In Will's mind her question seemed more like a demand. He suspected he knew who was going to run the operation, if they still had in mind staying here. "Yep, I'm good for my word. I got no plans to arrest you." His answer brought a smile to her face. He asked her a question then. "Are you still thinkin' about tryin' to run a legitimate business here?" When she answered that they were, indeed, he continued. "Well, it ain't likely to be easy. You're gonna need some operatin' money to get you started. So, I expect it'd be a good idea to go through Cobb's and Jace's pockets. They might have some cash money in their saddlebags, too." That brought four grins immediately and Bud and Teddy wasted no time in starting the search. "I'll take their guns and ammunition," Will went on, "and anything else that'll help identify 'em. I need something that will help confirm they're dead."

Considering there were two bodies lying on the floor, there was now a gala atmosphere in the former saloon called Mama's Kitchen. After the bodies were relieved of everything useful, Bud and Teddy, with Will's help, dragged each corpse out of the building to be deposited by the back door. Teddy said that he would be happy to drag them out of the yard to be planted somewhere. "Wherever it is," Etta said, "don't put no fertilizer with 'em. I'd hate to see what might grow outta them two." Even though the hour was late, she put on a fresh pot of coffee and warmed up some leftover biscuits in the oven. While Will enjoyed the coffee and biscuits, they served to remind him that he had left five prisoners in jail without any supper. He would have made arrangements to feed them, had it been possible, but there was no way it could have been safely done. There was no one there he would ask to risk dealing with the likes of Ward Hawkins and Tiny McGee. It wouldn't hurt them to go without supper. He would have Lottie fix up a big breakfast for them to make up for his neglect. He said good-bye to the new operators of Mama's Kitchen and wished them luck. Then he loaded their weapons and ammunition on one of the horses he selected from the corral to pack them on and started back to town.

At about the same time Will left the four new partners in the Boggy Town Hotel, as Etta had suggested calling their venture, Ward Hawkins reined his horse to a stop and held up his hand.

"What's up, Ward?" Tiny asked when he pulled up alongside him. "Whadda we stoppin' here for? That looks like a creek or somethin' up ahead." He pointed to a dark image of trees ahead in the darkness.

"We need money and supplies," Hawkins said. "We can make camp up ahead, but we ain't got nothin' to cook. I ain't ridin' all the way to The Falls on an empty belly, and there won't be nothin' in that cabin when we get there."

"Maybe we'll see a deer or somethin' else to hunt," Harley suggested, "or maybe we'll strike a store or tradin' post between here and the mountains."

"And maybe we won't," Hawkins replied. "There ain't no store between here and the hideout. But I know where we can find supplies, and a coffeepot, and some money. I shoulda thought about it and gone straight to Boggy Town when we left Atoka. I'm goin' back to get my packs and pick up Cobb and Jace. It ain't that far back to the saloon."

"Hell, I thought about the money when we was at the stable, but I reckon I just started thinkin' about headin' for the mountains," Tiny said. "I'll go with you."

Harley and the two wagon drivers were not anxious to return to the saloon, now that it was so well known to the law. When he saw their obvious reaction to his plan, he said, "You three can go on to that creek and make camp. It won't be long before me and Tiny get back with somethin' to cook, maybe somethin' to drink if they ain't drank it all up." That suggestion suited the other three, so they continued on to the creek in the distance. Hawkins and Tiny turned back toward the east, on a line that would take them back to Muddy Boggy Creek.

After a ride of close to seven miles, they struck the creek a quarter of a mile downstream from Boggy Town, so they followed it upstream until they came to the burnt remains of the barn and stables. The site served to rile Tiny, since he was the one who had built it. "I hope that rat is here." They had considered the possibility that Tanner had gone after Cobb and Jace and might still be there because he had been gone from town all day.

"That would put the icin' on this cake, wouldn't it?" Hawkins replied. With that in mind, they rode slowly across the darkened barnyard toward the main building. There was no horse tied at the rail, so they rode on up to the front porch and dismounted. Being careful not to alert anyone inside, they moved up to the front window and looked to see who was in the saloon. All four of Tiny's hired hands were there, but he didn't see Cobb or Jace. "Looks like they're havin' a damn party," Hawkins muttered.

Still celebrating their bold venture together, Ida

opened a bottle of whiskey she had hidden in the pantry. Holding it up, she started to propose a toast when she suddenly stopped in midsentence and stared glassy-eyed at the front door. When her three partners turned to see what had stopped her, there were now four glassy-eyed gawkers. Being keener of wits than the other three, Etta sang out, "Welcome home, Tiny!" Following suit, the others attempted to make a show of welcome.

"What the hell's the big celebration?" Hawkins demanded.

Continuing to carry on with the farce, Etta answered, "Why, because that lawman finally left here, and we're still alive." She would not tell them that it had been a very short time since Will had left. And she could not help wondering how they had not bumped into each other.

"Where's Cobb and Jace?" Hawkins asked. "Didn't they come back here?"

"Tanner killed 'em," Teddy answered him. "Tanner came here after 'em. They're layin' out by the kitchen steps. I'm fixin' to bury 'em in the mornin'."

Hawkins and Tiny exchanged a long glance, both thinking the same thing. While they were obviously considering what to do about that last piece of news, Ida asked the question she and her partners were vitally interested in. "Are you back here to stay now?"

"Hell, no," Hawkins answered sharply. "This

place is too hot for us now. Every lawman in Texas and Oklahoma will know about Boggy Town. As soon as we pack up some supplies and collect our possibles, we're puttin' this place behind us." He cocked a sharp eye at Ida. "My saddlebags and other stuff better be in that room I was sleepin' in."

"Oh, they are, they are," Etta answered.

"There's a roll of cash money in one of those pockets in my saddlebags," Hawkins said. "I reckon that's still there, right?"

"Well, I don't know if it is or not," she replied. "We ain't bothered none of your things. But that deputy took money outta Cobb's and Jace's pockets, and he went back there in the bunkhouse to look around. So he mighta found your money, too."

"Damn!" Hawkins cursed. "Start gatherin' up some food," he told Tiny, then headed toward the bunkhouse to get his personal things. When he returned with his saddlebags and a canvas sack that held his shaving things and spare clothes, he announced, "My damn money's gone." He stared at Etta with an accusing eye.

"Oh my," she said, "that is sorry news. Was it much?"

"It was enough," he said stony-faced.

"I wish I'da looked in your things and beat him to it," she said. She could feel Ida's wide-open eyes focused on her, but she dared not look at her for fear they would give the whole farce away.

Anxious to change the subject then, she asked, "If you and Tiny are fixin' to leave here, are you wantin' us to pack up and get ready to go with you?"

"No, we can't take you with us," Hawkins said at once. "We'll be movin' too fast. Looks like the lot of you are gonna have to fend for yourselves. It's tough, but that's the way it is sometimes. Besides, we'll be stayin' in an outlaw camp up in the mountains. Ain't no place for women." He looked at Bud and Teddy, who were both watching, speechless. "Won't have much use for a bartender or a hired hand, either." That said, he went to the storeroom to help Tiny empty some of the shelves of flour, salt, coffee, dried beans, and anything else they thought they could turn into food.

The four of them watched as Hawkins and Tiny carried out everything they could load on the two packhorses they had taken from Stanley Coons's stable. It put a sizable hole in their stored supplies, but they were secure in the knowledge that they had a ready supply of cash money, courtesy of Cobb, Jace, and particularly Hawkins. Once their horses were loaded, Tiny and Hawkins wasted no more time in Boggy Town and set out to join their companions, waiting at the creek for them. "Those boys oughta be glad to see us 'cause they ain't got nothin' to cook," Tiny said as he climbed up into the saddle.

CHAPTER 13

It was well past suppertime when he rode into town and everything looked all buttoned up for the night. The dining room next to Doug Mabry's boardinghouse was dark and there were only a few lights burning in the boardinghouse itself. It would have been too late to pick up any food for his prisoners even if he had arrived an hour earlier. He thought to ride straight to the stables first, but glancing ahead toward the jail, he was surprised to see a jail wagon standing alongside the building. The odd thing about it was the fact that the team of horses was still hitched up to the wagon, and a saddled horse was tied to the back of it. His first thought was it must have just arrived, and that was odd, that whoever the deputy was, he had pushed on to arrive this late at night. *It couldn't be Ed,* he thought, thinking he would not have had time to get back. He bypassed the stables and went directly to the jail. As he approached, he saw there were no lights inside the jail, in the front office or the cell room.

It wasn't until he pulled Buster to a halt and stepped down from the saddle that he noticed what appeared to be two prisoners sitting down inside the wagon. That was more than enough to alert him that something was dreadfully wrong.

He reached for his Winchester and advanced cautiously toward the jail wagon. Walking past the front door of the jail, he noticed that the door was not closed but was slightly ajar, as if the last person in or out was careless about closing it. He was only a few feet from the back of the wagon when the still form sitting in the corner spoke. "Will? Is that you?"

He recognized the voice at once. "Ed? What the hell? What are you doin' out here? Who's that?" he asked when the other form stirred.

"It's me, Horace Watson," he answered. "They locked us in here."

Feeling as if he had been struck dumb, Will didn't have to ask who had locked them in the jail wagon, and he didn't have to ask if his prisoners were still secure inside the jail. He looked around him, halfway expecting to find himself surrounded, but there was no threat forthcoming. "All five of 'em?" he asked, simply.

Ed nodded slowly. "All five," he confirmed.

"Ed, how the hell did it happen?" Then before Ed could answer, he asked, "Are you all right? How 'bout you, Horace?" He was working hard to remain calm, but he wanted details of how five prisoners locked in a secure cell room could escape and lock the arresting officer in his own jail wagon.

Horace answered first. "We're all right now that you finally got here," he said. "They left us here and didn't even tie the horses. We was afraid the horses would get spooked and take off to who knows where. I'm all right, but Ed took a bullet in the shoulder when he tried to stop 'em."

"How bad is it?" Will asked Ed then. "You need to see Doc Lowell."

"It ain't that bad," he said. "There ain't no bullet in it. It just tore a rut right across my shoulder. I stuffed my bandanna over it and got the bleedin' stopped. It'll hold till mornin'." He shook his head slowly, obviously reluctant to admit that he had once again been ambushed by a felon. "I swear, Will, it looks like I'm snakebit when it comes to takin' prisoners in custody."

"With the pair you were dealin' with, it could happen to anybody," Will said, knowing how ashamed Ed felt. "How long have they been gone?"

"Since after suppertime," Ed answered.

Will took hold of the padlock on the jail wagon and tried it, in case it wasn't fully engaged. "They take the key to this lock with 'em?"

"No," Horace answered. "That one feller, the one they called Hawkins, he took it outta Ed's pocket, so he could unlock it and put us in here. Then he just threw it toward the corner of the buildin'. I heard it hit the side of the buildin'." He pointed toward the right corner.

"Maybe I can find it," Will said, knowing it would be hard to break them out of the wagon.

242

"If you heard it hit the sidin', maybe I can find it in the dirt." He went over to where Horace had pointed. Striking a match, he looked around in the dirt by the building. After striking two more matches, he spotted it and was able to free them. Looking back to Ed, he asked, "How the hell did you get back here so fast?"

"Dan Stone had already sent another jail wagon. We met 'em along the way and I swapped with 'em. They took the prisoners back and me and Horace came back to help you."

"You say you got here at suppertime?" Will asked.

"Yep, or maybe a little after. I know that one feller was complainin' about wantin' to eat. Said you'd been gone since breakfast and you shoulda been back to feed 'em." He began to recount then, starting with when they arrived and found the jail locked up with Will nowhere around. "Well, I figured we could feed 'em, so Horace got him a fire started and I went to the telegraph office to see if that Barnet fellow had another key to that building. Me bein' a deputy, same as you, he gave me the spare keys to the outside door and the cell door, too, before he went home.

"Horace cooked up supper and when it was ready, I went in and unlocked the door to the cell room and let one of 'em out at a time, so I could keep my gun on him the whole time. When he got his plate full, I'd walk him back to the cell and take another 'un out to get his." He paused to shake his head, apologetically. "It went pretty well till it was time to take that big one out, the one with a wounded shoulder. He got his plate all right and was ready to go back in the cell. Right there is where I ain't sure what happened. The big galoot musta stubbed his toe or somethin', because before I knew it, he fell against me and pinned my arm straight out against the doorjamb. Trouble is, that was the hand I was holdin' my gun in, so it was stickin' straight out there where I couldn't pull it back. His partner was standin' there, next one to go for his plate. All he had to do was grab the gun outta my hand. That big ox had me pinned against the jamb. I pulled the trigger, but I didn't hit nobody. Horace come runnin' in to help me, but it was too late. That Hawkins fellow forced my gun outta my hand in time to cock it and stop Horace in his tracks."

"I didn't have no idea what was goin' on in there til I heard the gun go off," Horace declared. "It was too late to help Ed. That feller stuck his gun in my face and told me to back off, so I did."

To Will, it was like two actors giving a presentation on how not to handle dangerous prisoners, but he didn't express that impression. "How did you get nicked on the shoulder?" he asked Ed.

"When that big 'un finally let me off the doorjamb, I made a try to get my gun back, but Hawkins saw me come at him and he shot at me. I was lucky he missed. I don't know why he didn't go ahead and finish me. Didn't wanna wake the town up, I reckon. You'da thought somebody woulda come to see what the shootin' was about, but they didn't. Then they locked us up in the wagon, instead of in the jail where it was warm. Acted like they thought it was kinda funny, lockin' us in our jail wagon. One of 'em, the one that was doin' all the bellyachin' about missin' supper when we first got there, told me to give you a message." He looked at Horace for help. "What was it, Horace?"

"He said, 'Tell Will Tanner that Harley was sorry he weren't here when he got back, but he decided to go out for supper.'"

Will grunted, amused, even in the face of the disastrous jailbreak. "I don't reckon you've got any idea what happened after they left here."

"No, we don't. They headed for the stables, I reckon," Ed offered.

"I reckon you're most likely right," Will agreed, thinking it was too obvious to even ask. That was where their horses were. "Did you hear any shots down that way after they left here?" Ed said that they did not. Will was worried about Stanley Coons—he wasn't cut out to face up to men like Ward Hawkins and Tiny McGee. "We'd best get over there and see if Stanley's all right."

"I ain't got no weapons," Ed said. "They took mine with 'em."

"Look on that packhorse there," Will told him, "and pick out whatever you need."

After all that had been said about the jailbreak, a question just then occurred to Ed. "Where were you, anyway?"

"I was busy down in Boggy Town," Will said. "Let's go see if Stanley's all right." The three of them walked up the street toward the stables. Will led Buster and the packhorse, planning to leave it with Stanley.

There was no evidence of Stanley, but due to the lateness of the hour, he didn't expect to find him still working. His real concern was that he hoped he would not find his body. There were a lot fewer horses in the corral and none in the stalls, which was a bad sign, so they lit a lantern and started a search of the stable. They found Stanley in one of the back stalls. Luckily, he was alive, not hurt, but tied up securely. "Will!" he exclaimed when he saw who it was. "Man, am I glad to see you!" He struggled to flip his body around to face them. "I hollered my head off for about an hour, but nobody could hear me back here in this stall. So I finally just quit when my throat started gettin' hoarse."

"Are you all right?" Will asked as he untied the knots holding Stanley's hands and ankles. "They trussed you up pretty good. Any injuries?"

"No, I didn't try to put up a fight. They were a pretty rough-lookin' bunch and there were five of 'em, so I didn't see much sense in gettin' myself shot. They were in a hurry to get outta here, I reckon. So they just tied me up, got their horses and saddles—and anything else they fancied—then took off. They stole four horses and saddles from the tack room. One of 'em belongs to Doug Mabry—he ain't gonna like that."

Will and Ed helped him to his feet. "Did you hear 'em say anything about where they were goin' or what they were gonna do?" Will asked. "I noticed they didn't bother to take the wagon." He could understand why the two men who had delivered the load of "molasses" had no desire to be slowed down driving a heavy freight wagon.

"Like I said, they took horses and saddles, but left the wagon. I heard two of 'em talkin' when they came back to the tack room for something. I couldn't hear everything they said, just caught a few words. There was something about goin' to some camp somewhere, sounded like they called it The Falls, or something like that. Sorry I didn't hear much more," he said. Then after a short pause, he added, "The one he was talkin' to said they should go back and get some money."

That was enough to give Will a place to start. He remembered a hideout in the Arbuckle Mountains he had found on his first job as a deputy marshal. He would never forget the cabin near the bottom of a seventy-foot waterfall, because it was the place where Fletcher Pride was killed. He was the man who persuaded him to join the Marshals Service. Outlaws had a name for that camp. They called it The Falls. Not only Pride lost his life in that place. His cook, Charlie Tate, was killed as well. It figured that the five outlaws might head for that hideout, and they would have no reason to believe he knew of its existence. The other remark Stanley mentioned, about their need to get some money, was of interest to him as well. There just might be a chance that Hawkins would risk a visit to Boggy Town before he ran to the mountains. When Will had arrested Hawkins and Tiny, Teddy Green had saddled their horses, but there were no saddlebags out there on the porch with the other gear. Hawkins might want his saddlebags and personal belongings bad enough to go to Mama's Kitchen first. The one thing that refuted that idea, however, was the time frame. If Hawkins had gone straight to Boggy Town after they left the stable, they would have arrived there while he was still there. The hour was late when he left Boggy Town. Had they waited for some reason, he might have met them on the trail from town. He couldn't let go of the idea, however. If they were heading for The Falls, they needed supplies and the only place to get them right away was Boggy Town. Hawkins would think that Cobb and Jace were still there. He decided that was going to be his first call. He told Ed and Horace what he had in mind. They talked it over for only a few minutes before Ed agreed that it was worth a try, thinking Hawkins and the others might still be there. "There is one more problem," Will said. He looked at Horace and shook his head. "If we're gonna try to catch up with those outlaws, it ain't gonna be easy with a wagon. So I expect we'd best leave it up to you to decide if you wanna jump on a horse and go with us and leave the jail wagon here. You don't have any obligation to join in a posse."

Horace stopped him right there. "I ain't nothin' but the cook, right? Well, I'm goin' with you, anyway. You're gonna need all the help you can get to go after five of 'em."

Bud Tilton paused and turned to exchange glances with Ida Simpson when he heard horses approaching the front porch. "Damn, they've come back," he muttered, and quickly put the whiskey bottle back under the bar where it had been hidden before.

Alarmed as well, Ida alerted Etta and Teddy. "They're back! Hide them glasses. They find out we had another bottle hid, they ain't gonna be too happy about it." Their celebration had continued on after Hawkins and Tiny had left them. It was going to be hard to explain why they were still celebrating. The four of them stood silently watching the front door then until Will walked in, followed by Ed and Horace. "Damn," Ida swore, "we thought that was Tiny and Hawkins comin' back." She held her sigh of relief, however, not sure if the deputy's return was good news or bad.

"They were here?" Will asked at once.

"Yeah, they were here," Teddy spoke up, " 'bout an hour ago. They loaded up a couple of packhorses with half our supplies and lit out."

"All five of 'em?" Will asked. Teddy said no one but Tiny and Hawkins showed up.

"Well, you were right," Ed said. "Too bad we couldn'ta got here sooner." He turned to Ida then. "Did they say where they were headin'?" She started to answer but hesitated. She didn't know Ed as well as she had come to know Will. She knew only that he was a deputy marshal and she was suddenly reluctant to give out information to the law about her former employer. Too long a prostitute working with outlaws, she was troubled by a sense of loyalty.

Etta, however, was not troubled by such nonsense. As far as she was concerned, the outlaw code flew out the window when Tiny and Hawkins discarded the four of them without so much as a fare-thee-well. She saw that Ida didn't want to reveal Tiny's plans, so she volunteered. "They told us they weren't takin' us with 'em because they're goin' to some place in the mountains, called The Falls." As soon as she said it, she had a second thought and added, "I'd just as soon you didn't tell anybody I told you that. I don't particularly want a reputation as the person who spilled the beans on Ward Hawkins and caused him to get arrested—if you do arrest him."

Will couldn't suppress a smile for the feisty old woman. "No need to worry about that. Fellow that owns the stables in town heard 'em mention The Falls. He turned to Ed then. "We've got some decidin' to do. Looks like they've only got an hour's head start on us, but we're gonna have to pick up their trail. They didn't head back toward the road to McAlester 'cause we woulda run right into 'em. So they took off in some direction west, but we ain't got much chance of findin' their trail in the middle of the night. We might as well make camp for the night and wait for daylight."

Ed was in agreement, since the night was already half-gone. "It wouldn't hurt to rest our horses up, too," he said.

"Hell," Etta blurted, "you boys can stay right here. We got an empty bunkhouse wing on the back, and we'll fix you somethin' to eat." She looked around at her partners and saw nothing but grins. "You'll be the first customers in the Boggy Town Hotel, and we won't charge you nothin' for the night. That all right, partners?" The other three gave their nods of approval immediately.

"I reckon that'll be hard to pass up," Ed responded. "Ain't that what you say, Will?"

"Yep," Will answered. "We thank you for the

offer. It does feel kinda funny, though. We ain't exactly the kind of customers Tiny and Hawkins built this place for."

"Maybe we oughta call this place the Hotel Reform," Teddy offered, "on account we've all reformed to change our old ways."

Teddy's suggestion brought a chuckle from all of them and caused Will to silently hope they could somehow make a success of their business, even though he didn't see much chance of it. Now that it was settled, the two lawmen and Horace Watson brought their personal gear into the bunkhouse, then took care of the horses with Teddy's help. Etta offered to make breakfast for them, but Will said they would leave before breakfast and stop to eat when they rested the horses. She insisted on frying up some ham and corn cakes for them to eat before they went to bed, an offer they found hard to refuse.

Will was up at first light the next morning and was down at the corral saddling the horses when Ed and Horace came out to help. They attempted to get the packhorses loaded and ready to ride without disturbing their hosts, who were trying to recover from the late night of celebrating. They were joined by Etta Grise, however, who came out the kitchen door to see them off. Walking past the two cold corpses of Cobb and Jace, she came out to wish them luck. Going up to Will's stirrup, she said, "You be careful, Will Tanner." She paused, then added, "I never thought I'd be sayin' that to a lawman." Before she turned to go back to the kitchen, she said one more thing. "I found that money you left on the kitchen table."

"That was just a little something toward the room rent and the supper last night," he said, then gave Buster a gentle nudge and started down the creek. He knew by the smile she gave him that the gesture pleased her. It might not have meant as much if she had known that it was money he had taken from the two drivers who had delivered the "molasses." *What the hell,* he said to himself, *it's the thought that counts.*

Although Will was sure the outlaws were going to the hideout known as The Falls, he preferred to follow their trail in case they went someplace else. With Ed in agreement, they decided to split up, with Ed and Horace searching the commonly used trail that followed Muddy Boggy Creek, while Will led a packhorse along the bank of the creek. The hope was to find tracks that were fairly fresh. Knowing Hawkins had to strike a heading due west, if he was going to the Arbuckles, Will crossed over to the other side of the creek. He knew the two outlaws had to cross Muddy Boggy at some point, so he watched for tracks entering or leaving the water. He had not gone far before he found what he was looking for when he crossed a wide gap in the trees lining the creek. The ground in the gap was not covered with leaves and limbs, like the biggest part of the creek bank. Several distinct prints were evident, suggesting the two outlaws had approached the saloon from behind it on this side of the creek. But he saw no prints heading in the opposite direction, so they must have come back on the other side of the creek. To go west, they had to have crossed back to the side he was searching at some point.

They had to cross somewhere, he thought, *so if I keep going along this creek, I'll find where they came out of the water, and we'll have a trail to follow.* He continued on along the bank for less than a quarter of a mile when he reached the clear tracks of four horses where they left the water and scrambled up the bank. He drew his Colt and fired two shots in the air to signal Ed. In a few seconds, he heard an answering shot and figured it to have come from the common trail on the other side. After another couple of minutes with no sign of Ed and Horace, he fired another shot in the air. A few moments later, he saw them making their way through the cottonwoods to come out on the creek bank. Sighting him then, they crossed over to join him.

"This is where they came across," Will said when Ed and Horace came up to him. "They left a pretty plain trail for us, headin' that way."

He pointed dead west toward a gap in a low line of hills in the distance. "I figure it's about fifty-five or sixty miles to the Arbuckles from here, wouldn't you say, Ed?" Ed agreed, so Will continued. "I'd figure, if they stay on this line, it's about twenty-five or thirty miles to Blue River. We could make it there before we rest the horses, if we push 'em a little. Whaddaya think?"

"That's fine by me," Ed said, aware that Will was trying to make sure this was a joint operation and he respected his opinions. But as far as he was concerned, he was content to let Will call the shots.

With Will leading, they followed the trail across an empty, rolling land until coming to Clear Boggy Creek, which was about halfway to Blue River. There they found a campsite. "They didn't go very far before they stopped for the night, did they?" Horace remarked.

"No, they didn't," Will said. "But it was gettin' pretty late at night when they were ridin' across here, so I reckon they didn't wanna take a chance on injurin' a horse. I'd say it was a pretty good idea to rest 'em. Judgin' by the tracks, they were workin' those horses pretty hard." He took a good look at the campsite. "This is where they caught up with the other three. They were waitin' for 'em here on Clear Boggy." They waited there only long enough to let the horses drink before starting out again for Blue River. By the time they reached it, horses and riders were ready to rest and get something to eat. When they figured the horses were ready, they started out again, riding another twenty miles before camping for the night.

CHAPTER 14

Up at first light, the three riders readied their horses for what Will and Ed figured to be a ride of between ten and fifteen miles before reaching the base slopes of the Arbuckle Mountains. There was no question in Will's mind about the destination of the men they followed. The outlaws' tracks led to an old Indian trail Will had followed before, and when they struck the trail, the outlaws stayed on it. They were going to The Falls. "Whaddaya think?" Horace asked. "Reckon I oughta fix a little breakfast before we start out this mornin'? You say it ain't but about ten or fifteen miles before we get to them mountains. We might be pretty busy when we get there."

"We might at that," Ed replied, and turned to Will. "Whaddaya think, Will?"

"I could use some coffee and a little something to eat," he answered. He was no longer concerned about catching up with the five outlaws. He was mainly concerned with how he was going to capture them. He remembered the camp the outlaws called The Falls. A cabin built up at the top of a narrow gully, it was not an easy place to approach without being seen. So, convinced that they would find Hawkins and his gang there, he no longer felt the need to hurry. He figured the outlaws should have gotten to the cabin last night, and they weren't likely planning to go anywhere else for at least a little while. And it was obvious that both Ed and Horace wanted to eat first. "We might as well go to work with a full stomach," he said, and Horace got busy immediately to revive last night's campfire.

A little over fourteen miles west of the deputies' camp, at a point where a lively stream came down between two twin mountains, the five escaped prisoners followed Ward Hawkins. In single file, due to the narrow path, they climbed up a game trail beside the stream. "You sure this is the way to that cabin?" Tiny called out to him. "This trail is pretty damn grown over. We oughta have got to that gully by now."

"I'm sure," Hawkins shot back over his shoulder, although he was not really that sure. Tiny was right, the path had grown over since he had first made his way up it. "We ain't halfway to that gully," he added confidently.

"I hope to hell we're on the right trail," Harley piped up. "I'm so hungry I could eat the south end of a northbound mule." They had spent the night in a camp near the base of the mountain they were presently climbing. This morning, Hawkins had insisted on starting up to a cabin that was supposed to be near the top before thinking about breakfast.

"If we run across a mule runnin' wild up here, we'll know which part to save for you," Pete Jessup japed. "You ain't the only one needin' breakfast. My belly's makin' sounds like a tornado goin' 'round in there."

"A belly the size of yourn, it's a wonder we all ain't heard it," Harley cracked, then the joking stopped as they suddenly became aware of a noise coming through the fir trees above them. "What the hell is that?" Harley blurted. Like Pete and Ernie, he had never been to the outlaw camp before.

"It's The Falls," Tiny answered. "Water comin' down from a cliff up above the cabin." A few dozen yards farther brought them to a narrow gully and the game trail left the side of the stream and went up the gully. After another short climb, Hawkins held up his hand, signaling them to stop.

"We'd best lead the horses from here on up," Hawkins said, and climbed down out of the saddle. "It gets pretty steep in spots and you're liable to catch yourself doin' a backflip, and your horse landin' on top of ya." Everyone followed suit and they led their horses up another dozen yards before Hawkins signaled another stop. When they all caught up to him, they could see the simple log cabin through the branches of a large fir tree. It was built beside the source of the noise they had heard, a small pond, formed by the stream cascading down from a cliff, some seventy feet above it. "Best check to see if there's anybody in there right now," Hawkins said. He turned to Harley, who had moved up beside him to take a look, and pointed to his left. "Climb up on the side of the gully yonder. You oughta be able to see a little corral behind the cabin. See if there's any horses in it."

After a minute, Harley reported, "I see the corral. There ain't no horses in it."

"It don't look like there's anybody there," Tiny said, but they continued to wait there and watch for a few minutes more until Hawkins started walking again.

"Hello, the cabin!" Hawkins called. "Anybody home?" He walked out into the clearing where the cabin stood up close to the cliff and the waterfall. There was no response from the cabin, so the rest of the party followed up behind him.

Noticing a fire pit in front of the cabin, Harley was inspired to ask, "Ain't there no stove inside the cabin?" It had been cold enough on the way from Atoka and it was bound to be colder still near the top of this mountain.

"Fireplace inside," Tiny said, "but it's easier to do most of the cookin' out here. Ain't much room inside that cabin." That prompted everyone to hurry inside to claim sleeping places before thinking about taking care of their horses.

"Man," Ernie blurted, "it's cold as a whore's heart in here."

"Ain't quite as fancy as Boggy Town, is it?" Harley was quick to point out. "Ain't much bigger'n that jailhouse we just broke out of."

"You're damn sure welcome to move on to find you a fancy hotel," Hawkins answered him.

"I would, but I don't wanna miss all this high-class company here," Harley replied. "The first thing we need to do is collect some wood for a fire and get us somethin' to eat."

"Amen to that," Pete said at once. He looked around him inside the one-room cabin. "Looks like ain't nobody been here in a good while. I sure am glad they left us an ax, though," he said when he saw the ax leaning against a small stack of wood. " 'Cause we're sure gonna need more wood than that."

After the packhorses were unloaded, the riding horses unsaddled, and the sleeping arrangement settled, enough wood was gathered and fires were built outside as well as in the fireplace to warm the cabin. Figuring he would starve to death if he depended on any of the others, Pete took over the cooking, but declared he would only do it if somebody else kept the firewood plentiful. While they settled in to their new quarters there was very little thought, and no real discussion, about the posse that might, or might not, be on their trail. But after everyone's belly was satisfied, the topic was quickly brought up for discussion. "How long you figurin' on stayin' here, Ward?"

Harley asked the question, but everyone else was immediately interested to hear the answer.

Before Hawkins could answer, Ernie commented, "Yeah, we ain't got supplies enough to make it here for very long, and it ain't even real winter yet. It's gonna get cold as hell up on this mountain."

"There's a feller name of Jeremy Cannon that runs a tradin' post on Blue River, halfway between here and Tishomingo, which would put it about fifteen miles from here," Tiny said. "We can get supplies there when we start to run out. We can also get a drink of whiskey there."

"Well, we're sure short of that. I might wanna ride down to see that feller pretty soon," Harley commented.

"There's deer up in these mountains," Tiny said. "There was plenty of sign on that game trail up here. We ought not to starve."

Ernie, alone, was the only doubtful member of the gang, as well as the most practical. "That's all well and good, that tradin' post on the Blue River," he commented. "But what are we gonna use for money? I don't know if any of you fellers were able to hold on to any cash money, but that deputy cleaned me out."

His remark served to remind the others that they were in a similar situation. They had all been relieved of their money when arrested. The lighthearted air they just enjoyed suddenly vanished. After a moment, Harley declared, "Well, it looks to me like I'm gonna have to go back to practicin' what I'm good at, takin' the other feller's money."

"Yeah?" Tiny responded. "Where you gonna do that? There ain't nobody nowhere around here that's got any money to steal. That's the reason this is such a good hideout. There ain't nobody, and there ain't no banks or stores or railroads to hold up."

Ward Hawkins made no comments while the banter continued between his four partners in the jail escape. But their concerns were the same ones he had thought about ever since he had left Boggy Town. And he did not intend to be without money for very long, which meant he might as well go ahead with his plans to rob the bank in Sherman. He had decided that to be a job two men could handle, especially when one of them was as good with a gun as Bill Todd had been. *Before he met Will Tanner,* he reminded himself. He would talk to Tiny about it, now that he had nothing else holding him. He wasn't as fast as Todd, but Hawkins didn't expect to run into Will Tanner in the bank in Texas. He had not told any of the four now with him because it was a two-man job and he didn't feel like sharing the money with four others. That thought caused him to look at Tiny, still with his arm in a sling. If he didn't heal up pretty quick, Hawkins was going to have to consider cutting one of the other three in on his plan. And he was not impressed by any of the three. *Damn,* he thought, *I owe Will Tanner for all this mess. I don't care how long it takes, I will settle that score before I'm done.*

The man Hawkins was cursing was at that moment talking the situation over with Ed Pine and Horace Watson. "There ain't no doubt, that's their tracks," Ed commented as they looked at the fresh prints crossing the stream to continue on the game trail leading up between the mountains. "Looks like they're headin' right where you said they were."

"Goin' up that trail, they couldn't be goin' anywhere but that cabin," Will said. "There ain't but one cabin up there. The problem we've got to solve is whether or not we oughta climb up that trail to try to surprise 'em. We'd have to go up it single file and the higher it gets, the steeper the trail gets."

"That don't sound like too good an idea," Horace was inspired to say.

"It might help us if we could get a look at that cabin and see what they're up to before we decide what we're gonna do," Will said. When Ed asked how they were going to accomplish that without walking up the path, Will explained. "This ain't the first time I've had to get to this cabin. But to do it, I had to circle about halfway around this mountain and climb to the top from there. You come out over that cabin right on the edge of a cliff. That's where this stream goes over the cliff and makes a waterfall. From the cliff, you can see the cabin about seventy feet below."

"Let's do that," Ed said. "That sounds better'n climbin' up this trail, yellin' *Shoot me, shoot me, I'm a lawman.*"

Will responded with a forced chuckle, then climbed back aboard Buster and led the way around to the back of the mountain. As best as he could determine, he made his way up a series of game trails that had taken him to the waterfall before. His memory proved reliable because just short of the top of the mountain he reached a ledge that looked familiar. He dismounted and followed the ledge back around the mountain until eventually coming to the stream where it came out of the top of the mountain and flowed down over the cliff. After crossing over the rapidly flowing water, Will inched up to the edge of the cliff where he could look down on the cabin below. Ed moved up beside him. "There they are, all right," he muttered. Although there was no one outside the cabin, their horses were in the small corral beside it.

"Be careful," Will warned. "Some of that loose gravel will give way with you if you get too close to the edge." Ed nodded and moved up a little closer to the edge. "I ain't ever been able to find a back way outta that place, at least one where you could ride a horse," Will said. "If there is one, they've got it hid pretty good."

"I see what you mean," Ed said. "Don't look like there's but one way out of that place." They continued watching in silence for a few moments before Ed gave voice to what they were both thinking. "They've got 'em a fire goin' outside, must be thinkin' about cookin' out there instead of inside. Be kinda easy to pick two or three of 'em off when they came outside, wouldn't it?"

"Yeah, it'd be temptin', all right," Will replied.

Horace crawled up between them to take a look for himself. "Dang," he blurted in a loud whisper. "That's a pretty fair drop, ain't it?"

"I'll say it is," Ed answered. "So watch yourself on that loose gravel, or you'll be takin' dinner with 'em."

Horace nodded in reply but continued to crawl up a little closer to the edge of the cliff, trying to get a better look. Up even with Will and Ed then, he grinned at Ed as he placed his hand on the wrong rock to withstand the weight of his body. Suddenly, the rock gave way, loosening a shower of small rocks and gravel down on the cabin below. Unable to catch himself, Horace went over the edge with the rocks, saved only by the quick reflexes of Will and Ed, who each grabbed a leg to catch him. He dangled over the cliff for only the few seconds it took for the two deputies to pull him back up to the top. "Oh hell!" Ed gasped as he and Will dragged the hapless cook away from the edge of the cliff, his face white as a sheet from the close call. "They sure as hell know they got company now."

Will's initial reaction was the same as Ed's, but on second thought, he changed his mind. "It might not be as bad as it looks," he said. "They had to hear all that stuff landing on the roof, but they might not think it was ol' Horace fixin' to make a call." He glanced at the shaken man to receive a sheepish look in return. "We've been tryin' to figure the best way for us to go after them and maybe Horace's way is our best chance." Ed wasn't sure what he meant, so Will explained. "There wasn't anybody outside the cabin to see Horace, so they won't know what caused the rocks to fall. Might think it's just the mountain dirt givin' way, but it oughta give 'em something to worry about. And they'll most likely wanna know for sure, so somebody'll have to come up here to see what caused it. Seems to me that's the best thing we've come up with to draw some of 'em outta that gully."

"What if they don't think nothin' of it, and nobody comes up here to check on it?" Ed asked.

Will shrugged. "Then I reckon Horace is gonna have to come up with another idea to bring 'em outta there." Ed offered half a chuckle for Will's attempt to be funny. Horace, still shaken by his near-death experience, could see no humor in their dangerous situation and invited them to kiss his behind. "If it was me down there in that cabin," Will continued, "I'd sure wanna take a look up here, just to make sure the mountain wasn't fixin' to come down on my head."

"Most likely, that's what they'll do," Ed agreed. "So we'd best get ready for 'em." With that said, he looked to Will to set up their welcome party.

"More than likely, whoever comes up here is gonna take the shortest way, and that means they'll come up here pretty much the same way we did. So let's move our horses a little farther around the mountain, so they don't see 'em." He paused to look around him then before continuing. "That clump of fir trees where the stream comes outta the ground looks like the best place for us to hide. Then, if they do what I would expect, they'll walk over to the edge of the cliff to take a look. That way, they'll be backed up to the cliff and a helluva drop behind them. Whaddaya think?"

"I can't think of anything better'n that," Ed said.

"All right, then," Will said, "let's go hide these horses. It's gonna take a little time for anybody to get up here, so we oughta have plenty of time to get back here and get set up for 'em." The only thing he could not anticipate accurately was how many of the men down there would come up to find the cause of the rockslide. And they would still be left with the problem of how to arrest the ones who didn't come up to check on the rocks.

"What the hell was that?" Harley blurted when the rocks and gravel landed on the roof of the cabin. Sitting around the small table in the center of the cabin moments before, all five were standing now.

"Somethin' fell on the roof!" Tiny exclaimed. "Sounded like the damn mountain is fixin' to fall on us." He followed the others, who were already running out the door to take a look.

Of the five men, only Hawkins picked up his rifle as he went out the door. Obsessed with a feeling that the relentless lawman had somehow found this outlaw hideout, his first thought was to protect himself. He found his companions standing in front of the cabin staring up at the cliff above them. Tiny pointed to what appeared to be a broken place at the top edge of the face. "Yonder's where that stuff broke off. I hope ain't no more of it fixin' to turn loose."

Still suspicious, Hawkins stood staring at the little pile of dirt, rocks, and gravel that had just missed the roof. Pointing to the pile, he said, "That's just what landed on the ground. That ain't what we heard landin' on the roof. Look around, there ain't no other rocks and stuff on the ground down here—just that one pile that fell a minute ago. Seems kinda funny to me, kinda like somethin' musta caused that stuff to fall."

This alerted Tiny. "You think somebody's up there?"

"I don't know if there's anybody up there or not," Hawkins replied. "I'm just sayin' the damn mountain ain't just started to crumble on its own."

"If that was the law up there, they'd be shootin' at us right now, standin' out here in the open like this," Harley said, and took a nervous look up at the cliff. "Why don't we just go up there and see what's up there?"

"That's a good idea," Ernie said. "I'll go with you, Harley. I know I'll feel better about sleepin' tonight if I don't see no sign of anybody up there lookin' down at this camp. How 'bout it, Pete, you goin' with us?"

"Well, I don't have any plans scheduled for this afternoon. I reckon I could go along with you," Pete answered. He always partnered with Ernie on just about everything.

Ernie turned to Hawkins, but before he could ask, Hawkins told him that he was satisfied to let the three of them scout the cliff. "Me and Tiny will keep the coffee warm for ya." He was looking Tiny straight in the eye when he said it. His gaze seemed to tell the big man to stay there.

"How we gonna get up there, walk?" Pete wanted to know.

"Hell, no," Harley answered him. "We're gonna have to ride down the gulch, then go around the mountain till we find a place that ain't too steep to climb. That's the reason I bought a horse, so I wouldn't have to walk."

"You mean that's the reason you stole a horse," Pete told him.

The three of them walked out to the corral to saddle their horses. Behind them, Tiny asked, "Why'd you give me the bad eye when I started to get up and go with 'em?"

"Because we might be leavin' this place right away, and if we have to leave, I need you to go with me on a bank job." When Tiny was obviously confused, Hawkins explained. "This was a bank I scouted out with Bill Todd on our way up here from Texas. We didn't say nothin' about it because it's just right for two men to get in and out of there without the rest of the little town knowin' it was happenin'. Todd got himself shot, so now I'm offerin' it to you. You were too busy runnin' Boggy Town before, or I woulda offered it to you instead of Todd. I wasn't gonna hit that bank until next spring, after I was satisfied that you were gettin' along with the saloon all right. But the fix we're in right now, needin' cash money, changes that plan. We need to hit that bank right now. Are you up for it?"

"Hell, yeah," Tiny replied at once, but he

didn't understand the sense of urgency Hawkins appeared to have, so Hawkins explained.

"This Tanner is harder to shake than a case of the itch and I've got a feelin' he's tracked us up here," he said. "Now, maybe that ain't nothin' a-tall, them rocks fallin' on the roof, just a piece of the cliff that's broke loose. But what if it ain't? What if it's somebody wantin' to smoke us out of this cabin? They come ridin' up that gully and they'll get shot, sure as hell. But if they get us to come outta here, go up there to see what's what, then we're dead meat."

Never known for his quick perception, Tiny nonetheless was beginning to understand. "You think Tanner might be waitin' for Harley and them up there?"

"I think he might be and it's gonna take them a little while to go around that mountain and climb up there. So I'm gonna saddle my horse and get ready to go if I hear the first sound from up there on that cliff. Are you wantin' to go with me?"

"I sure am," Tiny said. "I don't like bein' holed up here on this mountain, anyway. Let's get saddled up." He paused a moment to think. "What if there ain't nothin' up there and they see us gettin' ready to leave?"

"We'll just tell 'em we changed our minds and was fixin' to come up there with 'em," Hawkins said.

"Right," Tiny responded, "we'll tell 'em that."

"We might as well load up a packhorse, too," Hawkins said. "If they get ambushed up there, they ain't gonna be needin' any of these supplies we've got."

CHAPTER 15

Lying flat on his belly, holding a short branch from a fir tree next to his head to hide behind, Will watched the cabin below. Ed and Horace stood back from the edge, waiting for his report. Below him, he saw the three men come out of the cabin and go to the corral to saddle their horses. "So far," he said softly, "there's only three of 'em. Hawkins and Tiny stayed in the cabin." He continued to lie there after they had saddled their horses and disappeared down the gulch toward the stream. "Looks like they're on their way." Disappointed that Tiny and Hawkins were not with them, he started to back away from his position but halted when he saw them come out of the cabin and go to the corral. "Wait a minute, maybe they're coming up, too." He watched a few minutes longer, knowing he had some time before the first three could make their way up to the cliff. "Oh hell," he uttered when he saw them loading a packhorse, "they're not comin' up here, they're runnin'."

His initial thought was to pull his rifle up beside him and try to stop them from escaping, but he knew he couldn't. That would warn the three already on their way up. All five of the men were wanted and if he gave away the ambush by firing at Hawkins and Tiny, it might result in all five getting away again. Knowing time was running out, he quickly explained the situation to Ed, and they decided it best to stick with their original plan and arrest the three men on their way up the mountain. They would just have to pick up the trail of the other two after Harley, Pete, and Ernie were secured. Resigned to the fact that things don't always work out the way you want them to, Will pulled back from the edge of the cliff and went to the clump of firs on either side of the opening in the rocks from which the water flowed. With their rifles at the ready, Ed and Horace were already selecting their hiding spots in the trees. Will picked a spot where he was sure he wouldn't be seen until he was ready to spring the trap. Satisfied, he looked to see that Ed and Horace were ready, then said, "All right, nothin' to do but wait and see if we can catch these three."

It was not more than twenty minutes or so before the three outlaws showed up, although it seemed longer to the men waiting in ambush. They heard them when they dismounted and led their horses the rest of the way up to the ledge. Moving cautiously at first, until he saw no one on the top of the cliff, Harley walked over to the edge and looked down at the cabin below. He was holding a rifle in his hand. Behind him, Pete and Ernie followed and walked over to take a look, too. "Lookee yonder," Harley said, "there's that pile of stuff we heard hit the roof." They all peered over the edge at the rocks on the roof seventy feet below them.

"Just stand right there and you won't get shot," Will said as he stepped out of the little clump of trees. Following his lead, Ed and Horace came out from the trees, too, all three now with rifles held on the three surprised outlaws. "I reckon I don't have to tell you that you're under arrest again," Will said. "We're gonna have to add on charges of breakin' outta jail to the charges I arrested you for the first time."

Realizing they were caught in an impossible situation, they turned to face him, shaken by having been lured into ambush. With three rifles facing them, and nothing but a seventy-foot drop behind them, there was nothing they could do. "Will Tanner," Harley finally declared. "I shoulda knowed you'd turn up on our heels." He chuckled softly. "You know, my life has been a helluva lot more troublesome ever since you came into it."

"All of you," Will ordered, "unbuckle those gun belts and let 'em drop on the ground." They did as he said. "I'm gonna need you to lay that rifle on the ground, too, Harley."

"This?" Harley asked, as if he had forgotten he was holding it. "It ain't even loaded. I was usin' it mostly as a walkin' stick to help me up the hill."

"Drop it, Harley. I ain't gonna tell you again," Will warned.

"All right, all right," Harley responded. "I thought you knew by now that I don't look to cause you no trouble." He crouched down. "Look, I'm puttin' it on the ground real gentle-like." His move was sudden, when he raised it to fire, but slower by a fraction of a second than the .44 slug from Will's Winchester. The shot struck him just below his neck, and he reeled backward off the edge of the cliff.

In a panic then, Pete and Ernie both dropped to their knees, their hands raised high over their heads, as all three rifles were aimed at them. "Who's next?" Ed asked.

"You ain't gonna get no trouble outta us," Pete was quick with an answer.

Below them, Ward Hawkins yelled, "Go!" when they heard the rifle shot, followed a few seconds later by the dull thump of Harley's body when it landed on the roof. Hawkins kicked his horse violently as he and Tiny raced down the path in the gully, with no thoughts of caution for the steep, treacherous path. They lay low on their horses' necks with the sounds of .44 slugs ricocheting off the rocks and embedding in the sides of the gully behind them.

Unfortunately for the deputies, they didn't have a clear shot and they would have to settle for the arrest of the two luckless men who had driven a wagonload of whiskey into Indian Territory. They could add a jail break on to that, but they were not the prize Will most wanted to win. "I reckon that worked out all right," Ed commented. "We ain't got but two sets of handcuffs with us." He took it on himself to cuff the prisoners while Will looked over the edge of the cliff at the body lying sprawled on the roof of the cabin below. He couldn't help feeling a little disappointed that Harley had attempted to shoot him. Of the five prisoners, Harley was the only one who was kind of amusing. That thought was a fleeting one, for his mind came immediately back to the larger problem of Ward Hawkins and Tiny McGee. Until a few minutes ago, he knew exactly where they were, although they were not easy to get to. Now it was a question of how good a job he could do to track them. And even before that, something had to be done with the two men they had just arrested. He didn't know what Ed had in mind as far as going on from here, but he knew what he was going to propose. First, however, they would have to get Pete and Ernie ready to travel.

They retrieved the horses and went back around the mountain through the gully up to the cabin. With their hands cuffed, the prisoners were allowed to collect their personal things. What food supplies were left after Hawkins and Tiny took their pick of them were loaded on the packhorse standing in the corral. Ready to ride, they left the cabin and started back down the mountain at once. Pete looked at Ernie as they set out and complained, "Didn't even get to stay one night."

Ernie shook his head in response. "We was talkin' about cuttin' ourselves loose from Hawkins and Tiny, but this ain't what I had in mind."

They rode no farther that day than a few miles back out of the mountains. It had been a busy day and everybody was feeling the effects of it. As soon as they made camp, Will secured the two prisoners by handcuffing them to a tree, as was his usual custom. Horace built a fire and was soon preparing supper, while Will had a little meeting with Ed to discuss their plans from that point on. There was general agreement between the two deputies that they had captured a couple of minor lawbreakers while the big game had gotten away. Ed complained that their predicament was awkward. "What are we gonna do with these birds?" he asked Will. "It's five days or more from here back to Fort Smith on horseback. Hell, it'll take longer'n that when we put 'em in that jail wagon in Atoka. I know it was Hawkins and McGee we wanted, but I can't see any sense in tryin' to track them down with two prisoners to worry about." He paused briefly when another thought struck him. "I reckon we could put these two in that jail on the railroad tracks in Atoka while we come back here to pick up the trail again. But you know Dan Stone ain't gonna approve reimbursement money for the time we keep 'em there. He's gonna pay for the cost to bring 'em back to Fort Smith. By the time we got back here, we'd have a mighty cold trail to try to follow."

Will let him have his say before replying. "You've pretty much summed it up, all right." He knew if he was riding alone on this job and faced with this situation, he would be inclined to cut Ernie and Pete loose. He would tell them to get out of Indian Territory and warn them they would face a prison sentence if he ever caught them here again. With Hawkins and Tiny on the loose, it would be a waste of time and money to escort Pete and Ernie back to face minor charges. The only crime of theirs he knew anything about was accepting money to drive a wagon of whiskey to Indian Territory. He would opt to go after the real criminals while there was still a chance to pick up a fresh trail. However, he couldn't tell Ed to release prisoners who had broken the law, no matter how minor. "There is another way we could handle this thing," he began. "You and Horace could escort these two back to Fort Smith, pick up your jail wagon on the way. I don't think they'll give you any trouble. I can see if I can track Hawkins and Tiny while there's still a chance to pick up their trail. Whaddaya think?"

Ed answered with a wry smile. "Well, there ain't much doubt about which job is the hairiest, is there? Maybe it ain't fair to stick you with the most dangerous job. Maybe we oughta flip a coin for it. Both of them coyotes have a grudge against you and I expect they'd love to know you're comin' after 'em all by yourself."

Will was afraid Ed might take that attitude. He preferred to go after the two outlaws alone. It was the way he most often worked, but he also knew that Ed might let his pride influence his decision. "Maybe you're right," he said. "Maybe we oughta flip for it." He reached in his vest pocket and pulled out a silver coin he kept as a lucky piece. "Heads, I go after Hawkins and Tiny. Tails, you go after 'em. All right?" He flipped the coin in the air and let it drop on the ground. "It's heads. Looks like I'll go after 'em." He reached down, picked up the coin, and showed it to Ed, then quickly put it back in his pocket so Ed wouldn't see that the coin had a head on both sides.

"Your luck ain't too good today," Ed remarked. "I sure hope it improves if you're goin' after those two." He was not ready to admit it, even to himself, but he was happy that coin landed heads up. "I reckon me and Horace can take care of these two hombres." He glanced over at the two prisoners shackled to the trees. Back to Will then, he said, "You be extra careful, Will. Those two are mean clear through."

"You don't have to worry about that," Will replied. "I've got important business back in Fort Smith." Why it came to mind at this moment, he was unable to explain, but he had an immediate thought of panic. "Say, what's the date today? Do you know?"

Ed looked puzzled. "Why, I don't know, hadn't thought about it." He looked at Horace. "You know the date today?"

Horace shook his head. "Hell, I'm lucky I can remember what month it is." He paused. "It's December, ain't it?"

Ed turned back toward Will. "Why? Is it important?"

"No," Will answered. "I just wondered." It was important, all right. He was supposed to get married on Christmas Day. Already gone long enough to forget what day it was, he was not at all certain how long it might be before the business with Hawkins and McGee would be finished. He suddenly formed an image of Sophie Bennett, her face twisted into a dark visage of anger if he arrived a day late. Compared to that, an encounter with Hawkins and Tiny seemed tame.

They broke camp early the next morning. Will stood by as Ed and Horace guarded their prisoners while they answered nature's call, then got them in the saddle with their hands cuffed. Before they left, Ed asked Will if he might want to change his mind and give up on Hawkins and Tiny. "They're sure as hell gonna get outta Indian Territory," he said. "Might as well let 'em go."

"No, I reckon I'll go back to the mountain, just to see if I can even pick up a trail," Will said. He was not so sure they would leave the territory, not for long, anyway. He remembered that Hawkins had made him a promise that he would settle the score with him. And he believed Hawkins had not made the promise casually. *Better to hunt him than have him hunting me,* Will thought. They said, "So long," and Ed and Horace started back to Fort Smith, their two prisoners and their packhorses on lead lines behind them. Will climbed aboard Buster and turned the big buckskin back toward the mountain they had just left the night before.

At the bottom of the gully that led up to the cabin, there were many hoofprints, some as fresh as last night's and some a little older than that. It was not a simple task to determine which prints were the ones he searched for. He could, however, rule out those that led back to circle the mountain, as well as those heading east toward the camp he had just come from. When his search failed to discover any tracks other than in those two directions, he had to assume the two outlaws had ridden down the stream to keep from leaving a trail. So, he rode Buster down to the bottom of the mountain, keeping a sharp eye for any trace of the fugitives' tracks coming out of the stream. He found what he was looking for when he noticed one hoofprint at the edge of the stream where it ran through a grassy clearing. Hoping to hide their exit from the water, they had ridden out onto the grass. On the other side of the meadow, he found their trail again. After following it for a while, he decided they were heading south to Texas, for their tracks were in the direction of a commonly used Indian trail that ran straight north and south. It made sense that they would return to Texas, since that was where they had come from. Thinking that he should have thought of that last night, he decided to waste no more time scouting their trail and rode straight to the Texas road. He struck it after a short ride and turned Buster to follow it. If his memory served him, there was a trading post about twenty miles south of where he now rode. It sat on a creek where the north–south road crossed an east–west road that led to Tishomingo to the east. It might be that the two outlaws he chased had stopped there. He remembered the fellow who owned the store as a friendly man, but he couldn't remember his name. All he could remember was that he had a funny-sounding name. So he asked Buster for a lively pace, one he could maintain for twenty miles, and promised to rest him at the trading post.

By the time he reached the crossroads and

spotted the store sitting back by the creek about thirty yards from the road, he was ready for some coffee and some breakfast to go with it. Buster issued a little whinny when he sensed the horses behind the store as Will pulled up to the hitching rail. He was surprised to see the owner step out on the porch, holding a shotgun, evidently having heard the horses communicating, too. "Jasper Johnson," Will greeted him, as the name popped back into his memory upon seeing the slight little proprietor.

His greeting caused Jasper to crane his neck forward to peer at Will over a pair of spectacles parked at the tip of his nose. "Deputy Tanner?" he asked, not certain he could trust his memory. When Will answered with a nod, Jasper set his shotgun down and leaned it against the wall. "You're too late, if you're after that pair that held up my store last night."

"Sorry to hear that," Will said, and stepped down. "Anybody hurt?"

"A few bruises and a cut lip," Jasper answered. "The only things that got hurt bad were my cash drawer and some of my stock off the shelves. I heard you come ridin' in and I thought it mighta been those two comin' back for more."

"Your wife all right?" Will asked.

"She's the one with the cut lip," Jasper answered, "but she was up and workin' first thing this mornin'. What are you chasin' them for?"

"About everything that ain't lawful," Will answered. "Murder, robbery, breakin' outta jail, sellin' whiskey to the Indians." He paused then when Erma Johnson came out to see who Jasper was talking to. "Mrs. Johnson," he greeted her. "I'm really sorry you had to get a visit from Ward Hawkins and Tiny McGee."

"Will Tanner," she said, remembering his name, and gave him a smile that looked lopsided, due to her swollen lip. "From what I heard you tell Jasper just now, I count us lucky we just lost the money and some stock, nothin' we can't recover from. One of those fellows was big and the other one was bigger'n him. I was afraid Jasper was gonna try to fight 'em when one of 'em smacked me in the mouth after I told him to get outta our store."

"I think it's a smart thing that he didn't," Will said.

"Dad-burn right," Jasper said. "I ain't no dad-blamed fool. Those two were killers and I didn't have my shotgun handy when he hit Erma."

"Did you see which way they went when they left here?" Will asked. "Did they stay on the road to Texas?"

"No," Jasper answered. "I saw 'em start out to the west on the road toward the Texas Panhandle."

"You sure of that?" Will asked. He would have bet the two outlaws were heading to Texas as fast as they could get there. And that would be straight south. By taking that road west, they wouldn't be out of Oklahoma for a few more days. If they had continued south, they'd be in Texas now. He tried to stir his brain to remember the country west of where he now stood. There was nothing between there and the Panhandle, and not much more in the Panhandle. He had to consider, of course, that wild country was what they wanted. It was not totally empty, for in recent years there had been settlers moving in to use the vast prairies to raise cattle. He looked up then and realized both husband and wife were studying him while he was lost in thought. "Well, I'll head west, then. I have to rest my horses, though, so I'll stop long enough for that." He looked at Erma hopefully. "Last time I was here, I bought some supper from you. Any chance I could buy some breakfast while my horses are restin'?"

"Yes, sir, you sure can," Erma responded. "I'll rustle you up some breakfast, you go take care of your horses, and I'll have you somethin' by the time you get back."

She was as good as her word, and after breakfast, he set out again after the two fugitives. The trail he now rode was no more than about thirty miles north of the Red River, which was the Texas border. Once again, he was risking the limits of his authority if he crossed the Red and went into Texas. It had caused headaches for his boss on the occasions he had not stopped at the border when on the trail of an outlaw. Dan Stone had dressed him down proper on more than one occasion for operating outside the Oklahoma border. Yet, Stone had been known to brag about his young deputy's devotion to bringing the outlaw to justice, no matter the cost. Stone had, on occasion, threatened to fire Will for working outside his territory. But he never acted on the threat, and Will was satisfied that the reason was the shortage of deputy marshals in the Nations. So here it was again and Will had no thought of stopping at the river to watch two men as ruthless as Hawkins and McGee ride into Texas free as birds.

Although it was a commonly used road, it was obvious there had been very little traffic on it in the last few days. For that reason, he felt pretty confident that the tracks he saw along the trail were those left by the two he followed. They appeared to be left by three horses and when he had seen them leaving The Falls they were leading one packhorse. Just as they had, he stopped to rest his horses by a stream close to twenty miles from the crossroads. He saw the remains of a fire, so he figured they had themselves some coffee and maybe some side meat they had stolen from Jasper Johnson. After his horses were rested and he had some coffee for himself, he continued on the trail that never veered from its straight-west course. Constantly watching the sides of the road he followed, he hoped to spot any place where the outlaws might have left the road. As the afternoon wore on, he began to think the occasional track he saw might not have been left by the horses he trailed, for he estimated he had ridden at least twenty-five miles. Seeing what looked to be a creek or stream up ahead, he went on and was relieved to find traces of a camp.

Wanting to push on in an effort to overtake Hawkins and McGee before they reached their destination, wherever that might be, he knew he had to rest his horses. The sorrel he had taken for his packhorse looked especially in need of a good rest. *What the hell,* he decided. *I'm not likely to catch them before they get where they're going. So I might as well not kill my horses while I hunt for them.* With that settled, he unloaded the horses of their burdens and made his camp, with the intention of starting fresh in the morning.

CHAPTER 16

Always sensitive to Buster's signals of company coming to call, he woke right away when the buckskin gelding nickered a greeting to the two horses that stopped in the trees on the creek bank, short of his camp. He rolled over on his side and pulled his rifle up beside him. He couldn't see who his visitors were, but he knew they had to be approaching his camp from downstream. Never forgetting Hawkins's promise to settle with him, he couldn't rule out the possibility that he and Tiny, suspecting he was trailing them, had doubled back to look for him. When he had climbed into his bedroll, he had taken precautions for just such an unannounced visit. He had built his fire close to a clump of laurel bushes that grew at the foot of a line of oak trees. With his bedroll up against the bushes, he was close enough to the fire to feel its heat, but also able to roll out of the bedroll into the bushes. Clutching his rifle now, that's what he did, quietly enough so he could then crawl behind one of the oaks. He waited for his visitors to make their move.

In a few minutes, a couple of shadows separated from the stand of trees lining the creek bank and moved toward his fire. It was obvious they had not seen him escape his bedroll, and they were approaching very cautiously, hoping to surprise him. They were close enough now that he could see it was not Hawkins and McGee. He eased away from the tree and moved carefully along the bushes until he could circle around behind the two men, both holding rifles. They stopped then, realizing there was no one in the bedroll. "Best you just stand right there and lay those rifles on the ground," Will warned. "If you don't wanna get shot, you'd do well not to make any sudden moves." Both men jerked visibly upon being surprised by the voice behind them, but they slowly laid their rifles on the ground. When they had done that, Will said, "Now turn around and state your business in my camp." They did as he instructed.

Since neither man was wearing a sidearm, Will took a moment to look them over. One of them, obviously the elder, spoke out. "I reckon you know what our business is, since you've been thinnin' out our cattle for the past couple of weeks."

"Where's the rest of your friends?" the younger man spoke up then. "They workin' on somebody else's herd tonight?"

"I hate to disappoint you fellows," Will said, "but I ain't one of the men you're lookin' for." He let his rifle drop to his side, and with the other hand, he pulled his coat aside to expose his badge. "My name's Will Tanner. I'm a U.S.

Deputy Marshal outta Fort Smith. Right now, I'm tryin' to track two fugitives, so I'm a little too busy to rustle your cattle."

Not sure if they could believe him or not, they were reluctant to accept his story, even though he no longer aimed his rifle at them. "All right if we pick up our rifles?" the older man asked.

"Sure," Will said, "as long as you ain't thinkin' about usin' 'em." He watched them carefully. "You raisin' cattle on this land?"

"Tryin' to," the older man answered, "leastways between this creek and the Red River. But it looks like that bunch of rustlers across the Red in Texas have decided we've got too many cows."

Will was surprised. "You own land from right here all the way to the Red River? That's a long way from here, ain't it?"

"It ain't that far," the younger one said. "Ain't but about eight miles. And we don't own the land. It's all free range, and there's three families grazin' cattle on it. We got together and wrote the Texas Rangers about those rustlers, but they ain't done nothin' about it yet. So we've been tryin' to watch our herds as best we can till they do. Ain't that right, Cal?"

"Everybody knows it's that damn Hawkins family that's doin' it, but ain't nobody been able to catch 'em at it," Cal said. "They come over the river, cut out a part of your herd, and drive 'em back over to Texas to sell." He paused when

292

he saw that his statement had obviously caught Will's attention.

"Did you say Hawkins?" Will asked.

"Yeah, Hawkins," Cal answered. "They've been rustlin' cattle for years. Most of it was in Mexico, but since settlers moved into this territory in Injun Territory, I reckon they've found it's easier to just ride across the Red." He hesitated, but then decided to ask, "You looked like you got real interested when I said it was them Hawkinses."

"One of the two men I'm tryin' to catch up with is named Hawkins," Will said. "Helluva coincidence, ain't it?" There was suddenly some sense to the path Hawkins and Tiny had taken, instead of continuing south into Texas. Hawkins had to be a member of the family notorious for stealing cattle. Odds were too much against it being a coincidence. "Do you know where this Hawkins family is located in Texas?"

"Not exactly," Cal answered. "Somewhere not too far from Wichita Falls is what I've heard." He paused then to say, "I reckon we owe you an apology for tryin' to sneak up on your camp, but we thought we'd caught one of those scoundrels alone. My name's Cal Wiggins." He nodded toward the younger one, "He's my brother, Sonny. We're sorry for wakin' you up."

"That's all right," Will replied, "no harm done. Nobody got shot." He figured it a good deal to get the information about the Hawkins family, anyway. "Sorry to hear about your trouble with rustlers. There ain't much I can do to help you right now. I'm on the trail of two pretty dangerous outlaws and I'm tryin' not to get too far behind 'em. When I can get to a telegraph office, I'll wire my boss in Fort Smith and tell him about the trouble you folks are havin' out here. Sorry I can't offer you much more right now." They were disappointed, but said they understood the problem, so Will pushed for more information. "I know where Wichita Falls is, but I don't know how far it is from right here."

" 'Bout fifteen miles," Sonny said. "Wouldn't you say, Cal?"

"That's about right," Cal answered. "It's 'bout eight miles to the Red where the Wichita River empties into it and follow the Wichita 'bout seven." He turned and pointed. "Yonder way," he said. He turned back to face his brother. "I reckon we've done messed up this man's sleep enough. We'd best get along back to the house. Looks like the Wiggins cows ain't scheduled to get stole tonight." He offered his hand to Will and they shook. "Good luck with catchin' those two outlaws."

After saying good luck with their cattle problem, Will watched them disappear into the shadows of the tree line to get to their horses. He didn't feel like trying to go back to sleep.

He had a decision to make. Should he continue along the common wagon road, hoping to find the hoofprints that would lead him to Hawkins? With a strong hunch now that Ward Hawkins was a member of the Hawkins family of Wichita Falls, or at least close kin, would his best bet be to go directly to Wichita Falls on the hopes that someone had seen Hawkins pass through? He wrestled with the decision for a while longer, telling himself that he might even be able to cut the distance between himself and the two outlaws if he went directly to Wichita Falls. In the end, he decided to leave it to chance. He reached in his pocket and pulled out his lucky silver coin. "Heads, I go straight to Wichita Falls. Tails I stay on the road." He flipped the coin in the air.

Fanny Hawkins walked out to the front porch of the large two-story house to watch the sun set behind the trees on the other side of Bobcat Creek. Pulling her favorite rocker over closer to the edge of the porch, so she could see the setting sun at a better angle, she sat down heavily. She reached into the pocket of the sheepskin vest she wore against the cold and took out her corncob pipe and knocked the ashes out of it on the heel of her boot. From another pocket of the vest, she pulled a small drawstring sack of tobacco and carefully filled her pipe. Next, she fished around in her pants pocket for a match. Finding one, she reached down to strike it on the floor of the porch, then lit her pipe and puffed a few times to get it started. Giving it a minute or two to burn, she used her finger to tamp the burning ashes down again. She found another match and relit the tamped-down tobacco, satisfied now that it would burn evenly and provide her with a good smoke. Inhaling the strong tobacco smoke deep into her lungs, she prepared to enjoy her favorite moment of peace. It was then that she saw the two riders approaching along the path that followed the creek. Knowing that her boys were still sitting around the supper table, she wondered what varmints were coming to disturb her peace at this late hour.

Puffing steadily on the corncob pipe, she watched the two riders, unable to identify them at that point. It was of no serious concern to her, for she feared no one. And for that reason, she gave out no shout to alert her sons, but unconsciously dropped her hand to rest on the Colt .45 she wore. When the riders grew closer, she thought there was something familiar about one of them, the way he sat his horse, maybe. She wasn't sure. There was a big man with him, his arm in a sling. "Now, who the hell . . . ?" she started, curious, but not concerned. If it was another one of those Texas Rangers coming to ask her a bunch of questions about her cattle business, they'd get the same answers as the last one. Could be they wondered if she knew anything about why that last one suffered a gunshot wound on his way back to Houston. She had already told them that he was fine when he left her ranch.

The two riders left the creek and rode directly toward the front porch. *Without so much as a call-out to say who the hell they are,* she thought, *they're acting like they don't need an invitation to just ride right on up to my door.* Without waiting for an invitation to step down, they did so. It was not until that moment that she recognized the one she had been trying to place. A wry smile formed on her weathered face and she reached up to take her pipe out of her mouth. "Well, well," she clucked sarcastically, "what the hell are you doin' here, Ward?" He had changed his appearance with a heavy mustache and beard, but she knew she should have recognized him.

"How you doin', Fanny?" Ward Hawkins responded. He, like his three brothers, had always called his mother by her given name. "I thought it was high time I paid the old homeplace a little visit—see my mama and my brothers."

"Haw," she huffed. "What for? Ain't nobody around here said they wished they could see good ol' Ward again. It's been about three years since you left here and went off to be a big shot somewhere. Where was that?"

"Houston," Ward answered.

"Yeah, Houston," Fanny went on. "Well, I don't

remember any big story in the newspapers about Ward Hawkins bein' elected governor of Texas. Last I heard of you, the Rangers were lookin' for you for robbin' a bank."

"You ain't ever bought a newspaper in your life," Ward said. "If you had, you wouldn't have read it 'cause you can't read."

"I can read a feller's face good enough to know when he's come runnin', lookin' for a place to hide. Who you runnin' from, the Rangers? Have you led a bunch of Rangers to my door?" Her standing with the Texas Rangers was poor enough without adding on some of his trouble.

"No, I ain't led no Rangers to your door," he insisted. "I just had some business I was carryin' on in Indian Territory that ran into a little trouble. I decided to leave till it cooled down. And since I was so close to Wichita Falls, I figured it'd be a good time to see how you folks over here are doin' without me."

"Pshaw," she spat. "We've been doin' just fine since you left. We're runnin' more cattle to market now that you ain't here." She shifted her attention to Tiny then. "Who's this puny little feller you got with you?"

"Tiny McGee," Ward said. "He's a business partner of mine."

A dumbfounded spectator to that point, Tiny had stood by his horse, witnessing the strange reunion between a mother and her son. With the sarcastic woman's gaze fixed on him now, he attempted to respond. "Pleased to make your acquaintance, Miz Hawkins."

"I'll bet you are," Fanny replied. "A business partner, huh? How come you're carryin' your arm in a sling? Sometimes business ain't so good, is it?" She turned her focus back on her son. "In Injun Territory, was you? You got them deputy marshals after you, so you had to skip outta Oklahoma, so they couldn't follow you. Now you expect me and the boys to take you back?"

"No, I don't," he replied. "I don't expect you to do nothin' for Tiny and me except let us sleep in the bunkhouse for a couple of nights, and maybe give us a little grub if you think you can spare it. If you don't, we can cook our own grub. We've got supplies. I've got a big job we're fixin' to go on and I'll pay you for your trouble. I'd pay you up front, but we had a little bad luck when the Oklahoma deputies found our cash supply." He preferred not to tell her that he and Tiny had been thrown in jail and that was when they lost all the money they had.

"You're broke, ain'tcha?" Fanny asked. A satisfied smile spread across her rough features.

"Hell, no, I ain't broke," Ward came back right away. "If you've got to have your money up front, I'll pay you up front. I'd just druther we waited till after we cash in on the job we've got lined up. I'll be a lot more generous then." He reached in his pocket and pulled out a roll of bills to let her get a glimpse of it. It was money he and Tiny had stolen from Jasper Johnson, and there wasn't much, at that.

There was still much resentment for her eldest son from the rest of her sons, as well as herself. He had thrown his nose in the air and walked away from the workaday world of rustling cattle, the only world his brothers knew, and his father before him. When her husband was slain, knocked out of the saddle by a Mexican rancher's bullet, she and her other sons had expected Ward to take over his father's role and continue to build the Hawkins brand. But Ward figured he was too good to work cattle, especially other people's cattle, because it was too much work, and most of it at night. Luckily for the Hawkins family, Fanny was tough enough to step in and run the business of cattle rustling, herself. Her first impulse at this moment was to tell her eldest to go to hell and get off her ranch. On second thought, however, she thought she might enjoy letting him stay for a while to let him see how little they missed him. She decided it would give her great pleasure to rub his nose in the failure of his grand plans and the success of the family business in his absence. She got up from her chair and walked to the edge of the porch, taking a moment to knock the ashes out of her pipe, using a porch post. Then, straightening up to her full height, she looked down at her wayward son and his friend at the foot of the steps, looking much like an evil queen, although a queen wearing men's trousers, boots, and a sheepskin vest. "All right, Ward, I'm gonna let you stay for a day or two. You're too late for supper, so you'll have to feed yourselves, if you've got any food. There ain't nobody in the bunkhouse, so you and Tiny can bunk in there. Your brothers sleep here in the house, since they're still members of this family. You can take breakfast in the house in the mornin'. The boys ain't got no run planned for tonight, so breakfast won't be till six o'clock. I'll tell Maudie to set a place for you."

"Much obliged, Fanny," Ward said, trying not to exhibit the relief he felt. "We'll take our possibles down to the bunkhouse and turn our horses out."

"I'll tell your brothers, so nobody takes a shot at you goin' in the bunkhouse," she said, a pleased smile on her face now, feeling that he had come begging. She stood on the porch, watching the two of them walking down to the bunkhouse. "The prodigal son's come home, John Henry," she announced to her late husband as she went back inside.

"Damned if that ain't the most tender homecomin' I've ever seen," Tiny remarked as they led the horses across the barnyard. "It almost had me in tears."

Ignoring his sarcasm, Hawkins said, "Hell, I was happy she didn't draw that Colt .45 she wears. At least we'll have a place to hole up for a few days while we plan how we're gonna take that bank." He shrugged and added, "I never said Fanny was gonna welcome us with open arms. After we turn the horses out, we'll build a fire in the stove. There used to be a coffeepot in the bunkhouse. We'll make some coffee and eat some of that jerky we brought."

"Who was you talkin' to, Fanny?" Lemuel Hawkins asked when his mother came into the dining room where all three sons were sitting around the table. "It sounded like you was talkin' to somebody out there on the porch."

"Ain't you boys the sharp ones," Fanny answered him. "Good thing it weren't the Texas Rangers or renegade Injuns, ain't it? Maybe the house would be on fire with you still settin' around the table."

Her comments caused Caleb, her youngest, to chuckle. "That's the reason we sent you out there, Fanny. So you could keep a lookout while we make sure we finish off all the coffee in the pot." That brought a laugh from the other boys.

"So, who was you talkin' to?" Lemuel still wanted to know, afraid his mother might be getting to the age where she talked to people you couldn't see. He wasn't sure, but he thought he might have heard her speak his late father's name as she was coming in the door.

"Why, I weren't talkin' to nobody but your older brother," she answered, then waited to see the reaction. She was not disappointed.

"Who?" Arlie asked, not sure he had heard her.

"Your older brother," she repeated. "Ward."

"What are you talkin' about?" Lemuel demanded. "You been smokin' rotten tobacco or somethin'? You sure you didn't just think you saw Ward? You most likely saw a shadow or somethin'."

"I hate to disappoint you, son, but I'm a helluva long way from goin' crazy. And if that weren't your brother Ward I was talkin' to, then I reckon it weren't him I just saw go in the bunkhouse."

She had them all worried then, much to her enjoyment, and she chuckled at Arlie when he went to look out the kitchen door toward the bunkhouse. She laughed heartily when he reacted. "Good Lord," he exclaimed. "There's smoke comin' outta the bunkhouse stovepipe." He was quickly joined by Lemuel and Caleb, wanting to see for themselves.

"He's right," Lemuel said, and turned to face his mother again. "Who the hell's down in the bunkhouse, Fanny?"

"I told you who it was," she answered. "Go see for yourself."

"I think I'll just do that," Lemuel said, and

went out the back door with Arlie and Caleb right behind him.

Inside the bunkhouse, Tiny looked out the open door and announced to Ward, "Looks like a welcomin' party comin'." He watched for a second more before commenting, "Maybe it looks more like a lynch mob."

Ward walked over beside him. "That's my brothers. Fanny musta told them about us." He unconsciously reached down to make sure his .44 was resting easy in his holster.

Noticing the move, Tiny took his arm out of the sling and removed it from his neck. "You sure this was a good idea, comin' back here?"

"Nothin' to worry about," Ward assured him. "They've just gotta see for themselves. Course, it always pays to be ready. These ain't the brightest boys ever stole a cow. I don't mind sayin' I got all the brains in the family." With that said, he stepped away from the door and positioned himself beside the stove. Following his lead, Tiny took a position on the other side of the stove. He rotated his shoulder several times, testing it, in case he was forced to use it.

After only a few seconds, Lemuel came through the door, stopped at once by the sight of Ward and Tiny standing there, waiting to receive their visitors. Caleb and Arlie pushed in behind Lemuel to stand there, uncertain as well. "I'll be damned . . ." Lemuel finally drew out, startled by his brother's obvious change. "What the hell are you doin' here?" he asked, just as his mother had.

"Come to see my brothers," Ward answered. "Wanted to see if you'd gotten any smarter since I left here."

"Things are different around here since you took off," Lemuel declared. "So, you're wastin' your time if you think you can come back and take over. I'm runnin' things now, and we're likin' it that way." Caleb and Arlie nodded in support of his claim.

Ward smirked. "You mean Fanny's runnin' things around here now, don't you, little brother?" Before Lemuel could react, Ward continued. "I've got no notion to come back to this broke-down ranch, so don't get yourself riled up. Me and Tiny are just gonna be here a couple of days, then we'll move on. We've got bigger things to do. So, you might as well just keep a cool head and we'll be gone before you know it."

There was a silent standoff for a few moments with none of the party really knowing what their reaction should be at this unexpected reunion. Arlie, who had always been the biggest and the strongest since they were all grown, was inclined to ask a question. Unable to ignore Tiny's size, he wondered, "Who's this feller with you?"

"Tiny McGee," Ward answered with a grin, knowing his brother could not resist comparing himself to his giant-sized companion. "He's a big 'un, ain't he?" He chuckled then and made a show of introducing them. "Tiny, these are my brothers, Lemuel, Caleb, and Arlie," he said, pointing to each one when he said the name. "Now, I'll tell you how it's gonna be for the next few days around here. Me and Tiny will mind our own business, and you can mind yours. We'll take our meals with you in the house, Fanny's already said that, so there shouldn't be no trouble between us. Anybody got any problem with that?" He aimed his gaze at Lemuel, since he knew he was the one who would feel challenged.

"I reckon not," Lemuel replied after a moment's pause to decide if there was any problem. "Long as you know who's runnin' things around here and don't try to stick your foot in it."

"Fair enough," Ward responded. "Now, me and Tiny ain't had no supper. So, since this stove has finally started to heat up, we're gonna make some coffee and find somethin' to eat in our packs. You boys are welcome to hang around if you want to. Ain't no reason we can't be neighborly."

In spite of the bad feelings that had been generated when Ward decided to leave the family band of rustlers, there was a natural curiosity about their oldest brother. Caleb, the youngest, was the first to express it openly. "Where have you been for three years?"

"It'd be an easier question to answer if you'da asked, *Where haven't you been?*" Ward said.

"I've been all over the state of Texas, Oklahoma, Kansas, too."

"We know you've still been sellin' some cattle in Houston," Arlie commented. "Thought you didn't like rustlin' cattle."

"I never said I didn't like rustlin' cattle. I just didn't like doin' it on the small scale you boys are doin' it. But I'm into bigger operations, too. Me and Tiny just opened up a big hotel-saloon operation in Indian Territory." He didn't see fit to mention its fate at the hands of the U.S. Marshals Service.

"Well, this cattle operation is plenty big enough for us," Lemuel remarked. He was not comfortable with any sign of a reunion with his older brother. "We're doin' all right with the way things are right now." He took a step toward the door. "I expect we'll go on back to the house." He didn't leave, however, until Arlie started for the door and Caleb followed him, just to be sure they didn't linger while he wasn't there. No matter what Ward had said, Lemuel was wary of an attempt by him to take over the top spot.

CHAPTER 17

Following the directions given to him by Cal and Sonny Wiggins, Will came upon the fledgling town of Wichita Falls. They had been accurate in their estimation of the distance as well, at about fifteen miles from his campsite of the night before. There were only a few buildings on the main street, but he saw posts driven in the ground that served to stake out the whole street in building lots. At present, he saw what appeared to be a store selling general merchandise, a blacksmith next to a stable, what appeared to be a saloon, and that was all. He decided to try the saloon, thinking he might be able to buy breakfast there, since he had started out that morning without eating. Although almost midmorning, there was no activity on the street that he could see. As he rode along the deserted street, a hound dog ran out from the blacksmith shop and started snapping at his packhorse's hooves, causing the sorrel to hop around in response. When the dog left the sorrel's heels, he made a pass at Buster's and received a solid kick that sent him flying. Will nudged the buckskin into a trot and they went on to the Wichita Saloon, a large tent, faced with a wooden facade. Will stepped down and went inside.

There was no one inside the tent, so he stood next to the bar and waited. After a minute, a sandy-haired little woman came in the back and stopped when she saw him. She stuck her head back through a canvas opening and called, "Howard, you've got a customer in here." When she heard Howard answer her, she turned to Will and said, "He'll be right in."

"Maybe you can help me, ma'am," Will replied. "Any chance I could get some breakfast here?" She didn't answer at once but looked at him as if he was asking for a handout, so he explained. "I'd like to buy breakfast, if you sell it."

"If you'll settle for corn cakes and coffee," she replied. "We ain't got our kitchen set up yet and we ain't got any eggs. But I can fix you up with some good coffee and corn cakes I fried up this morning." She just finished talking when her husband came from the smaller tent behind. "Fellow here is wantin' somethin' to eat," she said to him. "I told him I'd fix him some corn cakes and coffee." She turned to Will again. "You reckon that'll do ya?"

"I reckon it would, ma'am, dependin' on how much you want for it," Will answered. He figured if she asked too much, he'd just go ahead and cook his breakfast, himself, just like he typically did.

"Is twenty-five cents too much?" she asked.

"I reckon that's fair enough," Will said. He

pulled his money out and laid two bits on the counter. She promptly picked it up and disappeared out the back of the tent.

"You'll have to bear with us a little, mister. We're tryin' to get the place set up. We ain't been open but two weeks. When we get our permanent saloon built, we'll serve regular meals. My name's Howard Blaylock. That was my wife, Margie. 'Preciate you stoppin' in. I've got rye whiskey and corn whiskey, if you're wantin' a drink."

"Will Tanner," Will said in introduction. "I reckon it's a little too early in the day for me—maybe later on sometime."

"You from around here, Will, one of the cattle ranches, maybe?"

"Nope, I'm just passin' through town, tryin' to find somebody." He was disappointed to hear that Howard and Margie were almost as new in town as he was. He was not likely to get much information about the Hawkins ranch from them. Maybe the general store would be a better bet. At least that building had been there long enough for the lumber used for the siding to weather. In the meantime, he could eat some corn cakes and drink some coffee. "I'm hopin' to catch up with two other fellows. Any chance you mighta seen two other strangers come through town yesterday or last night?"

"Can't say as I have," Blaylock said. "And I reckon I wouldn't have unless they came in here for a drink. I've been workin' out back, building tables and chairs, so there coulda been a whole parade pass down the street and I wouldn't have known it."

"I reckon I woulda told you, if that had happened," Margie cracked as she entered the big tent, carrying a plate of cakes and a cup of coffee. She set them down on the bar in front of Will. "I wish a parade would come through here. We could use some business."

"You know anybody named Hawkins that might have a ranch around here somewhere?" Will asked, just on the chance they might know. Both husband and wife said they did not, but reminded him that they had not been in town very long. They left him to eat his breakfast while they returned to their chores. He accepted a refill on his coffee when Margie came back with the coffeepot and he didn't waste much time drinking it before saying good-bye and walking out the door.

Outside on the street, Will led his horses toward the building standing alone that claimed to be Brown's Store and advertised general merchandise. If the proprietor of this business had no knowledge of Hawkins, he didn't have much confidence in ever finding the men he hunted. As he tied Buster's reins to the rail in front of the store, he promised the buckskin, "As soon as I make a stop here, I'll take you to water."

"Does he ever talk back to you?"

Surprised, for he had not noticed when the slight feminine figure opened the door, he chuckled and replied, "Not so you'd recognize it as talkin', but he definitely lets me know what he's thinkin'."

"Well, I hope we've got whatever he needs," she said. "What can we help you with?" She stepped back and held the door for him to enter. When he was inside, she said, "That's my husband over behind the counter. We're Frank and Frances Brown." She paused to smile before adding, "I'm Frances, he's Frank."

"Howdy, stranger," Frank called out cordially. "Ain't seen you in town before. You just passin' through, or are you gonna be workin' at one of the ranches?"

"Will Tanner," he said. "Just passin' through, but I'm lookin' for one of the ranches near here."

"That so?" Frank asked. "Which one you lookin' for, the Double-D, the Broken Spur, the Rocking-T?"

"Don't know what they might call it," Will said. "The fellow that owns it is a man named Hawkins."

"Oh," Frank responded, and exchanged glances with his wife before answering. "I don't know if the Hawkins ranch has an official name or brand. 'Fraid I can't help you much."

Seeing how fast their tone went from cordial

to stone cold and guarded at the mention of the Hawkins name, Will decided to take a chance and play it straight with them. "You folks seem like honest people, so I'm gonna lay my cards on the table." He pulled his coat aside to reveal his badge. "I'm a U.S. Deputy Marshal out of Fort Smith, Arkansas. I was out of my jurisdiction the minute I crossed over the Red River. But I'm trailing a man named Ward Hawkins and another man with him. The two of 'em are wanted for some serious crimes in Oklahoma Territory. And I'm doin' my best to see they don't get away with 'em just because they crossed the river before I caught up with 'em." He was pleased to see the Browns' expressions transform back to the friendly facade he had seen at first.

"Mister," Frank declared, "I'd be happy to help you any way I can. That whole Hawkins clan is a pretty nasty bunch. We've had enough dealin's with 'em to write the governor for help, but up to now, there hasn't been any sign of the Rangers."

"Or anybody else," Frances finished his sentence for him, "till you showed up."

"Well, there was one Ranger a while back that called on the Hawkins ranch and he ended up gettin' shot on his way home," Frank corrected his wife. "But it's gonna take more than one lawman to do anything about that bunch of outlaws. Clive Smith, the blacksmith, told me there was an older brother that left the ranch a few years back—might be the man you're chasin'. But the family's run by the old man's widow, Fanny Hawkins. She's got three sons that do all the dirty work." He threw his hands up in frustration. "Everybody around here knows they're nothin' but a gang of cattle rustlers and Fanny might be the toughest one of 'em."

"Tell him about the brand," Frances prompted.

"Right," Frank responded. "I said I wasn't sure what their brand was, but that ain't exactly true. Folks around here say they're the Full Moon Ranch. Their brand ain't nothin' but a round moon that covers any brand that was there before."

Will said nothing for a while, overwhelmed by the outpouring of information from the couple. He had never expected this much to be offered so freely. When they paused for breath, he asked, "Can you tell me how to find that ranch?"

"Never been there, myself," Frank replied. "But I'm told it's on Bobcat Creek somewhere. So I reckon the best I can tell you is to find Bobcat Creek where it empties into the Wichita River and follow it till you get to the ranch." Anticipating Will's next question, he said, "Clive said Bobcat Creek is about two miles down the river from his stable. That's about as much as I can tell you, but I feel like I have to warn you, that ranch is a dangerous place for a lawman. It might be a good idea to get some help from the Texas Rangers."

"You say downriver?" Will asked. When Frank confirmed that, then Will realized the creek was back the way he had just come, between the town and the Red River. He had evidently passed Bobcat Creek somewhere that morning, probably paused to let his horses drink there. "I'm much obliged for the information," Will said. "Maybe at least I can find their ranch. Then we'll just have to wait and see what happens." In a gesture of appreciation, he decided the least he could do was to buy something from them. "I could use five pounds of coffee, some sugar, and some salt." He didn't really need any of the three items, but he knew he would eventually use them up. Remembering his promise to Buster, he tied his purchases on his packhorse, bid the Browns farewell, and took his horses to water.

After his horses were rested, he started out on the same trail he had ridden in on, this time trying to estimate the distance traveled as he proceeded. In an effort not to miss it, he kept a sharp eye on the banks in case the confluence between the creek and the river was not that obvious. He found that not to be the case, however, when he came upon a creek emptying into the river at what he guessed to be close to two miles from the stable. With some idea now of what he was up against, he followed along the creek with a new sense of caution. From what he had learned from Frank

Brown, he realized he faced not only Hawkins and Tiny, but also three more Hawkins brothers. He was going to have to be careful while he searched for some way to get to Hawkins and Tiny when they were away from the others. If he was found out before he made his move, it was going to turn into one big hunt and he would be the hunted. He couldn't let that happen. The thought ran through his mind that Jim Little Eagle would call him crazy, and Will found it hard to disagree.

He rode for a distance he judged to be about six miles, sighting small groups of stray cattle and no sign of anybody tending them. It was winter and everyone's cattle were on winter range, but there should have been some sign of a line shack or feeding sites where hay was dropped to keep the cows from starving. It was apparent that the Hawkins ranch preferred to make the spring roundup on someone else's herd. Out of curiosity, he rode into the midst of a group of six mangy-looking strays to check the brands. Four of the cows had different brands and two of them had the "Full Moon" brand, which was no more than a round, flat brand that burned out the previous one. It was not very sophisticated.

Following the creek around a sharp bend, he pulled Buster to a sudden stop when he spotted the ranch house in the distance. A big, two-story frame house with a wide porch that ran all the way across the front, it sat on a treeless yard, with a barn, bunkhouse, and several other outbuildings clustered around. He sat looking for a long while, watching the house, but there was no sign of anyone working outside or around the barn. There was smoke coming from two chimneys on the house. He shifted his concentration to the bunkhouse, where there was also smoke coming from a lone stovepipe. Frank Brown had made no mention of cowhands working for the Hawkinses, only Hawkins brothers, so Will naturally wondered who slept in the bunkhouse, the brothers? Or was it the new arrivals? Even if he knew, what could he do about it? At this point, he was forced to admit he didn't know. He decided that while he was making up his mind, he could try to move in a little closer to the ranch house to better be able to watch them. As he looked over the open area before him, he could see only one spot where he could get close in. And that was where the creek ran close by the back corner of the barn. There was a thick growth of trees on both sides of the creek there, so he wheeled Buster around to ride in a wide sweep around the ranch and approach it under cover of those trees.

Reasonably certain he hadn't been discovered, he guided Buster into the trees and paused to watch the barn and house for any sudden activity that might tell him he'd been spotted. There was nothing to indicate that he had been, so, after a few minutes' wait, he urged the buckskin on into the water. As soon as he crossed the creek, he dismounted and tied the horses to keep them from wandering. Then he moved up closer to the outer edge of the trees, picking a spot where he could watch the back door of the ranch house as well as one side of the barn and the corral. He would have liked to be able to watch the door of the bunkhouse, too, since there appeared to be a fire going in the stove. Once again, he found himself thinking it would have been handy if he had brought Jim Little Eagle to help him. As soon as he thought it, he knew he would have never asked Jim to come with him. He was going to catch enough hell as it was for operating in Texas. If he had persuaded a Choctaw policeman to cross the line with him, Dan Stone might hang him. He would fire him, to say the least. *And that would please Sophie and her mother.* That thought slipped into his brain unintentionally, causing him to caution himself to keep his mind on the business he was risking his neck to do. It was an unnecessary warning, however, for the back door of the ranch house opened, capturing his attention at once. A large man with many of the physical traits that Ward Hawkins exhibited, came down the steps from the kitchen. One of his brothers, Will easily decided, even though this man was thinner of face and had darker hair.

He was wearing a heavy coat, so Will guessed he might be intending to do some chore outside, maybe check on their cattle. From what he had witnessed on his way up the creek, it was high time somebody did. With one stop at the side of the barn to relieve himself of the quantity of coffee he had no doubt been drinking, he went inside. A few minutes passed, then two more men, bundled against the weather, like their brother, came from the kitchen and headed for the barn.

"Bring that sorrel you like, too," Lemuel said to Caleb when he met him and Arlie coming in the barn. With his saddle on his shoulder, he paused to give his brothers instructions. "We won't come back till about suppertime, so we'll need some coffee and somethin' to eat, too. Soon as I get saddled up, I'll go back to the kitchen for the coffee, and I'll see if Maudie's got any of those biscuits left. We'll go up to that old line shack and build us a fire, if it's still standin'. Fanny won't know the difference. As long as we're gone, she'll think we're roundin' up strays."

Upon hearing the conversation among the brothers, Will could not help but have a feeling of disgust for their lack of responsibility to take care of their stock, even if it was stolen stock. It was easy to deduce, from their conversation, that they planned to ride out to lie around in a line shack until suppertime in order to fool their mother. Then it occurred to him that his disgust for the men had caused him to fail to realize the opportunity they were about to provide for him. As far as he could determine, there were no other ranch hands working there. He remembered Frank Brown saying the ranch was run by Fanny Hawkins and three sons. With that being the case, there should be no one left on the place, but Fanny and maybe a cook. *Unless,* he thought, *that fire burning in the bunkhouse meant Ward Hawkins and Tiny McGee had come here, and they were camping out in the bunkhouse.* Up to this point, he had not figured out how he could possibly ride into a party of five gunmen and arrest two of them without getting shot full of holes. It now became possible to pull it off with these three getting ready to ride out and not return for hours. If Hawkins and Tiny were in the main house, however, he might have the old woman, Fanny, to worry about—maybe the cook, too. He had no way of knowing. Call it luck, or fate, whatever, it was an opportunity he hadn't expected to be handed to him and he couldn't afford to waste time to act. *Get moving,* he found himself silently badgering the three brothers to get saddled up and out of the way.

After what seemed an inordinate amount of time, the three brothers finally rode out of the barnyard. Will watched until they were out of sight to see that they continued in the same direction they started out in. When they were gone, the next thing he had to find out was whether or not Hawkins and McGee were actually in the bunkhouse. If they were not, he was going to have to come up with a whole new strategy to invade the main house. He went back to get his horses, then walked along the creek past the barn, where he could now see the bunkhouse. Leaving his horses in the trees again, he crept up to the edge to take a good look at the bunkhouse. It was a simple building with wood siding, one door on one end and one window on the other, designed no doubt to provide a draft through the bunkhouse when needed. He moved silently along the side to the window at the end.

Confident that there was no one outside the house to surprise him, he eased his head up to look in the window. So dirty that it was almost opaque, the glass in the window was just possible to see through, but it was enough to show him what he hoped for. Closer to the other end, the two men he sought were sitting beside the stove. Having pulled straw ticks and blankets from the bunks, they had fashioned lounges upon which to take their comfort. *Made to order,* he thought. They didn't look like they were going to go anywhere anytime soon, so he was ready to take the first risky move. It was important, if he was going to pull this off successfully, to have their horses saddled and ready to ride as soon as

Hawkins and Tiny were captured. That meant he was going to have to go back to the barn to saddle two horses and hope Tiny and Hawkins stayed put while he did.

Still cautious, although he felt sure there was no one left to see him, he walked in the barn to find the tack room. The two saddles in the corner were obviously the property of the two now taking their ease in the bunkhouse. Seeing a coil of rope hanging on a peg near the door, he pulled it over his arm to rest on his shoulder. Then he picked up a saddle in each hand, holding it by the horn, and walked out to the corral. With no concern for which horse belonged to which outlaw, he picked out a couple of stout ones. Both horses accepted the bridle without protest, so in a matter of minutes, he had two horses saddled, and so far, no indication that anyone from the house had taken notice. He led the horses around to the back of the barn, where he fashioned a lead rope from one horse to the other, with enough left to tie to his packhorse. When that was done, he hurried back into the trees to get his horses. Once he had tied the two saddled horses to his packhorse, he proceeded to complete the dangerous part of his plan.

"Hell, I could get used to this," Tiny declared as he reached up to get the coffeepot from the stove. He filled his cup, then gestured toward Hawkins, but Hawkins declined. Settling back down beside the stove, he said, "I was hopin' they didn't expect me and you to ride off with 'em to round up strays."

Hawkins grunted, unconcerned. "I didn't come back here to nursemaid no cows. Besides, Lemuel don't want me workin' with him and the other two, anyway. He's so damn scared I'm comin' back to take over this ranch."

When the door opened, both men turned their heads to see who was coming in. Unable to believe their eyes at first, both men could only gawk, wide-eyed at what appeared to be an apparition standing in the doorway, a rifle leveled in their direction. When Hawkins started to make a motion to get up, Will warned, "Don't even think about it. Sit right there."

Regaining his wits after those first few moments of shock, Hawkins snarled, "You've got to be crazy as hell, walkin' in here like this." He automatically dropped his hand to his hip, only to be reminded that he had not strapped on his handgun.

"You're right," Will responded. "I am a little crazy. So you'd do well to believe me when I tell you, you make one funny move and I'll put a bullet in your chest. I came to arrest you, take you to trial, but if you make any move to resist, I've got no choice. I'll blow you to hell without thinkin' about it twice."

"All we got to do is holler once or twice and

you'll have Fanny waitin' for you to come outta here. And she'll be waitin' with her Henry rifle," Hawkins said.

"Like I said," Will countered. "That would be the last sound you'd ever make. The best chance you two will have is to go back to Fort Smith for trial. It's a long trip back there, maybe I'll get careless. That's your best bet. Anything else, and you'll most likely end up dead right here and I won't have to bother with transportin' you back." He looked at Tiny, who was still trying to believe it was happening, then looked back at Hawkins. "So what's it gonna be? Execution right here, right now, or go back for trial?" They both looked uncertain, so he continued. "You can think about tryin' to jump me, if you think you can jump up from there before I put a bullet in both of you. But I don't think you can. Even if you could, which one of you wants to volunteer to take that bullet, so the other one can jump me?"

Neither man could supply an answer until finally Hawkins spoke. "All right, you mongrel, you're holdin' all the cards right now, but like you say, it's a long way from here to Fort Smith." He still remembered the first time he had decided to call Will's bluff, and he was convinced Will meant it when he said he would execute them on the spot.

"Tiny?" Will looked at the big man again. When he reluctantly agreed with Hawkins, Will said, "All right, both of you roll over on your belly with your hands behind your back." When both men rolled over, he quickly tied their wrists together. Tiny was first because he was the bigger man and the most likely to try something if his hands were free while Hawkins's hands were being tied. When each man was tied with their hands behind them, Will rolled them over with their arms pinned beneath them and made a quick search for any pocket pistols or knives. In the process, he came up with cash money taken from Jasper Johnson's store at the crossroads. "All right, get on your feet." He stood back and pointed toward the door with his rifle.

"What about our coats?" Tiny complained. "It's cold as hell out there."

"You're right," Will said. "I wanna make sure you're comfortable." He saw a couple of coats on one of the bunks. "Who belongs to which one?" When Tiny identified his, Will picked it up and draped it over Tiny's shoulders. Then he picked up the other one and put it on Hawkins's shoulders. He marched them out the door and around to the back of the barn, where they were disappointed to find two saddled horses waiting for them.

"That's my saddle, but it ain't my horse," Tiny complained upon seeing the gray wearing his saddle. Will told him it was his horse from now on. Then Tiny said, "Well, I can't climb up in that saddle with my hands tied behind my back."

"I'm gonna help you," Will told him. Then, with a cautious eye for Hawkins, in case he thought that an opportunity to make a break for it, he steadied the big man while he stepped up and threw a leg over the saddle. When he was settled, Will repeated the procedure with Hawkins. With both prisoners sitting calmly on their horses, Will climbed aboard Buster and led his procession out from behind the barn. So far, his luck had been good. He had not thought to count on Hawkins's three brothers to conveniently be away from the ranch. Nor had he expected to capture both of his prisoners without a shot being fired. His luck took a turn for the worse, however, when he led them away from the barn and started across the open barnyard toward the trail back to the Wichita River. He turned when he heard the kitchen door open and the cook stepped outside to empty her dishpan. She took one look at the parade leaving the barn and rushed back inside. *Oh hell,* he thought, and gave Buster a firm nudge. The buckskin responded and they started off at a gallop.

Seeing the alarm in Maudie's face, Fanny Hawkins did not wait for an explanation. She grabbed the Henry rifle she kept by the kitchen door and rushed outside in time to see Will leading his column toward the creek trail. There was no hesitation on her part as she raised her rifle and tried to set the sights on him. Her target was rapidly galloping out of her effective range, but she managed to get off two shots. The first one missed her target and the second one struck Tiny right between the shoulder blades. He slid from the saddle to land heavily on the ground. "Damn!" she swore. "It's shootin' a little bit low." Already they were out of range for the Henry, so she dropped it to her side and watched the strange procession riding out of sight. Not sure who she had just shot, she went down the steps and started out across the barnyard with mixed emotions for who it might be. Maudie was right behind her.

"Well, it ain't my son," Fanny announced when she got to the body. "It's that Tiny feller." She was at once struck with indecision, not sure how she felt about this sudden invasion upon her territory, and from the looks of it, by a single lawman. Already estranged from her son, she was not sure if she really cared that he had just been snatched right out from under her nose. It was obvious to her that the only reason he had returned to the family he had chosen to abandon was because the law was after him. On the other hand, she was not willing to stand for the law trespassing on her property, and there was a strong desire to teach them a lesson. For that reason alone, she considered having her boys go after their brother when they returned to the house. She looked at Maudie and remarked, "Just bad timin' that feller slipped in here when my boys were gone." Looking back at Tiny's body, she said, "Let's see if he's got any money on him. We'll let the boys drag his big ass outta the yard when they get back."

CHAPTER 18

Once out of rifle range, Will reined Buster back to a fast walk and kept him at that pace for about two miles before he pulled up to take inventory of what was left of his jail party. "I reckon that was your mother that done for Tiny," he said to Hawkins. "Seems like a gentle lady. I figure she musta missed when she knocked him outta the saddle. Reckon who she was aimin' to hit, me or you?"

"Too bad she missed," was Hawkins's sullen response. He was not inclined to confess to Will that he wasn't certain, himself. "You didn't bother to see if Tiny was dead or alive. He mighta needed help."

"He might have, at that, but I figured my primary responsibility was to transport you safely to Fort Smith, so I had to get you outta harm's way as quick as I could. I reckon your mama will take care of him, if he is alive, or finish him off if it was him she was shootin' at." When looking back at the time the shots were fired, he saw Tiny when he was hit, and he didn't stir after he hit the ground. There was no way to tell if he was dead or alive, and there was no percentage in favor of stopping to see. "It's a good thing you managed to hang on to that coat 'cause I wouldn'ta stopped to pick it up, either."

His comment caused his prisoner to snarl once again. "You're lucky I didn't fall off, with my hands tied behind my back." He had been forced to hang on to his coat by clamping his teeth around the collar and holding on until his jaws ached. He didn't think Will was aware of it, so he didn't confess it. "It wouldn't hurt nothin' if you tied my hands in front of me. It'd be a helluva lot easier to stay in the saddle."

"I expect you're right," Will said. "Don't know why I didn't think of that." Since Hawkins had evidently escaped his mother's attempt to shoot them, Will climbed back into the saddle with the intent to put as much territory as possible between them and Bobcat Creek. When they reached the Wichita, it would be only a few miles from that point before reaching the Red River and Oklahoma Territory on the other side. He had wanted to bring Tiny back to trial along with Hawkins, but it should make his task quite a bit easier to deal with one prisoner, instead of two. He had to assume that Hawkins's brothers would come after him, even crossing into Indian Territory to chase after them. Will's challenge was to simply leave no trail for them to follow. He would have been surprised had he known that Hawkins was not at all confident that his brothers would follow them.

By the time they reached the Red, Will had decided it best to travel the east–west road leading to the crossroads where Jasper Johnson had his store. It was a fairly well-traveled wagon road and his tracks might not be so easy to distinguish. He remembered the difficulty he had when tracking Hawkins and Tiny on the road when going in the opposite direction. Johnson's store was a good fifty miles from the point where he struck the road, and it was approaching noon at present. So he decided to press on for another thirty miles or so before stopping to rest the horses. Then he would decide whether or not to camp there for the night. He was thinking he would be at Johnson's by midday the following day. From there, he thought it better to follow the road on to Tishomingo, then head to Atoka from there. He figured there was a better chance of losing the three brothers if he took the less-traveled way to Atoka.

Still fuming inside over the second time he had been caught by the unpredictable deputy marshal, Ward Hawkins promised himself that he would never end up in Fort Smith. He would get his chance, he told himself, if he was patient. His complaining earlier, about his hands behind his back, had fallen upon deaf ears and he was forced to ride that way for the most part of thirty miles before Will stopped at a shallow creek for the night. It was against his nature, but he decided his best chance of turning the tables on the deputy was to pretend he was beaten. So when Will helped him down from the saddle, he mumbled a soft, "Much obliged." He could see that Will was surprised by the words of thanks, but his sly smile also told Hawkins that he was suspicious as well.

"I reckon I know when I'm beat," Hawkins said. "Ain't no use to give you any trouble. I'm just ready to get to Fort Smith, get my trial over with, and get to the hangin'."

Will looked at the suddenly beaten man, even more skeptical of his sudden reversal of attitude, but he decided to play the game as well. "That oughta make the trip a little easier on you. I'll tell you what I tell every prisoner I transport to trial—you don't give me any trouble, I won't give you any trouble." He glanced around the spot he had picked for his camp and used the Colt .44 he was holding to point toward a small oak. "That's your tree right there. You can sit right there while I build a fire and fix something to eat."

"I gotta take a leak first," Hawkins said.

"Figured you might," Will said. "You can walk right over yonder by those other trees."

"I got a little problem," Hawkins replied. "I can't let it fly with somebody watchin' me. How 'bout if I just step behind them bushes on the other side of them trees?"

"Then I reckon I'll have to step behind 'em, too," Will said with a smile. "You just go where

I told you and turn your back to me. That'll work just as well. Either that or hold it till we get to Fort Smith. Now, stay still while I untie your hands."

Hawkins couldn't help a sly smile. It was worth a try, he figured, and stood obediently while Will untied his hands. Then with Will standing about ten yards away, holding his Colt ready to fire, Hawkins relieved himself without bothering to turn his back. When he was finished, he went to the tree Will had pointed out. "Now, sit down and straddle that tree," Will ordered, and when he did, Will took his hands and quickly tied his wrists together. "You can sit there and watch me do all the work." Then with Hawkins left hugging the tree, Will went about taking care of the horses and building a fire. It was a procedure he had practiced many times before when transporting one lone prisoner without the use of a jail wagon. He had a gut feeling that the prisoner he was dealing with on this trip was more dangerous than any he had dealt with before. For that reason, he made it a rule to have one eye on him at all times.

When the coffee and bacon were ready, Will untied Hawkins's hands so he could eat, but before his prisoner had time to think about it, Will took the rope and tied his feet together, still astraddle the tree. "When I'm transportin' a prisoner, I've got certain rules. One of 'em is about eatin'. I untie your hands, so you can eat, but I keep an eye on you while you're eatin'. And if I see your hands anywhere near that rope around your feet, you get a .44 slug in your shoulder. Then the next time I feed you, you don't get your hands untied." He shook his head to emphasize, "And it's a helluva lot harder to eat that way."

Unable to maintain his pretense of passiveness, Hawkins leered at him and asked, "What's your rule when my three brothers catch up with us and start throwin' .44 slugs at you?"

"Well, my usual procedure in cases like that is to put a bullet in your brain, then use your body for cover," Will said. "I hope I don't have to use that rule this time."

"Go to hell." Hawkins could hold it no longer. Fully angry again, he picked up the plate of bacon and tore off a mouthful. "This ain't much of a supper, even for a prisoner," he complained.

"Hell, I ain't gettin' any better food than you are, but I'll tell you what. If you behave yourself and don't give me any trouble, I'll buy us both a meal when we get to Jasper Johnson's place at the crossroads. You remember that place, don't you? I believe you and Tiny stopped in there on your way to Texas."

Hawkins scowled fiercely. "If we make it that far," he spat in defiance, even though he had no real hope that his brothers were coming after them. "The smartest thing you could do right now is cut me loose. You do that, and I'll ride back to meet my brothers, and we'll turn back and let you go."

"That would be mighty considerate of you, Hawkins, since I've put you to all this trouble. I'll think about your proposition."

"You know there's a lot of lawmen that ain't workin' for peanuts," Hawkins went on, trying another approach. "Whadda they pay you? Two hundred a month? Less than that? If you had your mind set in the right place, I could guarantee you a helluva lot more than that."

"I'll sleep on it," Will responded, "but I have to be honest with you. I just do this job to get to know interestin' people like you. I don't do it for the money. Now, I'll put you away for the night and we'll start out in the mornin'."

"They're back," Maudie called from the kitchen door. Not sure Fanny heard her, she went through the kitchen to the hallway. "They're back," she repeated to Fanny, who was already hurrying from the parlor. Not even waiting to put on her coat, Fanny rushed past her cook and went out the kitchen door.

In the process of taking the saddles off their horses, her three sons were surprised to see her hurrying across the yard to meet them. "Uh-oh," Lemuel muttered. "Wonder what's got her stirred up." All three paused to watch her striding toward them.

"Don't put them saddles away!" Fanny cried out as she approached. "You boys are goin' back out. Put them saddles on a fresh horse and get ready to ride!"

"What is it, Fanny? Where we goin'?" Arlie asked. Fanny turned and pointed to an object at the edge of the yard. They all peered in the direction she indicated to see a dark lump near the path leading out to the creek trail. "What's that?" Arlie asked.

"Tiny McGee!" Fanny fairly shouted. "That's what!"

"Ward?" Lemuel asked at once, thinking his brother must have had reason to shoot him.

"No, damn it!" Fanny replied. "Ward's gone. A damn lawman rode in here and took him and Tiny, and rode right out again. I only had time for a couple of shots at him when they was ridin' out, but Tiny got in the way of my shot."

"You want us to go after him and bring Ward home?" Caleb asked. "We been out workin' all day, and we ain't had no supper."

"I want you to catch up with that lawman and string him up to a tree, so any other lawman will know they ain't gonna ride in here on our ranch anytime they please. I want you to ride tonight and catch up with him. Maudie will fix you some biscuits to take with you, but you've got to ride tonight while he's stopped to camp," she kept repeating to be sure they understood. "He rode out on the creek trail, headin' for the river, goin' back to Oklahoma, for certain. You oughta be able to catch him when they stop for the night."

"What about Ward?" Lemuel asked, still not certain if his mother had accepted him back in the family or not.

"What about him?" Fanny answered with a question. "I don't give a cuss about Ward. I want you to get that lawman. Now, get movin'. I'll go to the kitchen to get you some grub. Throw them saddles on fresh horses!" She spun on her heel and headed toward the house.

"Boy, she's really hot about gettin' that lawman," Caleb said when she was out of earshot. "She never said nothin' about bringin' Ward home. You reckon she wants us to bring him back?"

"You heard her," Lemuel said. "She said to string that lawman up. We'll just have to see what happens to Ward."

"How the hell are we supposed to track him in the dark?" Arlie asked.

"I don't know," Lemuel answered. "Maybe Fanny thinks they'll be takin' the same road Ward said they came outta Injun Territory on. I reckon we can just ride like hell on that road and see if we catch 'em. If we don't, we don't."

"We might catch up with 'em, but if they ain't camped right by the road, we still ain't gonna see 'em."

"Dagnabbit, Arlie, we'll just ride up there in Injun Territory, and if we see 'em, we'll take care of 'em. Just throw a saddle on another horse and quit bellyachin' about it."

"There ain't no real reason to change horses," Arlie complained. "We ain't done nothin' but lay around that line shack all day. Hell, my horse is just as fresh as any of 'em here in the corral."

"Change horses, anyway," Lemuel told him. "You'll have Fanny comin' down on all of us." He jerked his saddle off his horse and turned it out in the corral. "That's Ward's horse," he said upon spotting it. "He ain't ridin' his horse. I'll throw my saddle on him." He didn't express it, but he was having thoughts about the possibility that his older brother might accidentally catch a bullet, like his friend Tiny had. That would end the possibility of the elder brother's return to run the family for once and all.

Maudie and Fanny were back at the corral with biscuits and bacon wrapped up in three cotton towels before the brothers had finished saddling new mounts. They were soon in the saddle with Fanny still giving instructions. "You make 'em know they can't ride onto this ranch and have their way," she said. "String the devil up where other lawmen can see him. Lemuel," she ordered him directly, "you bring me his badge, so I'll know you took care of him."

"Yessum, I'll bring it," he said, and wheeled

his horse toward the creek trail. At a fast lope, he led his two brothers out of the yard, riding past the dark lump at the edge that was the late Tiny McGee.

Lemuel led the search party of three along the east–west wagon road, holding their horses to as fast a pace as he could without breaking them down. After a couple of hours, he let up on them. "I'm thinkin' as fast as we've been ridin' we might be gettin' close to catchin' up with him. I mean, if he's gone into camp. Anyway, we'll let the horses walk easy now and we'll just have to keep our eyes peeled to see if we see any sign of a campfire. As open as this country is, he'd have to go a long way off the road to hide it."

So the search continued, walking easy now with three sets of eyes squinting into the darkness while downing the last of Maudie's biscuits. Whenever they came to a stream or creek, they spent a little extra time following it in both directions for a little way before deciding it was clear. Lemuel was considering calling off the search when Caleb suddenly blurted, "There! There's a fire up that creek a ways!"

"Where?" Lemuel responded, equally excited. "I don't see nothin'." They continued to stare in the direction Caleb had pointed, but there was no sign of a fire, not even a spark. "You're just seein' things."

As soon as he said it, Arlie pointed to the same spot. "There it is. I see it." As they all three peered at the trees lining the creek some forty or fifty yards upstream, a tiny flash of light flickered, followed by a faint shower of sparks up through the branches of the trees to fade away in the dark sky. "Like somebody just throwed a stick on the fire," Arlie said. His remark was met with the sound of three rifles cocking at almost the same time.

"Leave the horses yonder," Lemuel said, pointing to a couple of willow trees on the edge of the bank about halfway between the road and the spot where they had seen the fire. "We'll come up on him from three sides. That fire looks like he's camped on the other side of the creek, so Arlie, you cross over to that side. Me and Caleb will stay on this side, and when we get even with his camp, Caleb, you keep goin' for a ways. Then you cross over to the other side of the creek. If we're quiet enough, we oughta be able to blast him from three sides before he knows what hit him." He paused for a moment. "Any objections?" There were none, so they headed for the willow trees, anxious to get the party started.

Always a light sleeper, especially in the field, Will opened his eyes and listened. Something had stirred him awake. Then he heard Buster whinny and knew that was what had awakened him. Not only Buster, one of the other horses nickered as well. He raised up to look in the direction of his prisoner. If Hawkins had heard the horses, he showed no sign of it now. Slumped against the tree that imprisoned him, he had finally passed out after fighting his position for a considerable length of time. Satisfied Hawkins was secure, Will looked back toward the fire and the blanket roll he had formed to resemble a sleeping figure. About to look away, he was suddenly startled by a rifle shot from downstream that ripped into the blanket, causing the end of it to flap up. "I got him!" a voice sang out, then followed it with another shot. This time, however, Will was watching the darkness where he thought the first shot had come from, his rifle ready to fire. He saw the muzzle flash of the second shot and immediately squeezed off a round and heard a cry of pain.

Knowing his muzzle flash had likely given his position away as well, he rolled away from the edge of the tree he had been sleeping under and prepared to meet the next attempt, not sure if it would come from another direction. Peering into the darkness beyond the fire, he cranked another cartridge into his rifle, on his knees now. Before he could get to his feet, he felt a heavy blow on the back of his shoulder that knocked him down on his belly. He knew he had been shot. "By God, he's shot now!" Caleb called out triumphantly.

"I got him!" He threw another shot at the prone figure as he hurried to claim his kill.

Seeing Will go down, Lemuel came splashing across the creek to make sure he was dead. He stopped before reaching the fire when he heard Ward yelling, "Over here! Over here! Cut me loose from this damn tree!"

"It's Ward!" Caleb exclaimed as he rushed up.

"Go find Arlie," Lemuel said. "I think he got hit. I'll take care of Ward." When Caleb hesitated a few moments, Lemuel blurted, "Go on! Arlie might be needin' help." After a glance at the body of the lawman, he stood there, looking at his brother, his hands tied around a tree.

"Don't just stand there gapin' at me," Hawkins exclaimed. "Cut me loose."

"I swear, brother, damned if you ain't got yourself in a fix, ain't you? Tied to a tree, waitin' for me and the boys to come save you. You ain't such a big shot now, are you?"

"What's the matter with you?" Hawkins demanded, uneasy with his brother's attitude. "Cut me loose. You boys always knew I'd come back to the family just like Pa wanted me to. Ain't that right?"

"Yeah, I reckon that's right, all right," Lemuel answered. "But you see, things have been gettin' along just fine since you left, and I aim to keep 'em that way." He raised his rifle to take dead aim at his brother, chuckling at Ward's attempts to use the tree trunk to protect himself. "He oughta tied you to a bigger tree," Lemuel said, aiming his rifle at his brother's head. With the sudden crack of the rifle, Ward sank to his knees, but not from the gunshot. He could only gape, stunned by the sight of Lemuel's body sagging lifelessly. As the rifle dropped from his hands, another shot sent him sprawling to the ground.

Hawkins could only stare in shock as Will struggled to get to a sitting position against a tree. The deputy didn't look like he was going to make it. "For Pete's sake, man, cut me loose before you die! You can't leave me here tied to a tree."

Not sure how badly he was hurt, Will was thinking to be ready for the third brother. Although he was beginning to really feel the pain behind his shoulder, he knew that he was showing no signs that any vital organ had been hit. A quick look inside his coat showed no evidence that the bullet went clear through. But his shirt was already soaked with blood. In response to Hawkins's pleas to be set free, he said, "Just sit there and wait for your other brother to come rescue you. You might have two brothers still on their feet. We ain't sure if that first one is dead or not. Maybe they'll be more apt to welcome you back to the family."

The brother Will wondered about, Caleb, was at that moment kneeling beside his brother's body—Arlie, having caught a .44 slug just below his chest from Will's shot at his muzzle flash. When he had heard the two rifle shots fired back at the camp, he was not certain what to think. It sounded like Lemuel's Winchester, but was he shooting at the lawman who was already dead, or did he shoot Ward? Caleb knew that was a possibility, so he was anxious to get back there to find out. He looked down at his brother, who was clearly dying, and finally said, "There ain't nothin' I can do for you. I ain't no doctor." He got up then and hurried back to the camp.

Crashing noisily through the underbrush and bushes, he stopped abruptly just before reaching the clearing when he saw Lemuel's body sprawled on the ground and the lawman seated beside a tree with his rifle ready to fire. *Lemuel and Arlie dead!* The truth of that thought caused him to hesitate. *Now he's sitting there waiting for me to show up.* He checked his rifle to make sure it was ready to fire. *I shot him once. When I saw him a few minutes ago, he was dead.* Caleb decided to take another shot at him before getting any closer, so he raised his rifle and tried to aim without trembling. Finally, he jerked the trigger, missing the target a good two feet. His shot was answered immediately by three quick shots that snapped branches on the large laurel bushes close to his side. Already spooked by the demon lawman who wouldn't die, the barrage

344

was enough to make Caleb back away, stumbling to the ground in his haste. Afraid the lawman would be coming after him, he crawled as fast as he could to reach the trees along the bank. Then he scrambled to his feet and didn't stop running until he reached the horses tied in the willows. Once he was safely in the saddle, he did not spare his already exhausted horses, but headed back toward Texas as fast as the poor horses could go. As he rode, he tried to think of the best way to tell Fanny what had happened. He decided to tell her there was a posse of marshals waiting in ambush, and that Ward was already dead when they got there. It occurred to him then that he was the only man left of the Hawkins family, and the only one left to claim the role of boss. This business tonight with the devil might work to his advantage.

In the camp behind him, a totally dismayed Ward Hawkins sat on the ground, his hands still tied around the tree, his feet astraddle it, as he watched his wounded captor trying to tend to the wound in his back. "Untie my hands and I can help you with that wound," Hawkins offered. Will thanked him for his offer, but declined as he took his spare shirt out of his war bag and tried to stuff it down his back to stop the bleeding. "You might as well decide to let me help you," Hawkins persisted. "You're gonna end up bleedin' to death if you don't. And I ain't gonna double-cross you.

Hell, you saved my life. Lemuel was fixin' to shoot me, so I owe you for that."

Will paused to look him squarely in the eye. "Hawkins, let's get one thing straight. You're still under arrest. Ain't nothin' happened here tonight that changes that. I hurt, but I ain't crippled by the bullet in my shoulder, so this is how we're gonna play it from now on. When I tell you to do something, if you don't do it, I shoot you. I just ain't able to be bothered by taking any chances with you right now. So keep that in your head— you don't do what I say, I put a bullet in you. You understand?"

"Yeah, I understand," Hawkins grumbled, thinking Will was going to die if he kept bleeding and leave him tied to a tree somewhere between there and Fort Smith. *Well, that ain't gonna happen,* he said to himself. Tanner was bound to become weaker and weaker and before long he wouldn't be quick enough to tie his hands and keep a gun on him at the same time. It was just a matter of waiting for the right time.

"We've got a couple of hours before daylight," Will said. "You might as well go on back to sleep if you can. We'll be ridin' to the crossroads come sunup." With considerable effort, he got to his feet, took another look at Lemuel, then walked across the clearing to check on Arlie's body. As he walked, he tried to walk as steadily as possible, for Hawkins's benefit, knowing he was watching closely for signs of weakness. He found Arlie's body lying facedown on the ground. From the dirt on his hands and clothes, it appeared that he had dragged himself some distance before he died. Will continued walking down the creek a little way until he came to the willows where the Hawkins brothers had tied their horses. He could tell by the fresh droppings left there. The surviving brother had taken the horses and run. Will had a gut feeling that it would be the last he saw of Caleb. On his way back to the camp, he checked to see that his horses were all right. He could feel his shoulder stiffening, so he cut off another piece of rope to help him in the morning. After a check on Hawkins, he returned to his blanket and proceeded to fashion a small loop in the length of rope before closing his eyes for a short nap.

CHAPTER 19

When Will awoke with the first rays of the new morning, Hawkins was already awake, anticipating the process of getting back in the saddle. He was anxious to see how Will had fared the night. Knowing this, Will made an effort to seem as able as he was before being shot. It was not easy, but it was convincing enough to disappoint his prisoner.

With his shoulder throbbing in pain, he managed to saddle the horses and load the packhorse again. Conscious of Hawkins's constant gaze upon him, he led the horses up ready to mount, knowing this was going to be the first test by his prisoner. "I'm gonna let you ride with your hands in front of you this mornin' and we'll see how you do. If you make trouble, they'll be back behind you like before. Understand?" Hawkins nodded slowly in reply, anxious to see how Will was going to untie him from the tree, then retie his wrists and hold a gun on him at the same time. He would need three hands. Will drew his Colt and held it on Hawkins while he worked at the knot with his other hand. When the wrists were free, he let the ropes drop to the ground while he picked up the short piece of rope he had fashioned a loop in the night before. Hawkins's intense gaze was locked on him as he made each move, waiting for the chance he felt sure was to come. "Back away from the tree, but keep your hands out straight in front of you," Will ordered, with his Colt aimed squarely between Hawkins's eyes. Hawkins did as he was told, convinced that the deputy would have to put the pistol down before he could retie his hands. When he was clear of the tree, Will, still holding the pistol on him, slipped the loop of the short rope over Hawkins's left wrist. Then before Hawkins knew what he was up to, Will drew the loop closed and quickly lashed the free end of the rope around Hawkins's right wrist, drawing both wrists tightly together. Then he thrust the Colt under his belt and quickly finished tying his prisoner's hands together.

"Now that you see how it's done," Will said, "from now on, when I untie you from a tree, you can go ahead and stick your hand in that noose and lay the free end over your other wrists. And I'll finish it up for you."

"You must really be scared that I'm gonna try to make a break for it," Hawkins snarled. "It ain't easy haulin' a man to jail when you ain't got but one good arm. Right, Tanner?"

"The only thing I'm scared of is that you are gonna make that move and I'll have to shoot you, then I won't have any company for that long trip back."

Hawkins smirked and responded. "You are

smug, ain't you?" When Will simply smiled in reply, Hawkins reminded him, "It's a long way from here to Fort Smith. You never know what you're likely to run into."

"Climb up into that saddle," Will said. "You don't need my help now that you've got your hands in front of you." Hawkins did so and watched to see Will grimace with pain when he climbed up on Buster. Hawkins was convinced his opportunity would come.

Erma Johnson looked up toward the road when something caught her attention in that direction. Riders, two of them, leading a couple of horses behind them, were approaching from the east–west road. She gave the edge of the porch a couple more swipes with her broom as she waited for the riders to get close enough to identify. After a few more moments, she went to the door, opened it, and called her husband. "Jasper, come here. It's that deputy marshal, Will Tanner, comin' back, and he's got somebody with him."

Jasper came immediately. He stood staring at the two men approaching the store now. "It's him, all right. And that's one of those outlaws that robbed us ridin' with him." Not certain if that was a good or bad sign, he ran back inside to get his shotgun. But when he returned to the porch, Erma told him that the other man's hands were tied, and the deputy was leading his horse by the reins. He was plainly a prisoner. "Well, that's a good sign." He exhaled a sigh of relief. "There's more than a few lawmen workin' both sides of the law."

Jasper walked down the steps to meet Will when he pulled the horses to a stop. "Will Tanner," Jasper greeted him. "I see you caught up with one of those outlaws that robbed our store—his partner get away?"

"Depends on how you look at it, I reckon," Will returned. "He's dead."

"Glad to hear it," Jasper said. "Any man that would strike a woman like he did oughta be dead. Too bad this one ain't dead, too."

"I expect he'll get what he deserves at his trial. Right now, I'd like to see if Mrs. Johnson could sell me a couple of plates of breakfast for me and my prisoner. I could use a good meal right now and it would save me the trouble of cookin' something for him. I need to rest the horses, so I'll be a while, anyway. How 'bout it, can I buy us breakfast?"

Erma hesitated when her husband turned to get her reaction. "Well, I sure don't mind fixin' something for you, Deputy Tanner, but I ain't too thrilled about feedin' that animal."

"Would it help if we were bringin' back the money he and his partner stole from you?" Will asked. "Least, I reckon it's most of it, anyway. I don't think they had a chance to spend any of it since they took it."

Both faces lit up at the same time. "Well, I reckon that does make a difference," Jasper answered for him and his wife. "Erma will cook you up somethin' in a jiffy, won't you, hon?"

"That I will," Erma replied. "We didn't think there was any chance we'd see that money again, and we were hurtin' pretty bad about it."

"Good," Will said. "I'll just go take care of the horses and find a good tree to leave Mr. Hawkins, here." He threw a leg over and started to step down. It was only then, when his coat gapped open revealing his blood-soaked shirt, that the Johnsons realized he was wounded.

"Good Lord in heaven!" Erma gasped. "You've been shot! You're bleedin' to death!"

"Well, I hope not," Will said. "I did get shot, but it ain't too bad, more a nuisance than anything else."

Jasper turned to give Hawkins a harsh look. "Did he do that?"

"No, he woulda liked to," Will said. "It was his little brother that done it. Anyway, it oughta hold all right till I can get back to Atoka. There's a doctor there. I'll have him take a look at it."

"You'd do well to let Erma take a look at it. Have you done anything to clean it up or anything?" When Will explained that he really couldn't get to it to do anything but stuff a shirt down his back to try to stop the bleeding, Erma insisted that she take a look at it.

"I'd appreciate it," Will said. "But I've got a prisoner that I have to keep an eye on, and I wouldn't want to be in any position where I couldn't watch him."

"Hell," Jasper suggested, "put him in the smokehouse and you won't have to watch him." That sounded like a good solution to the problem to Will, but still he hesitated. "He'd have to have some dynamite to break outta there," Jasper declared. "Solid log smokehouse, it's got a stout oak door and a damn good padlock." He shot a sneering glance in Hawkins's direction and added, "Course, there's a couple of hams in there that might go bad, with the likes of him in there." He looked back at Will. "But I'm willin' to risk it to take care of a man that's been so nice to us."

After Hawkins was safely tucked away in the smokehouse, Will insisted on taking care of the horses before submitting his wounded shoulder to Erma Johnson's care. It was not the first wound she had attended, but it was her first bullet wound. For that reason, she was keenly interested in examining it and trying to clean it as best she could. For his part, Will was grateful for the medical attention. And it was not his intention, but his pain and discomfort were much more in evidence with Ward Hawkins locked in the smokehouse. Erma cleaned the area around the wound, but the bullet was in too deep for her to try to get it out. So she poured some whiskey in the wound and fixed a bandage over it and tied it on with strips of the same old sheet from which the bandage came.

When her first aid was completed, she went to the kitchen to cook something to feed him and his prisoner. Jasper invited him to stay on for a day or two to rest up before continuing on with his journey, but Will was bound to finish the job he had started and to see Hawkins stand trial for all the crimes he was guilty of. "No, I expect I'd best get along as soon as the horses are rested enough, but I do appreciate your kindness."

"We appreciate you goin' after those outlaws," Jasper told him, "and the return of our money." He didn't say it, but he was genuinely convinced that Will was a giant as far as character, for he felt certain any other lawman would have pocketed that money and claimed never to have recovered it.

After he saw to the feeding of his prisoner, then ate the breakfast Erma fixed for him, Will was persuaded to sit down in a rocking chair to rest a little. Before he knew it, he was asleep, sitting in the rocker by the stove. His mind released him to get the much-needed rest that had eluded him, so much so, that he was not even aware that one of Jasper's regular customers had visited while he slept. He would have been even more surprised had he known that Jasper had invited the customer to take a close look at Will while he related the story of the capture of Ward Hawkins.

The solid rest did help, and maybe Erma's nursing skills were partially responsible, too. But he had to admit that he felt more confident that he could go on. The problem was, they had let him sleep almost two hours longer than he had planned. And when he found out, he was in a panic to get his prisoner on his horse and get under way. It was a half-day's ride to Tishomingo and he had planned to get there early in the afternoon. Now he would have to camp overnight there. "I reckon I have to apologize," Jasper said, "but it was Erma's fault. She wouldn't let me wake you up—said it would help that wound to heal."

"I admit it," she piped up. "I'm the guilty one, but you needed to rest that shoulder a little bit." She shook her head and sighed. "We wish you luck—hope you get home safely. But it's not a very happy way to spend Christmas, is it?"

Her remark stunned him for a moment. "Christmas!" he responded. "What day is this?"

"Why, it's Christmas Eve," she said, marveling that he had to ask. "December twenty-fourth. Don't you even know what day it is?" Judging by his apparent distress, she had to ask, "Is it an important day for you?"

He didn't answer right away, his brain fairly spinning around inside his head. So much had happened since he had arrested Hawkins the first time at Boggy Town that he had lost track of the days. Aware then of Erma's intense gaze, he realized she had asked the question. "Ah yes, ma'am," he said, stumbling on the words. "I'm supposed to get married tomorrow." He paused. "About a hundred and seventy-five miles from here."

Their reaction was what he would have expected. Erma couldn't find words, so she just placed her hands over her mouth and gasped, wide-eyed, in disbelief that anyone, even a man, could forget his wedding. Equally shocked, but being a man, Jasper grinned. "Well, I'll be damned," he started. "Forgot your own weddin'. You might not wanna get back home a-tall. The most dangerous part of this trip might be when you get back." He gave Erma a grin. "If she's anythin' like my wife," he added.

"Shut your mouth, Jasper," Erma scolded. Back to Will then, she said, "If she's the right kind of woman, she'll understand." Then thinking some more on it, she asked, "Were you and your lady just gonna get married when you get back? Or was there a regular marriage ceremony planned?" Will then told her of the planned ceremony Sophie and her mother had arranged, with invitations to several friends, including Miss Jean Hightower, who had been like a mother to Will. After hearing that, all Erma could say was, "Oh my."

As for Will, he felt like a dog for not keeping track of the days. It would be hard to explain to Sophie, and especially her mother, how important it was to apprehend Ward Hawkins and Tiny McGee. There was very little chance of convincing mother and daughter that anything was as important as his vow to marry Sophie. Knowing how much Ruth had worked against the marriage from the beginning, he figured this was the trump card she needed to stop it completely. *Well, it is what it is,* he thought. *What's done is done, and there ain't anything I can do to change it.* To Jasper and Erma, he said, "I reckon I've laid around here long enough. I'd best get goin'. I 'preciate your help."

Hawkins was more than ready to be released from the smokehouse, even though his incarceration was of short term. He complained that in the little log structure there were living things that you couldn't see in the dark. He made no show of resistance when Will tied his hands again and got him seated in the saddle. His attitude was no doubt influenced by Jasper, standing by with his shotgun to watch the procedure. With Will and the Johnsons each wishing the other good luck, Will started out to Tishomingo, where he would rest the horses and eat supper. He had planned to go from there to Atoka, so he could put Hawkins in the railroad jail while he had Doc Lowell take the bullet out of his back. And he would have Jim

Little Eagle to help him there as well. He decided he would hold to that plan, since he was already so late returning to Fort Smith, the extra time wouldn't make that much difference. He was not looking forward to the reception awaiting his return.

It was late afternoon when they reached Tishomingo, a ride of about twenty-five miles, and Will went to a spot beside Pennington Creek where he had camped before. After he went through the usual routine of securing his prisoner, a process Hawkins had become familiar with, he took care of the horses. When they were grazing beside the creek, he gathered wood for a fire and soon coffee was boiling and bacon frying. To add a little to their supper, he used the last of the sack of flour he had to mix with water and some sugar to make slapjacks. He formed cakes with it and fried them like fritters in the bacon grease. There were other supplies he was getting short of and he would have called on Dewey Sams to buy them, since he had traded with Dewey and his wife oftentimes before. But with the ever-snarling Ward Hawkins to account for, he decided to wait until he reached Atoka. Hawkins had made very few comments throughout the afternoon. Will figured his mind was busy planning the best time to attempt an escape, but he appreciated the quiet, nonetheless. Hawkins was a dangerous man and not likely to accept a peaceful ride to the gallows. The test for Will was going to be how well he could prepare himself for whatever Hawkins tried. He wished he could honestly say that his arm and shoulder were better after Erma Johnson's care. But the truth was, it was becoming more and more stiff and painful whenever he tried to move it to any degree. It was getting difficult to disguise it under Hawkins's constant observation. He knew he could expect an attempt at the first sign of weakness. It came sooner than he expected, when Hawkins was eating his supper with his feet tied around the tree and his hands free.

"What did you call this mess you gave me to eat?" Hawkins began.

"Slapjacks," Will answered. "You like 'em?"

"No. Did you?" He didn't wait for an answer. "I reckon, that's the kind of crap you have to learn to eat if you're a deputy marshal. It tastes more like horse turds to me."

"I reckon I'd have to take your word on that," Will said. "I ain't ever ate horse turds. I most likely ruined your taste buds when I bought you that breakfast this mornin'."

"I'm done with this stuff," Hawkins said. "Come get this plate."

"All right," Will responded, and walked over to the tree. "Put the plate down on the ground and stick your hands out. You know what to do." He drew his .44 and waited until Hawkins dropped the plate. Will figured that was to have been his move if he had taken the plate from him. With his familiar snarl, Hawkins threw the plate on the ground, obviously having been thinking along the same lines Will had. But he was not through. He extended his hands on both sides of the tree and waited for Will to slip the rope with the loop over his hand. This time, however, when Will quickly drew the noose tight, Hawkins jerked the line out of Will's hand, thinking to overpower the one-armed lawman. He howled in pain and released the rope when the bullet from Will's .44 tore through his boot. Ready for such a move, Will grabbed the free end of the rope and took a few quick turns around Hawkins's wrists, pulling them up tight together. "You don't learn very fast, do ya? I warned you what would happen if you tried anything like that."

"Damn!" Hawkins roared. "You shot my foot!"

"Just like I said I would," Will replied. "You might as well get it in your head that every time you try something like that, you're gonna get another bullet. Maybe you don't get the picture. You're wanted dead or alive and it don't make that much difference to me. You'd be a lot less trouble dead."

With his prisoner's hands bound tightly together again, Will untied his feet, but there was no relief for Hawkins. "I need a doctor," he wailed. "You broke my damn foot."

"Ain't no doctor in Tishomingo," Will said. "Reckon you shoulda waited to try that little trick when we got to Atoka. After he takes that bullet outta my back, I might have him take a look at your foot—depends on how you behave between now and then."

CHAPTER 20

The wounded lawman and his wounded prisoner spent an unusually painful day in the saddle before reaching Jim Little Eagle's cabin on Muddy Boggy Creek. The pain in Will's shoulder showed no signs of easing, and Hawkins's foot had swollen to the point where his boot was going to have to be cut off before Doc could treat it. Will decided it best to go to Jim's cabin before taking his prisoner to the jailhouse. He could use Jim's help in transferring Hawkins from his horse to the jail. And at this point, he was ready to admit he needed the help.

Mary Light Walker came to the cabin door to see what had caught her husband's attention. "It's Will Tanner," Jim said, "and it looks like he's caught up with Hawkins." He stepped off the little porch and went to meet them while Mary remained in the doorway, watching. "Heyo, Will," Jim greeted his friend. "Looks like you had good hunting."

"I reckon," Will replied, "but it coulda been a lot better. I was hopin' to bring Tiny McGee back, too."

"Tiny get away?" Jim asked. Will shook his head. "You shoot him?" Jim asked.

"No, Hawkins's mother shot him." He turned in

the saddle and looked at Hawkins, who responded with a painful sneer. "When I get a minute, I'll tell you all about it." Jim asked if he wanted to step down, but Will said, "I reckon I'd better not. We both need some doctorin', and I think I'll ride on into town and put Hawkins in jail, so I can go see Doc Lowell."

"You have to use my jail," Jim said, noticing the dried blood on Will's shirt under his coat. "Sam Barnet take his key back. Say no more railroad jailhouse. You shoot it full of holes. You wait till I saddle my horse. I go in with you." He peered hard at Hawkins, then looked back at Will. Will didn't need to wait for the question. "He's got a bullet in his foot," he said, and Jim nodded his understanding, then promptly turned toward the barn to get his horse. Mary stepped out on the porch and asked if he wanted her to fix food for him and Hawkins. "No, ma'am, thank you just the same," Will answered. "I wanna get Mr. Hawkins settled in the jailhouse before it gets much later. It's still early enough to get some supper from Lottie Mabry's dinin' room. And I need to see Doc Lowell, too."

When Jim was saddled up, they rode the short distance into town, going directly to the old converted storehouse that served as the official Choctaw jail. The first obstacle they were faced with was Hawkins's wounded foot. It was so sore and swollen, he couldn't walk on it, but it was also enough to discourage him from attempting any sudden moves to escape. He was a sizable man, as well, so it was a struggle to get him off his horse, then half carry and half drag him into the jail. By the time they had accomplished that, Will's wound was bleeding again, so Jim insisted on taking the horses to the stable, so Will could go to the doctor's office. "What about me?" Hawkins demanded. "I need the doctor, too."

"I'll get him to take care of you," Will said. "Just hold your horses. I'll bring you somethin' to eat, too, so just relax and enjoy your rest."

"You SOB," Hawkins said, which was his standard reply to Will's sarcasm.

"I swear, I don't believe it," Dr. Franklyn Lowell complained when Lila, his Choctaw housekeeper and cook, came to tell him Will Tanner was waiting in his office to see him. "On Christmas, and like every time he needs a doctor, it's at suppertime." Lila shrugged helplessly. "Is it him, or did he bring a prisoner to get doctored?" She said that it was just him, so he took another bite out of a piece of corn bread, washed it down with a gulp of coffee, and got up from the table.

"I'll put your plate in the oven," she said as he left the kitchen.

"What have you got this time?" Doc asked as soon as he walked in his office. "It better be a bullet wound 'cause if you've called me away

364

from my Christmas supper for a bellyache, I'll let you sit here till I'm finished eating."

"Sorry 'bout the time," Will replied while he carefully pulled his coat off. "I just now got into town, so I came as quick as I could. I'm sorry to disturb your Christmas. Tell you the truth, I forgot about it bein' Christmas."

Seeing the trouble Will was having, Doc helped him out of his shirt. Once he got the wound exposed, he asked, "How long ago did this happen?" Will told him it was two nights ago, causing Doc to shake his head. "Shoulda gone to a doctor right away."

"You're the closest doctor to where I got shot," Will answered. "I got here quick as I could."

"Well, we need to get that bullet outta there," Doc said. "That wound's heating up like a hot stove. Lila!" he yelled. "I'm gonna need some hot water."

Will's surgery didn't take long. Doc probed in the muscle of his shoulder for less than fifteen minutes before extracting the lead slug and pouring iodine in the wound. "That's gonna feel a helluva lot better in a day or two," he said. "Just try to keep it as clean as you can."

"I appreciate it, Doc," Will said as he paid the three dollars Doc charged. "I meant to tell you, I've got a prisoner down in Jim Little Eagle's jail that needs some doctorin', too. He's got a bullet in his foot."

Doc bit his lower lip, about to explode into his usual rant about having his supper interrupted, but then he paused. "Shot in the foot, huh? Is he the one who shot you?"

"No, that was his brother that shot me," Will answered.

Interested now, Doc asked, "This fellow down in the jail, did you shoot him in the foot?" Will said that he did. Doc shook his head and declared, "Crazy—I don't know who's the craziest, the outlaws or the lawmen."

"I reckon it's about a draw," Will said. He thought he might have heard the comment before, and he was pretty sure it was Ruth Bennett who said it.

"All right," Doc decided, "I'm gonna finish my supper, then I'll come down there and treat your prisoner."

"Thanks, Doc. I'm gonna stop by Lottie's place and pick up some supper for me and my prisoner, then I'll be down at the jail. If I don't get there before you do, Jim Little Eagle will let you in." He plopped his hat on his head and went out the door.

Doc paused at the window and watched Will walk down the street toward the boardinghouse dining room. "Damn shame, nice young fellow like that, probably end up dead before he reaches thirty."

"Jim Little Eagle say Will Tanner damn good man."

Unaware Lila had come from the kitchen until she spoke, Doc turned abruptly and replied, "He'll be a damn good dead man, riding for the law in this territory."

"I'll get your supper out of the oven," she said.

"Will Tanner," Lou-Bell declared when she saw him come in the door. "You come for Christmas dinner? We're servin' it up all day today." She walked up to greet him when she realized he had one arm in his coat sleeve and the other one in a sling. "What happened to you?"

"I got in the way of a bullet," Will answered, then quickly changed the subject. "I need to buy two suppers, and I need to take 'em with me. One of 'em is for a prisoner, and the other one's for me. I'll bring the plates back."

"So we're gonna have some more jailhouse business, are we?" Lottie asked as she walked up to join Will and Lou-Bell. She, like Lou-Bell, wanted to know what happened to his shoulder. He gave her the same brief report he had given to Lou-Bell. "Who's the prisoner?"

"Ward Hawkins," Will answered.

"So you got him back," Lou-Bell commented, remembering the stern countenance of Tiny McGee's partner. "Reckon you'll hold him this time?"

"Reckon we'll just have to wait and see," Will replied. "I expect he's thinkin' he's liable to starve to death about now." Lottie chuckled in response to his obvious jibe and hurried Lou-Bell off to the kitchen to serve up two plates.

When he got back to the jail, he apologized to Jim Little Eagle for drawing him away from home on Christmas. "I gotta be honest with you, I plum forgot what day it was, what with me and Hawkins both grumblin' about our wounds." Jim assured him that it made no difference to him, Christmas being just another day to him. "I coulda brought you one of Lottie's special Christmas plates." He held the plates up so he could see. "Look there, she's even got some stuffin' on there. Course, she didn't have any turkey, but pig's just as good." Jim said he'd already eaten supper and it was beef, which he preferred. "Then I reckon I'll have to give it to the prisoner," Will said, "if you'll unlock the door for me."

"I think I better," Jim said, looking at Will's sling. "Doc fix you up with one wing."

"I don't think I'll be wearin' this very long, but he's comin' here to doctor Hawkins's foot, so I'd best leave it on at least till he's done with him."

Overhearing their conversation, Hawkins called out, "How 'bout bringin' my supper in here, so I can eat it before that damn doctor starts cuttin' on my foot."

Will glanced at Jim and winked. "Why, sure, Mr. Hawkins. It'll be a pleasure to serve you this fine Christmas supper." He put one of the plates down, freeing his gun hand, while Jim unlocked the door. Then with his Colt drawn, he stepped inside and held it on Hawkins while he offered the plate with his other hand. "Be real careful what you're thinkin'," he warned Hawkins. "The next shot ain't gonna be in your foot."

"You crippled me up good, damn you. There ain't much I can do. Just gimme the plate." He took it from Will's hand and started to devour the food immediately.

Will backed out of the jail and Jim put the padlock back in place and, ignoring the cold, they sat down on a bench in front of the building while Will ate his supper. "I don't think it's a good thing for you to take him back now, not with that bad shoulder," Jim felt bound to say. "Maybe you leave him here till Ed Pine comes back."

"I ain't as bad off as it looks," Will insisted. "And I've already spent a helluva lot of money takin' care of prisoners on this trip."

"You stay here," Jim continued. "Dan Stone send somebody to take this prisoner back." Further discussion was halted at that moment by the arrival of Doc Lowell.

Doc's visit was not a lengthy one. He took one look at Hawkins's foot and declared, "You're gonna have to take him to my surgery. I can't operate on him in this filthy storeroom. I shoulda known that in the first place." He didn't wait to hear their decision but turned abruptly and returned to his office. "Bring him on, if you want me to work on him," he tossed back over his shoulder as he walked up the street.

Lila White Bird opened the door when Will, with Jim's help, brought Hawkins to the doctor's office. "Take him in there," she said, pointing toward Doc's surgery. Then she stood aside, casting a stare of contempt for a man responsible for supplying firewater to the Choctaw men of her tribe.

Sensing her scorn for him, Hawkins growled, "Merry Christmas," to her as he limped by, laughing when she turned at once and went to the kitchen to get hot water for the doctor.

"You mind your manners," Will warned, "or I'll take you back to jail without any doctorin' on that foot." He and Jim helped Hawkins into the little room where Doc did his surgery. In a short time, Doc came in, ready to work.

"Put him on the table," Doc directed. "That foot's so swollen, I'm gonna have to cut the boot away." So he went to work right away, eager to be done with it. When he got the boot off, he found that Will's bullet had gone almost all the way through with the slug's nose stopped by the boot's heavy sole. "Shouldn't take long," Doc said. "I'll just pull the bullet all the way out."

Hawkins was content to lie patiently waiting for Doc Lowell to finish working on his foot.

He had no intention of leaving his office still under arrest. He figured his best chance, maybe his only chance, to escape was while he was out of the secure little smokehouse that served as a Choctaw jail. And there was enough distraction in the tiny surgery to offer an opportunity to get the jump on his captors. The opportunity came when Doc bound the injured foot and declared he was finished. Both Will and Jim had to move back toward the corner to give Lila room to pick up a basin holding the instruments Doc had used. When she started to turn around to take them to the kitchen, Hawkins suddenly sat up and grabbed a scalpel from the basin, shoving Lila to the floor. Before Will or Jim could get to him, he collared Doc around the neck and pulled him back against him. Locked in a stranglehold and the scalpel against his neck, Doc was helpless against the much stronger outlaw. "This is where we part company," Hawkins informed Will and Jim. "I've got nothin' to lose here, so if you two don't back up to that corner again and drop your gun belts, I'm gonna slice a nice big smile across this old buzzard's throat." He glanced down at Lila, who was on her hands and knees, the contents of the basin scattered on the floor around her. "Get up from there and get back in that corner. And you listen to me, you Injun witch. You pick up their guns and bring 'em to me, or you'll be workin' for a dead doctor."

He clearly had the advantage, but Will was thinking to get a shot at him before he had time to cut Doc's throat. "There ain't no way you can get outta here alive, Hawkins. Odds are against you, even if you do cut Doc, I'll get a bullet in you before you can finish him. So, drop the knife and we'll take you back to the jail."

"One quick slice and Doc's gone," Hawkins replied, holding the hapless little man in front of him for a shield. "Ain't nobody fast enough to keep me from slittin' his gullet, so let your belt drop to the floor if you want him to live." He pressed the knife against Doc's throat just hard enough to draw a little blood.

"All right!" Will responded. "We're gonna drop 'em." He propped his rifle against the wall and made a pretense of unbuckling his belt, hoping that Hawkins would provide an opening for him to take a shot. But Hawkins was wary of just such an opportunity, so he kept Doc pulled up tight against him, knowing Will would hesitate to shoot if he didn't have a clear shot.

"Get over there like I told you," Hawkins growled to Lila, who was still on the floor at his feet. She got up then, hiding the other scalpel behind her skirt. When she came up, she lunged into Hawkins, plunging the scalpel into his side as hard as she could manage. He yelped in pain, reeling back while still holding on to Doc, but not tight enough to keep the desperate doctor from bending his head slightly forward. It was enough. Will's shot smashed the side of Hawkins's head in and he dropped to the floor with one arm still wrapped around the doctor.

"You all right, Doc?" Will asked. Still shaken for the moment, Doc couldn't answer.

"Hell's bells!" Doc finally managed to spit out, but that was all for a few more moments.

"You can thank Lila for savin' your life," Will said. "If she hadn't gone after him with that knife, I wouldn't have had a shot."

Gradually recovering his sarcastic persona, Doc said, "I ain't sure you had one. I'm lucky you didn't blow my head off." He looked to his housemaid then. "You all right, Lila?"

"I think it a good thing we got rid of that man," Lila said. "I need to clean up the mess he made."

CHAPTER 21

He rode hard, asking Buster for the maximum each day, in an effort to complete the 110-mile journey in two days' time. The picture of what might be awaiting him in Fort Smith was the only thought spinning in his mind as he urged the buckskin on. At the end of the second day, after leaving Atoka early the day after Christmas, he pulled his weary horses to a stop on the banks of the Poteau River, less than ten miles from Fort Smith. To go farther that day seemed too hard on Buster and the horses he was leading. To his credit, the buckskin gelding showed no sign of quitting and would have willingly pressed on over the short distance left. There was another factor that caused Will to hesitate. The dread of walking into Boggy Town to face Ward Hawkins and Tiny McGee did not hold a candle to the dread he felt for the face-off ahead with Ruth and Sophie Bennett. It would be three days past the date of the wedding. He could explain the situation he had found himself in, but the explanation would fall on deaf ears. Through a miracle he could never explain, he had been granted the good fortune to have won the heart of a woman he had come to realize he adored. To lose that precious heart to a worthier suitor would be one thing he could more easily accept. But to lose her because he forgot what day it was, struck him with an urge to run. He pulled Buster's head toward the trees by the river and walked him down along the bank until he found a spot that suited him. Then he climbed down, unsaddled his horses, and prepared to make camp. He would deal with it in the morning.

He awoke the next morning before sunup, his eyes tired and heavy from a restless night but determined to face his firing squad. He would take care of his job-related responsibilities first. That meant reporting to U.S. Marshal Daniel Stone in his office. Since he would be at Fort Smith before Dan came to the office, his first stop would be the stables to make arrangements with Vern Tuttle for the extra horses he was bringing with him. After leaving the stables, there was still plenty of time before Dan usually came into the office, so Will decided he might as well eat. The only place he trusted the food this early in the morning was the Morning Glory Saloon, so he decided to let Mammy fix him some breakfast.

"Well, I'll be . . ." Gus Johnson started when Will walked in. "How you doin', Will? Didn't expect to see you here this early in the mornin'." He looked genuinely surprised.

"Why not?" Will responded, but Gus just shrugged and put his bar towel down on the bar and asked if he was drinking or looking for something to eat. "If Mammy's in the kitchen, I was thinkin' I'd like to buy some breakfast," Will said, still finding Gus's attitude strangely reserved. It was not at all like him.

"I'll tell Mammy you're wantin' some breakfast," Gus said. "I'll be right back." Then he turned and walked rapidly toward the kitchen, which, again, seemed mighty strange. He would normally stay right there at the bar and yell it out to Mammy.

After a few minutes Gus returned. Lucy Tyler followed him out, carrying a cup of coffee. She placed the coffee down on the bar before Will, all the while gazing into his eyes as if deeply searching for something. It occurred to him then. *They don't know.* They thought he was just married and were probably wondering why he was in a saloon looking for breakfast, while a new bride was at home. To make matters worse, Lucy offered empathy. "Sometimes it takes a little extra time for things to work out between a man and a woman, 'specially when the woman ain't never been with a man before." Will cringed, but before he could respond, she continued, "I'd be happy to talk with you about it, if you're needin' the woman's side of things."

"No, no . . ." Will started in a panic, then paused to say, "I thank you for wantin' to help, but you're thinkin' the wrong thing. I'm in trouble, all right, but it ain't what you think. I never made it back here in time for the weddin'."

"Uh-oh," Lucy reacted, having heard Will complain about the big church wedding Sophie and her mother had planned. "You ain't married?" He shook his head and she reacted again. "Uh-oh. What happened when you finally showed up?" She pictured the same reception he was picturing.

"I ain't yet," he answered. "I just got back in town this mornin'."

"She don't even know you're back yet?" Lucy asked. "When are you gonna' tell her?"

"Right after I check in with Dan Stone," he said. "I have to take care of that first."

Gus had held his tongue during Lucy's interrogation, listening with eyes wide in astonishment and his jaw hanging open, but he could hold it no longer. "Will, boy," he blurted, "your goose is cooked. You'd better have a stiff drink of whiskey with your breakfast."

Lucy turned to cast a disapproving frown at the bartender. "Yeah, that'd help, all right. Show up with whiskey on his breath."

"I ain't gonna drink no whiskey," Will said, wishing now he had never stopped in. "I just needed something to eat. I didn't come in here to talk about anything else."

Mammy came out of the kitchen at that moment, carrying a plate of food for him. "I heard all the fuss," she commented. "You folks was jawin' so loud." She placed the plate on one of the tables in the saloon. "She'd be damn lucky to get you. If she gives you any trouble, I'll marry you. Then you can eat a breakfast like this every mornin'." She turned abruptly and returned to her kitchen.

All three could not help laughing as the tiny, fragile-looking woman, her gray hair tied in a bun, disappeared through the kitchen door. "I'm gonna hold you to that," Will called out after her. "I've got two witnesses to back me up." He looked back at Lucy's smiling face and said, "I reckon things will work out like they're supposed to." He ate his breakfast and they wished him good luck when he left for Dan Stone's office. "If you see me back in here in a little while, you'll know how I made out, and I'll need that drink of whiskey then," he said in parting.

Like his friends at the saloon, Dan Stone knew about the planned wedding, but unlike them, he knew beforehand that Will wasn't there for the ceremony. "How bad is that?" Stone asked when he saw Will's arm in a sling. Will assured him that it was not bad and well on the way to healing, so Stone proceeded to a subject of equal importance. "Sophie came to see me the day before Christmas. She wanted to know if you were on your way back and I had to tell her that I had had no communications with you for several days. Frankly, I was hoping you were on your way back then. You could have broken off that business with Hawkins and McGee and gotten back in time for your wedding."

"I was too close," Will said. "I couldn't just let 'em go to get lost somewhere in Texas."

"I know," Stone said, well aware of his best deputy's tendency to follow a felon until he caught him, no matter where the trail led. With no more discussion on Will's private life, they went on to his report on the happenings that led to the deaths of Ward Hawkins and Tiny McGee. When the meeting was over to Dan Stone's satisfaction, Will left to face up to whatever awaited him at Bennett House.

Ron Sample got up from his chair and walked to the edge of the porch to tap the tobacco ashes from his pipe, taking care to stand so that the cold breeze didn't blow them back in his face. "Hot damn," he murmured, then turned to Leonard Dickens, who was sitting close to the door, where the corner of the house blocked some of that wind. "Look who's comin' yonder, Leonard. Ain't that Will?"

That was enough to get Leonard out of his chair to join Ron at the edge of the porch. He peered back toward town to see the familiar figure, striding purposefully, his saddlebags on one shoulder, his rifle in hand. His left arm riding in a sling. "It's him, all right. Reckon we oughta go tell the women?"

"I don't know," Ron replied. "Might be kinda interestin' to see what happens if he just walks in and surprises 'em."

"Might at that," Leonard admitted, then slowly repeated, "Might at that." They both waited at the edge of the porch for Will to come through the gate. "Mornin', Will," Leonard greeted him when he started up the steps. His greeting was repeated by Ron.

"Don't get too cold for you boys to sit out on the porch, does it?" Will returned the greetings.

"Set around inside by the stove all day and it'll weaken your blood," Ron replied. "Ain't that right, Leonard?"

"That's what I was always told," Leonard said, then nodded toward Will's arm in the sling. "Looks like you run into a little trouble."

"You could say," Will answered, and walked past them to the front door. They both followed close behind, not wishing to miss the homecoming. He stopped at the door to prop his rifle against the wall in order to free his hand to turn the doorknob. The sudden stop caused Leonard to bump into him, then again when Ron, in turn, bumped into Leonard. "You fellows that anxious to get inside?" Will asked as he opened the door, then stepped to the side to let them go on.

"Reckon it was startin' to get a little chilly out here," Ron offered. "You go right ahead."

The pause at the door was enough to attract Ruth Bennett's attention as she walked through the parlor on her way to the kitchen. "Were you two born in a barn? Or are you trying to heat all . . . outdoors?" Her voice trailed off almost to a whisper when she saw Will standing there. Momentarily stunned, she wasn't sure what to say. After a long pause, she managed, "I see you're back."

"Yes, ma'am," Will said. "Got back as soon as I could." When she responded with nothing more than an expression of pure shock on her face, he asked, "Is Sophie in the kitchen?"

Ruth's brow furrowed as she rapidly recovered from the surprise and began to remember the frustration and indignation she felt for having her daughter stood up at the altar. "I suppose so," she answered curtly. "I think Margaret's helping her with a little chore she's anxious to be done with." She waited for him to walk past her, then followed him into the kitchen.

When Sophie turned to see him standing there, unshaven, his arm in a sling, what she could see of his shirt stained with old blood, saddlebags on his good shoulder, his rifle in his free hand, she immediately felt relief to see he was alive. Just as quickly, her anger for what he had caused her resurfaced to consume her. "I'm sorry I got held up," he offered. She dropped the wedding gown Margaret was helping her fold and walked up to stand before him. He was about to say more in apology when she suddenly doubled up her fist and threw a punch that landed on his cheekbone. The force of the blow caused him to take a step backward. "I reckon I had that one comin'," he said. "Might as well take another one, if you want one." He would have been surprised if she had, for she was rubbing her fist and grimacing with the pain from the first punch. Had he not been focusing upon her, he might have noticed the smile on her mother's face when it occurred to her the times when she felt like doing the same to Fletcher Pride. There was not a sound in the kitchen, even though Ron and Leonard had inched into the room to join Will and the three women. After a few moments, Will broke the silence. "I'm sorry I didn't get a chance to clean up a little bit before I got here." Sophie did not reply but continued to shake her head as if addressing a wayward child. "I don't reckon you still wanna get married," he declared.

"You don't, do ya?" She stepped back as if to get a better look at him. "Well, I reckon it ain't on the top of my want list. What happened to your arm?"

"It's my back," he answered. "Fellow put a bullet in it. Slowed me down a little gettin' back here, but it's all right. I think I'm ready to take the sling off."

"So you come back here after leaving me to tell the preacher and the wedding guests that the wedding is off, expecting me to marry you?"

"No, ma'am, I came back *hopin'* you'd still wanna get married. Do ya?"

"Not until you clean yourself up," she answered. "And when you look better than something that just crawled out of a cave, we'll go to see the preacher and get it done. And another thing, I don't want to go live on your ranch in Texas. I like it here in Fort Smith, and my mother needs my help here in running this boardinghouse. Those are my terms, and I've known you well enough to know you're not ready to retire to a cattle ranch, either. Maybe later that'll come. So do you still wanna marry me?"

"Yes, ma'am, I sure do," he answered at once, and the onlookers erupted into a chorus of cheering. Even Ruth was smiling, having decided that she would not have missed her short time with Fletcher Pride for anything. It was Sophie's decision to make, Ruth realized, and as she looked at the smiling faces gathered around her daughter, she decided it was the right one. It was truly a happy occasion.

Center Point Large Print
600 Brooks Road / PO Box 1
Thorndike, ME 04986-0001 USA

(207) 568-3717

US & Canada:
1 800 929-9108
www.centerpointlargeprint.com